OFF THE WALL

To the Louthers,
    May American humor and
    English wit enjoy a
    happy union

        Best wishes,

            Ralph Bromley

        2003

OFF THE WALL

Ralph B. Murphy

To order additional copies of this book, contact:
Xlibris Corporation
1-888-795-4274
www.Xlibris.com
Orders@Xlibris.com
16342

ACKNOWLEDGEMENTS

For inspiration and keeping the faith, Paul Hastings and Helen Murphy, for technical assistance and derring-do, Paul Schlenker, Bill Marino, Kate Ramos, Tracy Festinger, Jacques Murphy and Rachel Davey

CONTENTS

THE CLIPPETY-CLOP DRIVER EDUCATION VEHICLE

(CC-DEV or just THE DEV)

Rudolph "Smokey" Maggart, called just "Smokey" by most people, drives old cars. It is hard to say how Rudy came by his nickname of Smokey; maybe it is because he smoked two packs of cigarettes a day. Some say that Smokey "smokes" along the highway in his car. At any rate he hears nothing but Smokey from parents, children and everybody who knows him well.

Smokey's old cars in his later years were not valuable classics lovingly restored and coddled, but just old, worn and used cars that excite no envy and no offers to negotiate. That way there is no hassle over an allowance at the time of trade-in because the car has long been depreciated to zero. The trick is to get a dealer who will accept Smokey's junker and haul it away as a condition for purchase of another car.

Smokey does like to modify his old cars. He doesn't add fancy gadgets, no turbo-chargers, no sexy hood ornaments, no horns playing "How dry I am!" About the flashiest car accessory that Smokey ever bought was a fine piece of drapery, a luxuriant Scotch plaid to fling over the front seat and cover the broken springs on the driver's side. Usually, Smokey's additions to old cars are practical aids to survival in today's heedless traffic and its avalanche of thoughtless and ill-tempered drivers.

Over the years and after many experiments, Smokey has developed a set of mechanical extras for his car designed to encourage safety and to educate drivers in the rules of the road, that is, other drivers, not the ones at the wheel of Smokey's modified jalopy. Smokey began to call his specially equipped car the Clippety-Clop Driver Education Vehicle, known by its acronym, the C-C-D-E-V, or more affectionately, just the DEV.

What driver has not burned inwardly as some lout in front of him going sixty brakes hard to twenty and turns left without so much as a flick of the turn indicator? What conscientious operator has not longed to be a temporary traffic cop when some yard bird in the left lane goes sailing through on the red while the legally responsible citizen comes to the required stop? These infractions, and the arrogance that goes with them, the DEV is equipped to penalize.

There are three non-standard devices that Smokey installs on the Clippety-Clop. Smokey is not mechanically proficient. Rather, he comes up with the functional concepts but has to turn to certain mechanics in his neighborhood that work in what are known as chop shops. These are back alley businesses that disassemble cars of unknown ownership to obtain salable items for the very lucrative spare parts trade. Without becoming involved in that activity in any way, Smokey simply utilizes the known expertise of individuals who have learned a great deal about cars and who will not ask too many questions about the installations they are hired to make.

The first device is mounted under the front headlights, a set of Thunderbolt Tire Spears. Coiled and invisible until a switch opens covering flaps, the spears are deployed against a car cutting in dangerously close in front of the DEV. Then, after Smokey has been obliged to jam on the brakes, Smokey lines up the offending bastard directly in front of him and activates with a touch, the spears, one on each side, ten feet of gleaming, one-inch, sharpened, steel rounds which shoot straight ahead into the rear tires of the offending vehicle. The spear points should be kept heavily greased for easy retractibility from the other's tire. If the target is not quite lined up for one reason or another and one spear hits the gas tank, so much the better. Smokey is on his way with a thumb of the nose, so to speak, to a discourteous driver with two flat tires or maybe one flat and a leaking gas tank. Either way he will be in no position to give chase on one or more rims. And with an inward smile Smokey visualizes that driver in the future. Particularly, if he is a stranger to Smokey's part of the country, he has no way of knowing how many DEVs there may be on the highway. Smokey nourishes the hope that the other will become a permanently better driver.

The second device is in two parts. It is for the defiant goon who, his car that is, almost climbs into your trunk while you both are doing seventy miles an hour. Smokey's deterrent is a Crab Claw Grill Snatcher with Boxing Glove. The first part is an accordion-type extension that shoots backward from the rear bumper with a claw at its end. A few quick swipes of the claw with the rotator control will neatly remove a piece of the grill, or maybe the entire grill from the car following too closely. The grill piece can either be placed in Smokey's trunk by the receding claw, or perhaps better, thrown to the side of the road. The second part of the device is mounted at windshield height in the rear. A boxing glove, attached to a second accordion arm, is propelled across the hood of the too-close vehicle just two feet, under the best circumstances, in front of the boorish driver's nose. The device is safe; the arm is too short to touch the windshield and small enough so that the moving driver may see around it. The glove has on its padded tip in white letters one and a half inches high and clearly visible, "WHOA, MR./MRS. OR MISS BUSTER!" The "whoa" seems to indicate a horse is being addressed which in a way it is, if the meaning of "horse" can be inclusive of "stud," "old mare" and "filly."

Occasionally, a driver may just wander a little too close without aggressive intent. In this case it is recommended that the Boxing Glove be tried alone as a warning. If the other driver backs off to a decent interval, no harm, no further arm and glove. Some drivers will appreciate Smokey's reminder and will give a pleasant wave that Smokey can see in the rear view mirror and acknowledge with a friendly flick of his fingers, a pleasant encounter on the highway with another well-meaning driver. But if he or she turns surly as many do and renews the assault, even touching Smokey's bumper, Smokey does not hesitate to snatch the grill and throw it as far as the device will permit. This kind of driver will desist only in order to recover his grill.

The third device is more defensive than positively educational. In fact, it is for the sort who can be taught nothing, can only be deterred by fear from getting too close to Smokey's car. It is intended to discourage pursuit by someone who is angered by Smokey's use of the Crab Claw Grill Snatcher or even for an overzealous traffic patrolman who tries to haul Smokey over for going through a stoplight on the yellow, Smokey's perfectly legal option.

Let's say an irate motorist, for whatever reason, draws alongside Smokey on the Interstate and from his car makes threatening gestures and is so close that he seems to be trying to get everybody killed by a side swipe. The device, a Car Body Slicer, can be thrust out from the side about two feet. It consists of a thin, rotary, cutting disc, six-inch radius, somewhat like an old-fashioned lawn edger, revolving at high speed and made of Sheffield steel. If the side of the other car touches the disc and either pulls past or draws back, the Slicer will leave a horizontal slash from fore to aft. The Slicer can be turned to make its cut vertical if Smokey holds his car to the same speed as the offender. So, if the other driver persists for long enough in his or her harassment at sixty miles an hour, Smokey, by expert adjustment, going faster or slower, shifting from vertical to horizontal modes, can actually cut a square out of the car next to him. Even with minimum skill one can slice the side of the other car to ribbons, leaving streamers of metal flapping in the wind.

One time Smokey cut the passenger side and by maneuvering he changed positions with his assailant and also sliced the driver's side. The sight made Smokey laugh aloud as he zoomed away. In the rear view mirror the be-ribboned car resembled an unruly Maypole or maybe an octopus engaging an octopussy. On the highway Smokey feels safe in the DEV. When approached in unfriendly fashion, whether from the front, rear or side, trustworthy DEV has a riposte.

Regrettably, there are limits on the use of the DEVs armamentarium in cities, unfortunate because some of the drivers most in need of education tool around heavily populated areas. They are unconscionably arrogant, provocateurs to outright mayhem by aggrieved, innocent drivers. But in lines of traffic, long waits at lights and in the presence of hundreds of unreliable witnesses, Smokey feels he must resist the impulse to educate the other driver and, generally, he does refrain.

Once in Florida, Smokey's rather careless use of the DEV was costly. Smokey had no one to blame but himself, certainly not his girl friend, Harriet, who is never very confident anyway when Smokey resorts to the special buttons on the DEV. The two of them were going to the World's Fair in New Orleans. To make time they had arisen in Savannah before it was light on a Sunday morning and had proceeded across the Florida panhandle at a good pace in the pre-dawn. Interstate 10 was deserted except for a full moon. The swamps on either side sparkled in the moonlight and the rotting tree stumps pierced the sky at weird angles. It was a beautiful, eerie setting as they hurtled down the highway alone— just Smokey, his girl friend, and the DEV.

Despite the pre-dawn hour, Smokey broke into his rendition of *Melancholy Baby*, a version that his girl friend has come to accept without protest. Smokey was going no more than ten miles an hour above the speed limit, as is the practice of all law-abiding citizens. Suddenly, in the rear view mirror, as he reached the line of the song, "I'll kiss away each tear", there loomed the lights of a vehicle rapidly overtaking them. The thought of cops did occur to Smokey but as the car drew up behind there were neither flashing lights nor blaring commands from a speaker. Smokey was reassured. Nevertheless, reflexively, Smokey slowed to about fifty-five. The car behind swung out to pass. I-10 is a broad limited access expressway and there wasn't the slightest excuse for the driver to almost clip Smokey's rear, and then slide perilously close on his way by.

Smokey's good spirits evaporated. Without a cautionary look he activated the Body Slicer. Smokey was maintaining a constant speed of fifty-five so the other vehicle, in effect, slashed itself as it buzzed by, much too close for comfort, a loss of comfort the other driver would soon feel, when he next inspected the side of his car. Perhaps it was the absence of other traffic noise that enabled the other driver to hear the whir of the Slicer and alarmed him. Customarily, the other driver, particularly with his radio blaring and the device motor unusually quiet, does not know that he has been sliced and Smokey can drive merrily on. But now the flashing lights did appear and the siren sounded. Too late Smokey looked over and saw the silhouette of the trooper's Stetson and observed on the side of the car that he had cut through the seal of the State of Florida.

Smokey stopped on command. There was a patrolmen, an older man definitely in charge and as cantankerous as a redneck cop in the movies, and also a younger, quiet one who could have been the other's son. The crusty, old trooper knew that the two cars had made contact but couldn't understand the clean gash on his car and the lack of even a scrape of paint on Smokey's car. The Slicer had been retracted, of course, and the flaps closed. It was dark but the trooper was suspicious and persistent. After all he couldn't show up before the magistrate and charge a driver in a car without any marks on it with inflicting a gash on an official vehicle—and he was determined to press charges.

To shorten the tale, the trooper bored in on Smokey with questions until Smokey had to explain the unique construction of his side panel and was forced to open the recess and disclose the Slicer, its blade slightly discolored with the same color paint as the patrol car. Smokey's car followed the trooper's to a nearby town where they routed out of bed a still-drunken magistrate in a Sunday morning stupor from a big Saturday night.

"This betta' be good, y'all," he warned the arresting officers, "not to wait 'til mornin', to a decent time a'day. If it ain't a good case, I'll jug the lota' y'all."

The magistrate never fully understood the charge. The spluttering officer had trouble explaining, he didn't really know how Smokey had done it. The young trooper remained silent and was no help. The magistrate was likewise baffled when they examined the device.

"This h'yer thing broke loose and hit yer patrol car?" the magistrate asked the officers at one point.

"Naw," he was told, "this guy used it on us." The judge blamed the alcohol fumes still in his head for his difficulty in understanding.

What the charges lacked in precision they made up in number—willfully damaging a State vehicle, reckless endangerment, intent to inflict bodily harm, speeding and so on and on. The magistrate was annoyed. Perhaps he detected a flaw in the multiple charges. Smokey thought the speeding charge was particularly unjustified since the troopers had overtaken *him* without any sign of apprehending him. Possibly, Smokey's girl friend influenced the magistrate. She did not flirt with him but was looking demure and appealing, and some men in their cups are highly susceptible.

The judge fined Smokey three hundred dollars but it could have been worse. Smokey was afraid that the Claw and the Spears would also be discovered and he would really be in for it. Smokey paid the fine in cash so as to leave no paper trail and the magistrate was glad to get rid of them.

"I could probably lock ya up fer what yer did, whatever it was, but y'all and yer lady look like ya' ain't been in much trouble before."

He leered at Harriet and turned gruffly to Smokey, "Get outta the State pronto, or I might change my mind and lock up yer ass." He dismissed them and returned to glare at the officers.

As Smokey went to his car, the silent, young officer, just a callow kid in appearance and demeanor, followed them. With a furtive glance over his shoulder at his fellow officer who was arguing furiously with the magistrate the youth pressed into Smokey's hand a piece of paper on which he had scribbled his name and address.

"Say, when you get home, could you please send me a description of that thing on your car and where you got it?" the young patrolman requested. He gave Smokey a sheepish, imploring smile. Evidently, he saw possibilities in the device.

Back in Pennsylvania, Smokey debated whether to provide the officer with data. Finally, without a return address or even a name, he sent him specifications on not only the Slicer but also the Claw and Spears. He imagined the surprise, and, he hoped, pleasure on the young fellow's face when he digested that packet.

Smokey drove his cars until they were good only for scrap. He developed an affection for them. Once when his most successful and treasured DEV was no longer able to take to the road, Smokey, himself, drove it to the junkyard. There, a wicked looking bucket scoop was fairly drooling at the thought of smashing the DEV and dumping it on a huge pile of flattened cars. It was nothing personal, the bucket enjoyed its work and welcomed all cars that were driven the last mile to his greedy scoop.

When Smokey got out of the DEV for the last time and fondly kissed it adieu, Smokey must have left the motor on or perhaps the worn wiring of the old controls shorted. As he averted his eyes and walked away from his DEV and as the eager bucket descended, all devices of the DEV sprang to life, the Tire Spears shot in and out, the Grill Snatcher went snapping in a wide arc, the Boxing Glove jabbed and hooked, and the Slicer whirred in an ominous high whine. The DEV had triggered like a cat surprised by a terrier. And like a terrier, the bucket was transfixed in its tracks. The operator climbed out of the cab and came around to watch from a respectful distance. Nonplused, neither he nor the bucket would approach the whirling dervish of a DEV. Finally, the operator retired, came back with a stick of dynamite, lighted the fuse and threw it at the DEV, then retreated behind his cab. The DEV exploded with a roar, one instant a beautiful thing, the next a falling tinkle of glass, a painful clang of a universal joint, hubcaps and motor innards, and the soft landing of a boxing glove. The auto graveyard was silent again. The bucket, too close to the blast, had a Tire Spear stuck in its teeth. The operator quit for the day and went home.

Smokey had many adventures in his DEVs. People urged him to put the best of these in a book. Smokey did produce a manuscript for the children's trade. He thought it might make a companion book to *The Bingety-Bangety School Bus* and *The Little Engine that*

Could. Also, it would give young children lessons in the rules of the road. Smokey is still interested in finding a publisher of children's books. He visualizes a boxed set of three, retailing in the twenty-five to thirty-dollar range.

SECOND FRESHMAN FOOTBALL

In 1935 two days after registering at Harvard, Reinhard Meyerhoff went out for freshman football. His classmates found the name "Meyerhoff" an unnecessary mouthful and seeing his blond and crew-cut good looks immediately dubbed him "Dutch", a nickname that stuck for all except his mother.

Dutch's father emigrated from Germany as a young man to Canton, Ohio in the Allegheny Valley region of Pennsylvania and Ohio. Hard work and a profitable automobile dealership had rewarded him and his family with a good income.

Born in Canton, young Reinhard had an outstanding academic record in high school, Valedictorian in his class of 180 graduates. He was also good enough to make the football team. As a youngster he had dreamed of going to Ohio State or the University of Pittsburgh, football powers in the Valley that was the home of legendary quarterbacks. But his high school career as an average player ended his expectations of playing for a top college team. He still wanted to go to Ohio State but for an education, not for football.

Mr. Meyerhoff, with the brashness of early success as an immigrant, wanted the American best for his family. He was more impressed with his son's scholastic accomplishments than with his athletic prowess, although Mr. Meyerhoff, too, was an avid fan of the sports of his adopted land, preferring baseball and football to soccer. When Reinhard became a high school senior his father looked around the country at college possibilities. He learned that many Eastern colleges had excellent reputations. After investigation he picked Harvard and suggested to Reinhard that he apply there. Reinhard was surprised and doubted that he would be accepted.

"Fiddle-de-dee," said his father in his American slang, "You certainly have the grades and we can afford it. Harvard claims it wants more Midwestern and Western students, it will make a better college, they say."

Reinhard sent in his application with an essay as required along with recommendations from his teachers. He was accepted.

"Told you," chortled his father. "They want you. Why, you might even play football for Harvard. I understand they aren't what they used to be in football."

Only Mrs. Meyerhoff was dubious. She didn't say much but she came from a strong Lutheran background and would have preferred a religious college rather than an Eastern college which she had heard were free-thinking and irreligious. She was prim and silent when Reinhard boarded the train to Boston.

Reinhard, now "Dutch", went out for the freshman team because it was a duty to himself to be a scholar-athlete, a duty to the Midwest to improve Eastern football, an obligation to his father who, despite his emphasis on scholarship, would appreciate an athlete son, and finally a call to enjoy his youth. Dutch *did* like football and he had performed well, if not remarkably for Canton High School. He enjoyed the linesmen's struggle in the trenches, his Teutonic love for combat said his father.

Dutch also had an idea that he just might be able to play varsity football at an Eastern college. He would not have had a chance at Ohio State. But, he might be able to make the Harvard Varsity some day; it was worth a shot.

He responded to the announcement for football tryouts along with about a hundred other hopefuls in ill-fitting uniforms on Soldiers Field, spacious green acres that accommodated the Varsity baseball team in the spring and intramural games of all kinds throughout the year.

The freshman coach, Staley, and his staff of a half dozen men in sweat suits, gathered the group around them and Staley greeted the candidates, "I'm glad to see so many of you out for freshman football. Last year we beat the Yale freshmen and this year about ten of last year's freshmen team are on the varsity squad. The varsity had a bad season last year." Dutch had seen a film the night before at freshman orientation showing the varsity losing every game of the previous season. It was the worst season in Harvard football history, no wins, and nine losses.

"With our good freshman teams coming along and a new varsity coach," Staley told them, "we are looking forward to a winning varsity again. So give it your best in these tryouts."

The assistant coaches took over. The group was divided up by positions—ends here, tackles there, etc. Dutch took his place with eight or nine aspiring ends and an assistant coach. The coach told them to pair off and work one-on-one, taking turns blocking each other. Dutch looked over his fellow ends. At 165 pounds, Dutch was almost as large as any of them. Dutch squared off with a guy about his weight but shorter. Green was his name. Dutch assumed the down stance of an offensive end and began to practice blocks on Green who simulated the defensive tackle. Green seemed lackadaisical, he didn't try very hard, and when it was his turn, he didn't block well. Dutch showed him how to do the wheel block, an illegal maneuver that Dutch had perfected in high school. In fact, Dutch had invented the wheel block and named it. It involved planting both hands on the ground and throwing both legs sideways in an arc like a wheel, across the legs of the tackle charging through the line, thus setting up the tackle for the upper body block of the wing back. The illegal hold occurred when Dutch clamped his arm behind the tackle's leg. It was hard for the referee to detect. A penalty had never been called in Dutch's three years of wheel blocking in high school. (Editor's note: nothing about the so-called "wheel block", a cut block and leg clamp, would be legal in modern football)

On the Harvard practice field, Dutch changed blocking partners on the command of the coach. His new opponent didn't even know how to get down in an offensive stance. His butt stood straight up in the air. And when Dutch charged into him, he fell over backwards and Dutch stepped on his face, unintentionally.

During the drill there was opportunity to go one-on-one with four or five others. Dutch was impressed with only one, a big rangy guy about 6'2" and 185 pounds. When Dutch tried to wheelblock him, the big guy slapped Dutch's head into the ground, picked up Dutch's leg, and threw him on his back. "Okay," Dutch thought, "this guy is a football player, must be from Michigan or Illinois. If I had a wingback to help, we could handle him two-on-two, but he will be competition for me for a place on the team." The assistant coach, who didn't seem to be watching, did come around and ask Dutch where he had played. "Canton, Ohio," Dutch replied.

"Where's that in Ohier?" the coach inquired.

"Down the Valley from Cleveland," Dutch told him.

"Oh, that must be in Pennsylvanier, then," the coach stated without conviction.

The Easterners are weak in geography, Dutch thought. Then he had the effrontery to ask the coach, "Where are you from?"

"Came from Bunstubble," the answer sounded like, and when Dutch looked puzzled, the coach elaborated, "That's on the Cape, son. I played varsity," except he called it 'vahsity,' "at Amust and that's all you need to know." He walked away, a bit miffed. I'd probably would know where he's from, Dutch thought, if he spoke English.

If Dutch had been surprised by his first day of practice, he was shocked on the second day. Staley appeared again, surrounded by his coaches.

"Men," he announced, "we are going to divide this squad into two parts. We have a game coming up this Saturday and we have to field a team. It won't necessarily be the team that we will eventually have, but it will be the team for this Saturday. The rest of you will still have an opportunity to make the freshman squad. The other coaches and I will come down and watch your progress, and those of you who demonstrate ability will be promoted to the freshman team. So, so long for now. Work hard and enjoy this great game of football!"

With that, Staley took a ball and punted it fifty yards into a temporary field enclosed by a wooden fence, a solid fence to prevent peeping. Staley ran toward the enclosed field followed by about forty freshmen, and with a whoop and a holler, they disappeared from view inside the fence.

Dutch was stunned. No names had been called. All of those selected knew who they were. The rangy end disappeared behind the fence but so did Green, the lethargic kid that Dutch had tried to teach to wheelblock. Dutch stood with the forlorn, ragtail group that was left, bewildered, realizing that he had been cut after one day, not so much a day of practice, just a day of standing around. He had been cut without even a scrimmage.

Thus began Dutch's season with the Second Freshmen, the official designation. He never saw Staley again except at a distance. He learned that the real freshman squad had been practicing daily, invited to come two weeks before school started. However, Dutch's first reaction to his assignment to the Second Freshmen was determination. In the back of his mind he muttered, "Wait until we scrimmage and they see me block and tackle."

The Second Freshmen were a cacophonic medley of ill-sorted leftovers and never-weres, marginal players like Dutch, also big non-athletic slobs who had played for unknown high schools by standing in as guards, and little shrimps whose families thought they should "go out for football" and who were terrified by the possibility of contact. The Second Freshmen had a corps of rotating coaches, graduate students who were seldom there two days in a row and who may or may not have ever touched a football. The Second Freshmen had three plays—end run, up the middle and pass. On the basic three the players were free to improvise, in fact had to improvise. One encountered the most unusual formations and plays. In running for a pass, Dutch would suddenly discover that he was competing for the ball with a center on his own team who was an ineligible receiver. There were often three quarterbacks in the same backfield. On offense you might find yourself running against a line of anywhere from six to twelve men. The rotating graduate coaches were no help, not one of them remembering the names of more than three players from week to week.

The Second Freshmen was a team that never jelled. No one was cut but many dropped out or played only on game days. So the mob of sixty dwindled to thirty by the end of the season. In the absence of fixed assignments, five or six guys who got to know each other would form little cliques, would try to get into the game together and function as a sub-unit. In the huddle, the clique would agree that two of them would be linemen, two would be pass receivers, one would block, and you hoped the guy who was left could pass the ball. Dutch volunteered to pass despite his weak arm. In the melee that followed, with bad snaps from center, blocking linemen running into each other, the wounded ducks that Dutch threw up would have doomed any future as a Harvard football player, had the regular freshman coaches been watching, which they weren't.

Strange to say the Second Freshmen did play a schedule. Stranger yet, they won about half of their games. Their opponents were high schools and the junior varsities of prep schools like Andover and Exeter. Dutch was contemptuous of these opponents. The Canton High team would have ground them up to the tune of 50 or 60 to 0.

Dutch was astounded at his teammates, the way that many of them cried when they got hurt. In high school he couldn't remember many players who had cried, a few perhaps in rage and disappointment, perhaps one or two who may have cried with a broken leg or similar bone. But scrapes and bruises, getting the wind knocked out or a jar to the head. Not that Dutch thought he was tough. Too many ignominious defeats and retreats were a part of his past. Ah well, some of these kids were not used to head knocking. He tried to picture what they had done on Saturday mornings in the little New England towns or New York apartments they had grown up in. Gone sailing probably.

One game the Second Freshmen played Dutch will always remember. It was against a suburban Boston high school. The field was behind the school, as so many are. A crowd of several thousand was there, not one of them rooting for the Second Freshmen, a lot of them brought up to hate Harvard. Maybe the school was Catholic, or worse, a public school full of Catholics.

The Second Freshmen went by bus to the suburban high
school. When they trotted out to warm up, the field itself grabbed
their attention. Was it a football field? The site of the school and
field had been formed by filling in a portion of a valley between
two residential slopes that passed for hills in the Boston area. The
composition of the field was urban debris covered with sod. At the
50-yard line one might land on a hunk of concrete or a bicycle
chain. The landfill had not quite been completed at the football
end, probably a contractor error. The field was too short. Each end
zone was eight yards deep. At one end, it terminated at the brick
wall of the school and the school had ground level windows. The
pass receiver who went too deep, or in this case, to the back of a
normal ten-yard end zone, was in danger of going through the
glass, probably to land on a band saw in the school shop. At the
other end of the field, the land broke sharply downhill, exactly at
the back of the end zone, that was too short. Then in the left
corner, the slope became a precipitous drop into a gully, twenty
feet below. The Harvard quarterbacks and ends barely had a chance,
before the game, to look down into this canyon. They vowed not
to go near it. The shallowness of the end zone was belatedly
recognized when the captains met at midfield before the kickoff.
The referee mumbled something about "the limitations of the
playing field" but in the excitement of the pre-game huddle, the
captain-of-the-day for the Second Freshmen, a kid from the Bronx,
did not communicate this fact particularly well to Southerners on
the team. The game began and the end zone was indeed a factor.
The high school boys knew every inch of their home "turf." When
they got within the 20-yard line a rangy end would head for the
left of the end zone and in the corner would plant himself, jump,
and pull down a neat lob pass for a touchdown, then pirouette
cockily along the edge of the precipice. The Harvard defender
would be left standing, wondering whether to hit the guy as he
caught the ball, probably knocking both of them into the gully, or
to jump high and try to knock down the ball and maybe find
himself alone in a swan dive toward the beer bottles, or to decide
he was not very good on defense and let it go at that.

Dutch had his chance at defending in the left end zone after three of those touchdowns passes caught by the rangy end. The crowd cheered wildly at each of these touchdowns, handclaps mixed with guffaws. The nice boys from the parish were showing these brainy, atheistic bastards from Harvard! However, despite the three touchdowns, Harvard led 21-20. But High School was getting near the goal line again and the rangy end would have a chance for a fourth touchdown. Dutch decided that the only way to break up the pass was to cold-cock the guy before he got to the deep corner. There would be a penalty; of course, Dutch would probably be ejected from the game. But it was the fourth quarter and with the ball Harvard could grind to a touchdown and put the game out of reach of High School. So the risk was worth it.

Dutch found a medium-sized piece of brick in the rubble of the end zone and stealthily tucked it under his jersey. He did not have to conceal it long. After an ineffectual thrust into the line, the opposing quarterback faded back to pass. Dutch dropped back to the goal line, took the piece of brick from underneath his jersey, being careful to clench both fists to conceal the brick and waited for the end. However, the damned end crossed him up. He did not run for the corner. He ran straight for the goal post at the back of the end zone, did a ninety-degree turn to the left and came tight roping along the edge of the chasm. Before Dutch could react, the end gathered in a low pass and was beginning to dance along that rim of disaster. Dutch was three yards away from the reception. It was too late to hit the end with the brick and it would be useless to shoulder him into the gully. The pass was complete, the touchdown would count, and Dutch would be ejected for unsportsmanlike conduct. Disgusted, Dutch threw the brick into the gully and received a compliment from the field judge for ridding the field of a hazard. High School made the point after and led 27 to 21.

Dutch was dejected. There was no scoreboard clock but there must be only a few minutes left in the game. Dutch looked at the scoreboard and snickered. These high school teams referred to the Second Freshmen as Harvard. It would look good in the high school yearbook: Codfish High 27, Harvard 21. As they lined up for the kickoff after that last touchdown, the head linesman informed both teams that there were five minutes left to play.

Harvard took the kickoff and moved down the field, six yards, thirteen yards, penalty against Harvard for offsides, thirty-three yards on a Harvard pass but a loss of fifteen yards on the play for crawling with the ball. (Editor's note: an outmoded penalty for scooting the ball forward when tackled and lying on the ground) There would be no penalties against Codfish High at this stage of the game. "Damn that goof ball!" seethed Dutch, referring to his teammate, not the referee, "A long pass completion and that non-football player pushes the ball forward so that everybody in the stands can see him do it. Jerk!"

Harvard picked up ten yards through the middle of the Codfish line, then fifteen yards around end and the ball was on the 22-yard line, twenty-two yards away from the winning touchdown, provided they could score the extra point. "We will probably run for it," Dutch told himself. The Second Freshmen could not be expected to get a good pass from center, a good hold, and a good kick all on the same play. But time was running out and no one on the field knew if there was a time-out left. There were only three per half and that included injury time-outs. No one in his right mind would call a time-out for an injury unless he had a broken leg or was prepared to go straight to the hospital with a fractured skull. However, a time-out was called by the coaches. Someone on the Second Freshmen sideline apparently could count to three. But this was the third and final time-out.

Dutch and his teammates flopped on the ground. Dutch's mind was beginning to wander, to forget this game, and look forward to tomorrow when the real Harvard would be playing the Princeton varsity and Dutch would be watching in the stadium.

However, the Harvard graduate school coaches had been meeting on the sidelines. There were some ten coaches that day, it being Friday, and all graduate students in need of pocket money for the weekend. They were paid only when they showed up. It seems that the ten coaches had been meeting during the Second

Freshmen drive and had come up with a play. They illegally signaled the captain-of-the-day to call time out. Fortunately, the captain had been looking in their direction. Now a substitute came in with information from the coaches.

The sub began explaining to the quarterback-of-the-day the strategy of the board of coaches. Ears perked up as the team overheard the sub's instructions. The coaches had indeed come up with a brilliant strategy, nothing less than turning the tables on this high school crew. Harvard would flood the forbidden left corner of the end zone, at the edge of the precipice, with five receivers. It was a perfectly conceived play. High School counted on visiting teams staying away from the left corner of the end zone, like stags at a dance sniffing the ugly wallflowers. On defense, High School didn't even bother to send a man there. The sheer audacity of the play appealed to the Harvard men, brawn cum intellect. The team smiled approvingly. The quarterback-of-the-day had a good arm. The teams lined up, atheists against nice parish boys. The ball was snapped.

Two ends and three backs, the maximum number of eligible receivers, took off for the left corner. Since the quarterback had no protection, he back-pedaled furiously and, as he fell on his butt, threw the ball up in a high arc. It drifted down, more like a seagull having a heart attack than a football. The five receivers were waiting at the edge of the end zone, the chasm a step behind them. No one had been designated a prime receiver, no time for such precision. All five soared high to meet the plummeting football. The Codfish defenders wisely stayed out of it. The receivers came down in quintuple, clutching at the football and each other, down, down, four of them and the ball disappearing into the gully, the fifth man knocked forward to the solid ground of the end zone. The dying pass, alas, had wobbled a bit too far. Dutch was playing guard or tackle, whatever, on this play because Harvard wanted its fastest men as receivers. When Dutch looked up and saw the four bodies disappear, he was appalled. It reminded him of Dante's Inferno which he was reading about in Freshman English. The Pit of Hell had opened up and swallowed four football players.

The teams, coaches, and most of the fans rushed to the edge of the crater fearing the worst or hoping for the best, depending upon whether they were High School or Harvard. They saw two receivers sitting at the bottom of the pit fingering their noses and ears, and beginning to bleed slowly from abrasions and lacerations. The slope was full of cinders. The other two men were fighting over the ball, in full agreement that the pass had been caught but disagreeing completely over who caught it. The issue became moot because the referee disallowed the touchdown, ruling that both receivers were out of the end zone. The coaches screamed that allowance should be made for the eight-yard, too-short end zone. They got nowhere.

The gun had sounded. The game was over. The officials disappeared. The crowd jeered Harvard. There was nothing left for the Second Freshmen to do but grumble and climb aboard the bus, the showers in the visitor's locker room had no water.

For a good half-hour it was a silent ride back to Cambridge. Then a few began to laugh and most others joined in. A boisterous busload of Second Freshman pulled into Harvard Square. That game was both the high point and the low point of the season, high for those who came out of it unscathed and began to ruminate humorously on the topography of the Codfish field, and low for the ends and backs who tried to explain to friends back in the dorms how all four of them had been cut and bruised on the same play while simultaneously catching, maybe, a touchdown pass, maybe, at the bottom of a gully.

For all their ineptitude, the Second Freshmen had some good athletes. One man later pitched for the varsity baseball team, another had a two-year stint with the Boston Red Sox during World War II. The coaches for the Freshmen Varsity were true to their word, after a fashion, and several times looked in on the Second Freshmen. This was usually when nothing was happening. In low tones they would talk to the graduate school coaches, whoever happened to be there that day. Late in November, one of the second freshmen got elevated to the Freshman Varsity. He was a small quarterback, sort of cocky and fast. Dutch didn't think he was much of a football player. However, Dutch discovered his speed when Dutch was playing end on defense in a scrimmage. The flashy kid came wide around Dutch on several end runs and twice got upfield, Dutch's fault, of course. But the kid, besides being too light, too mouthy, and with a Groton accent, had no stomach for contact. In a scrimmage one day the kid came out toward Dutch at end with the option to lateral to the wingback. He lateraled, but not in time to keep Dutch from burying his helmet in the kid's gut. The budding quarterback deflated like a punctured balloon and lay on the ground puking and retching for ten minutes. When the guy was promoted to the Freshmen Varsity, Dutch saw no more of him because the Second Freshmen had no opportunity to see the Freshmen Varsity, that is, unless they went to see them play on Saturday mornings, which Dutch didn't. Two years later when Dutch was a junior he saw the kid again at a Harvard Varsity game. Dutch was a spectator in the stadium. In a game hopelessly lost, Dutch's former teammate, the kid from Groton, was inserted at tailback. He got the ball and scampered around end for all of two yards and didn't get up. He was carried off as the crowd murmured its sympathy. Dutch did not care. The kid was a phony as a football player. Dutch never saw him again at Harvard or anywhere. He forgot the kid's name.

Freshmen lived in the enclosed Harvard Yard but as sophomores most Harvard men chose to live in the seven new Houses along the Charles, 300-man dormitories, each with its own dining hall, library, tutors, social life, dances, and athletic teams. Dutch applied for and was accepted by Winthrop House. Dutch learned that there was more to life than football—there was basketball, baseball, even softball, tennis, and some fifteen or sixteen sports that the excellent intramural program offered at Harvard. The teams were organized by and represented the Houses.

Dutch found satisfaction in playing intramural football for Winthrop House. He no longer felt the competitive pressure of high school football, or the frustration of the Second Freshmen team. For the first time since schoolyard days, Dutch could play for fun. There were a few marginal athletes on the Winthrop House team who, like Dutch, played for the exercise. Dutch could laugh at the antics of the inept. No one hit very hard. No one cared a lot. It was just like the playing fields of Eton, gentlemen scholars taking a break from serious study. Dutch was the quarterback of all things, and threw several touchdown passes. Dutch also played basketball and softball for the House.

Winthrop was known as the jock House, none of the effete intellectuals of some other houses. It was the chosen House of the Kennedys with the famous father who was Ambassador to England. In Winthrop House was Joe Kennedy's eldest son, Joe, Jr. who was captain of the Harvard varsity football team and younger brother, Jack, who was a varsity swimmer.

POINT COUNTERBLAM

He liked Mozart and the classical; she liked the Stones and hard rock. They lived in adjacent apartments and they both wanted to hear all the subtleties of their own music on their respective stereos. They didn't know each other and, of course, did not speak. It began without malice, but as the spring gave way to summer and windows stayed open, the contest was undeniable. His Chopin mazurka, wafting into the evening breeze, would be met head on by her James Brown's *Papa's Got a Brand New Bag*. Her Springsteen's *Thunder Road*, seeking the outdoors, would cut off the tail of his Brahms violin concerto; his Beethoven *Eroica* would be imposed on her *Yellow Submarine*. By August his *1812 Overture* with belching cannon could scarcely be heard over her ear-shattering Guns In Roses' *Welcome to the Jungle*.

They worked different hours. She went to work earlier and came home earlier. In the mornings she left for work grinding her teeth to his sickening melodies of Schubert and Strauss. In the evenings he would arrive home to an apartment saturated with Beatles and reeking of Madonna. It took fifteen minutes to purify the air with Brandenburg Concertos.

Once her stereo broke down and there was a week that she was hors de combat. He made the most of it, giving her Sutherland screeching at the top of her form, Callas twisting in the knife. Realizing she was at his mercy, he played soft German lieder and sadistically turned the volume down. She could only strain her ear against their common wall to detect his instruments of torture. When her record player was back in service he was almost glad that the battle was on again. Once they shared an elevator in the building. Her look told the story, a tight-lipped disdain for the way that he had musically raped her, satisfaction in the knowledge that he was a musical chauvinist pig, and determination that it would never happen again.

The stand-off continued for weeks. Then he stopped playing, he wanted to rest his esthetic sensorium. More accurately, the battle was wearing him thin. Unchallenged, her spirits rose. The Grateful Dead, the Rolling Stones, and Genesis boomed joyfully throughout and outside her apartment. But unaccountably, her enthusiasm flagged. While biting her nails one day she was seized by the horrible truth. She could no longer enjoy the strong rhythms of David Bowie without a soft accompaniment of DeBussy strings. The Dead sounded dull without competing timpani. She missed the French horn, the rich viola, the dry tinkle of the harpsichord. Finally, her annoyance could not be contained. "Is your stereo broken?" she blurted to him in the hallway.

"No!" he shot back, his lip curling superciliously.

She tried again, "Are you moving?"

"No, ... actually," he intoned, "I'm planning to stay here a long, long time." It sounded threatening. He was so indecently self-assured.

"Damn his eyes," she thought, "of all the possible neighbors I could have had, why does it have to be this bastard?"

She more or less put him out of her mind. "If he doesn't want to play, OK!" But one evening she became aware that there were no sounds from next door, no doors opening or shutting, nothing. At the apartment house desk she was told he was in the hospital. Probably a bad case of the clap, she mused, from one of those angular uptown broads who like to have balls with their Bolero.

Later she knew he was home from the hospital by the banging in his kitchen. But there was no sign of his going and coming, a long convalescence and no music. Then for two days there was not a squeak from next door. She inquired at the desk if he were back in the hospital. The clerk decided he wasn't.

She wondered, "Is it possible that a bad case of the clap can be fatal? Ridiculous!" But she had heard how single people often died in apartments and are not discovered for days. She sniffed at his door for an odor of putrefaction, smelling something like burned cabbage and dirty socks. At last she surrendered her pride. The Jewish mother in her put Campbell's chicken soup on the stove over a low fire and, thus prepared, she knocked imperiously on his door. "After all," she rationalized," even your classical snob doesn't deserve to have his pecker rot off without someone to empathize."

He opened the door looking perfectly healthy. "I smelled gas," she snarled, "thought you might have fallen asleep and were going to blow us all to Hell!" He checked his burners, came back and assured her that all was well. She stood there with her bare face hanging out, left without a leg to stand on but she tried anyway, partly succeeding.

"Well, I heard you were in the hospital," she said, planning to exit gracefully.

"Yes, I was!" he confirmed, "Hemorrhoids, you know."

She nearly retched at this intimacy from a man she didn't know, except she knew she did know all about him. Musically, he was an open book full of blank pages.

"Won't you please come in?" he offered and swear-to-God he made a half-assed courtly bow like someone out of *The Three Musketeers*. In a fog she stumbled forward while he wondered to himself, "Why is this dumpy broad asking me about my hemorrhoids?"

Yes, she would accept just one cup of coffee. At the coffee table, he waxed eloquent on the miseries of hemorrhoids. He squirmed in the chair. "No class," she gr1maced.

"Maybe it was the bike last summer," he explained, "rough roads in New Mexico." Then he asked her directly," Do you think that motorcycles can cause hemorrhoids?"

She would have guffawed in his face but she didn't want to encourage his lowbrow humor. "I haven't the most elemental," she assured him stiffly, "I've never been on a motorcycle and I'm not a rectal expert."

"You could have fooled me," he confided, then coloring, added quickly, "I mean I could have sworn you were used to motorbikes."

"Couldn't get me on one," she told him.

He extolled the virtues of motorcycles, worrying her like a

Jehovah's Witness attempting a conversion. Her eyes glazed over when his motor failed on the climb up Pike's Peak and he had it all disassembled at the summit.

"I got it back together because—," he wanted to convince her, "because I had all the parts laid out in the exact order I had taken them apart in. You know, if you do that, that is, lay them out in the same order as you take them apart in, the parts will go together, that is, they will go together in the same way you took them apart." She contemplated his verbal disaster and he hung his head.

"Why did you take the parts apart? Was all that necessary to get the damned motor started?" she wanted to know.

He realized that he had stumbled into the quagmire of female mechanical ignorance, so he contented himself with the observation, "Well, I did get the engine together," and ended triumphantly, "and here I am, living proof."

They gazed at each other across the chasm separating male from female logic. Suddenly, a smell like burning feathers drifted in from the corridor. She made a dash for the boiling chicken soup in her apartment and he followed. The soup had gone all over the stove. In her apartment he noted Matisse prints and a Picasso sketch of mother and child. When order was restored in the kitchen and she joined him over coffee, he remarked, "I never would have thought that you lived here."

She struggled with that but it eventually came clear that he had no idea that Matisse and Madonna could co-exist in the same apartment. Over wine they explored this and their other incompatibilities in each of their respective apartments but reached no significant conclusions.

She gave him a comprehensive course in world art from the drawings on the wall in the caves of France, through the Greek appreciation of the human form, the architecture of the Eternal City of Rome, the icons of the Greek Orthodox Church in every city and little hamlet in Russia, the Renaissance awakening of Michelangelo, Leonardo, Raphael, the treatment of light by Vermeer and the Dutch School, even the realism of the New York painters of the Hudson River School. He whistled at Whistler's Mother, he was indignant at the barbaric German School of Duhrer and his followers. He tried to appreciate the deadly dullness of the neo-classicists like Delacroix. The French landscape painters appealed to his bucolic nature on his mother's side, she had been born on a farm. He was ready for Manet and Monet and other impressionists. He exclaimed over the contrasting spires of Chartres Cathedral and applauded the lacy soaring of Rheims. He learned the pivotal role of Cezanne and rejoiced over Van Gogh's sunflowers. He was a sucker for Picasso's blue, rose, and classical periods. He loved Picasso until they came to the bulls and she could not convince him that it was more than the tired maunderings of a disillusioned and thoroughly commercialized hack. She quickly switched to the tranquilities of Matisse. He did well with the abstractionists like DeKooning, he accepted Jackson Pollack, Mondrian and their kind. His spirits rose higher with the emergence of Andy Warhol, Edward Hopper and the pure American magic of his *Night Watch*.

On her part she discovered that he fulfilled all three of her requirements for a husband:(l) He had killed a bear. In these days it is almost impossible to kill a bear. In this country they are a protected species. One would have to leave the country to kill a bear, someplace like Siberia or Chile. So one must accomplish an equivalent feat. For him it was not an animal bear but the human grizzly bear of his boss that he "killed." He politely asked for the raise to which he was entitled and was turned down, was disdainful of the efforts to get him back, joined a rival firm and promptly gave them all the secrets of his former workplace. (2) Knowing she was weaker than he and that they were bound to lose their tempers with each other, he permitted her to beat on him without hitting her back. He was a thoroughly civilized gentleman. When she noted to him his obvious refraining from retaliation, he merely smiled and said she couldn't hurt him anyway, gritting his teeth and massaging his jaw as he said it. (3) He kissed a baby that was not a blood relative. When her best friend arrived with a new husband and a new baby he took the baby in his arms, kissed it, patted it on the forehead, and mistakenly tried to get it to walk.

Its mother seized the child and stopped its crying but he had successfully passed the three tests. He would make a good father.

These vital matters resolved they lapsed into small talk which in the ensuing weeks became smaller and smaller. In due time he proposed and she accepted, or she proposed and he accepted, whatever, they arrived at an understanding and were married. The marriage service was strained, a Jewish service with Protestant undertones. At the reception the quartet of musicians was almost driven crazy by the mixture of light classical and Jewish cantor. To complete matters, the two families sniffed at each other more than is customary at weddings.

The couple had one child in ten months and others at decent intervals. She accepted rides on his motorcycle, then got a bike for herself and learned to do her own maintenance. He mastered the art of diapering in squirming, standing and climbing modes and took no offense at the circumcision of his man-children. Sometimes, in his affected Irish brogue, he would tell friends how they had happened to meet. He developed a reputation as a Scot who laughed uproariously at his own stories. She laughed, too, but it was more at his fractured brogue than anything else.

The moral of this story is: "strange music makes good bedfellows" or should it be "strange bedfellows make good music?" Or possibly—Oh, just drop it!

HOW TO COOK A DUCK

Succulent duck, good for any meal, is particularly welcome for elderly couples and other families who might like a treat on holidays, for Christmas or Easter dinner, perhaps. The traditional huge turkey or capon can be intimidating to small appetites. Then there are those who prefer moist, dark meat to the dry, crumbly white meat of turkey and capon. Roast duck also can be a gourmet surprise for one's young newly-wed guests who might be tempted to think that older couples can only go out for tasteless, carrot-and-pea early bird specials or sit at home and eat pizza delivered by bicycle.

Good cooking does not always come easily. Succulent duck does take time to prepare. First, erase from your mind the memory of the greasy, fatty dish called in many restaurants, "Long Island Duckling." The presence of orange sauce only compounds this disaster.

There is a cardinal rule in preparing duck—GET RID OF THE FAT—that's standard in NUTRITION 101. Fortunately, roast duck is improved, nay, its distinctive flavor made possible by removing the fat. There are two ways of doing this: the first and time-consuming but best way is to slice around the thawed-out breast, detach and slice back the skin, and remove the fat with a knife or poultry shears, the same with the legs, neck and back. Then restore the flaps of skin, skewering as necessary. This preparation will take about an hour, but it is worth every minute of it, unless you are one of those impatient cooks who never takes time to skin the squid, take the veins out of the jumbo shrimp, or who has never peeled and charred a roasted, green pepper. Cook the bird uncovered as any other fowl and the result will be a golden tender duck which will slice like a Thanksgiving turkey but taste three times as good, nice, moist but not greasy slices, with or without orange sauce. If sauce is desired it should always be made with fresh orange juice, see *The Good Housekeeping Cookbook*, 7th Edition, Revised, page 597: Hard Sauce, Orange.

The second way to prepare duck is much faster but there are definite hazards to this method. The technique is to punch holes all over the skin of the duck with an ice pick in order to let the heated fat melt and drain out as you roast. You will discover that there is a great amount of fat to melt. If the duck is placed in a shallow pan, as seems logical, the pan must be taken from the oven a number of times during cooking and emptied. One can see the danger of emptying the hot fat into another receptacle on the pulled-down oven door. But this absolutely must be done several times for there is even greater danger by letting the fat accumulate and rise to a high temperature—a flash fire in the oven.

If you simply want to enjoy roast duck, stop here and get busy in the kitchen. "Bon appetite!" Have you ever heard that expression used, either the English "appetite" or the French "appeteet?" Both certainly are better than the "enjoy" that a frumpy waitress throws at you as she scurries away from your table.

Continue reading if you'd like to hear a story of what could happen, not likely, but could happen, to a cook using the second method of preparation, punching holes in the duck's skin. Stop here or read on, as you prefer.

For continuing, intrepid readers, this account involves Smokey Maggart, yes, the same Smokey who modifies old cars. Somehow, it isn't surprising to hear that Smokey said one day that he once used the second quicker method of defatting the duck, punching holes in the skin. Smokey frequently says that a straight line is the shortest distance between two points. He often takes the shortest way home when he'd be better advised to take the sure and longer way around. People have said that Smokey lacks judgment. His wife takes a body bag when they go on a trip that has beautiful scenery and sheer cliffs to gaze from. Admittedly, Smokey is a stimulating companion and can, be amusing in relating his "hair-raising" escapades. Indeed, some are inclined to think

Smokey is more interesting for the slight whiff of danger that he brings to a drive in his car.

Be that as it may, Smokey confesses that for such a prosaic job as defatting a duck, he made a major mistake in judgment. Some people may find his story funny. That depends on one's perspective, perhaps one's sense of humor, possibly one's warped sense of humor. Others sigh and say the tale is even a little sad.

Smokey considers himself a busy man and wished to save time in cooking his duck. He also wanted to impress his son and French wife who prides herself on her French cuisine and cooking skills. Smokey invited them to dinner to savor his duck. He poked sizable holes in the duck with his ice pick, slid the duck into the oven in a roasting pan, and sat down to his computer. He resumed work on his autobiography, having reached that certain age when autobiography is a temptation. He was near page 600 and had barely got out of high school in Flint, Michigan, his hometown. Concise story-telling is not Smokey's forte.

The duck sizzled happily in the kitchen and Smokey typed happily in the living room, just a few steps away so that he could keep an eye on the kitchen. His eyes remained alert but, unfortunately, his ears failed him. Absorbed in the nostalgic recreation on paper of his own adolescence, Smokey lost contact with the outside world. Too late did Smokey hear the *comforting crackling* of draining duck fat replaced by a *steady roar*. It took an additional forty-five seconds or so to identify the roar as burning fat. Smokey responded with alacrity but tardily; he dashed to the oven and opened the door to find inside a raging inferno with tongues of flame darting out into the kitchen. He slammed the door shut and with great presence of mind phoned the front desk for help. With no mind at all Smokey barked, "Bring a fire extinguisher," forgetting there was one right outside his apartment door. The Apartment Manager, spurning the elevator, arrived on the run from six floors below carrying an extinguisher. Smokey rushed the Manager, Ken, into the kitchen, then seized the oven door, threw open the door and told Ken to start squirting. Smokey forgot that in the few seconds since he had first opened the oven door the oven handles had reached a blistering temperature. He seared his hands. The extinguisher smothered the blaze in about a minute. However, burning duck fat produces a copious, dense, black smoke that filled the apartment in seconds and seeped quickly into the hall. Ken left to call the Fire Department and direct it, maybe divert it, from the scene of the extinguished fire. The smoke was so intense that Smokey, choking and spluttering, had to open all three windows to avoid asphyxiation. The Fire Department, long nervous about the old building with some five hundred residents, got there without delay, sirens screaming and with dropped-off and unwinding hoses leaving a trail in the street.

The smoke from the sixth floor windows alarmed the Battalion Commander as he arrived on the street below. He instantly directed the operator of the cherry-picker to hoist his bucket to the smoking windows of Smokey's apartment. Smokey heard the bucket of the cherry-picker bumping along the building, and rushed to the window, staring into the face of a fuzzy-cheeked fireman in rescue mode and starting to crawl into the apartment. Smokey restrained the young man, pleading that the fire was out and now that the smoke was escaping there was really no need to evacuate anybody. Reluctantly, the fireman desisted and the cherry-picker retracted downward.

Despite Smokey's best efforts to keep his door closed, the hall also filled with smoke and the Manager and others would not let Smokey's girlfriend, Harriet, the apartment Rental Agent, go up to see Smokey. He was glad they did not let her for he didn't want her running down the hall alongside firemen with upraised axes that Smokey knew were on the way. The apartment management restrained her, afraid that she would be asphyxiated, or at least claim that her lungs had been damaged. The management was extremely nervous about lawsuits. They had every right to be in this old building. The fire exits did not comply with the building code even for renovated buildings, an oversight of City Licenses and Inspections. The Manager had to remind them of their needed oversight every year by visiting their office in City Hall and leaving fifty dollars to jog their memories. In those days, Philadelphia was *not*, I say *not*, noted for its municipal rectitude. But one had to "play the game" and fifty dollars was a pittance compared to the thousands that would have been required to meet the code. Some engineers even said it was architecturally impossible to meet the code; they advised tearing the building down and starting over. Engineers don't give a damn for historical landmarks. It would have been irresponsible to tear down this building, Chestnut Hall. It had been built in the 1920's when West Philadelphia was an elite residential area. Imogene Cocoa was born there and undoubtedly others who had gone on to fame. The building had attracted society with its unobstructed view of the Schuykill River, hosting weddings, debutante balls and political scheming, and had weathered many name changes from its original, The Pennsylvania Hotel, finest residential hotel in Philadelphia.

Smokey had another worry. He knew that firemen would be inside the building, running down the hall with fire axes at the ready and he was afraid that in the murky smoke they would smash his computer with their axes. Then he heard them outside his door. He flung open the door and barred the way. He was right. Two firemen with axes were ready to batter down his door. Luckily, they did not swing and decapitate him. He calmed them, took them in, and showed them that all danger had passed. He showed them his computer. In the kitchen, the oven door was open, exposing the charred remains of the duck, with tender little pieces of duck clinging to oven wire shelves. Then the fire alarm finally went off in the hall. Residents of the building were quite accustomed to the fire alarm, a huge blatting noise that might arouse them any hour of day and night. Because of the defects of the building the alarms had been made extra sensitive. Many of the alarms were false; many went off for minor accidents such as burned toast. The smoke detectors, wired to the alarms were so sensitive that cigarette smoke from apartments behind closed apartment doors would set them off, as would steam from the laundry rooms. Smokey did not broil a steak without throwing open all the windows. Often alarms sounded in the middle of the night. Residents were supposed to file down the fire stairs at every alarm. Most residents had learned to ignore the two A.M. blatting, to turn over and go back to sleep. Only the retarded folk of Elwyn Institute who lived at Chestnut Hall were obliged by their resident counselors to file out into the street in all kinds of weather.

In the present instance, Smokey couldn't suppress a rueful smile at the alarm sounding after the fire was out. The tension over, Smokey sat down at the kitchen table with the firemen. Smokey started to put his blistered hands in cold water but a fireman stopped him, "bear the pain as long as you can without putting your hands in water. It will make them worse." Smokey could not understand why a fireman whose business is fires and their serious aftermath would not know that the recommended modern treatment is to immerse burns in cold water immediately. Smokey was impatient for the firemen to leave so that he could ice his hands.

The fireman sat at the table while the Battalion Commander did his paper work. It took some time. Smokey could not understand why so much reporting was required about a fire that was out when they got there and which they had absolutely nothing to do with. Finally, they did leave. Smokey thanked them profusely, for what he was not sure, except that they had not smashed his computer.

Smokey got ice water for his hands. Too late, the blisters were great liquid-filled sacs along his fingers and inner palms where he had grabbed the red-hot stove handle. Smokey called his son and canceled the dinner date. Smokey and Harriet got busy on the soot that covered everything. Looking at the black soot in every nick, cranny, and wall surface in every room, Smokey, with a mirthless ironic laugh burst out to Harriet, "Maybe they should call me 'Sooty' instead of 'Smokey'." The stove was a lost cause, burned out. The yellow paint in the kitchen responded to soap, water, and Brillo pad but looked streaky. The green walls in the living room looked passable after scrubbing. The worst problem was the books in the bookcases, the exposed edges covered with soot.

Smokey and Harriet worked into the night. Next morning

Building Maintenance came and picked up the stove, laughing a little bit as they did so. It was the first of many titters, some of them behind Smokey's back. There seemed to be something inherently funny about Smokey's misfortune with the duck. As if nobody has ever before tried to cook a duck and fired up an apartment.

That weekend with Smokey's blisters ripe and hands still throbbing, he and Harriet went to a cookout at a nephew's party in the suburbs. There was almost no sympathy for Smokey's blisters, but hardly contained merriment at the very idea of burning a duck.

Smokey couldn't understand why his trauma was so falling-down-on-the-floor funny. Was it the sight of, later the thought of, his blistered hands? Or, maybe there is something inherently funny about ducks. An old-time comedian, Joe Penner, used to get a laugh by carrying around a quacking duck and asking his audience, "Want to buy a duck?" Smokey thought about carrying a duck, in this case a wooden, decoy duck, because the apartment didn't allow live ducks. And he would change the chant to "How *not* to *cook* a duck."

He became a kind of legend around the apartment, something to tell a prospective new tenant, demonstrating that life was not all grim in inner city. The management never charged Smokey for the ruined stove, as they were entitled to do. They installed a new and better stove. In fact, every time something happened to a furnishing in that apartment house, the new item was an upgrade. Otherwise, one could live forever with rugs with holes, refrigerators that wouldn't cool properly, cracked light fixtures, etc. To get a new paint job, one had to leave the furniture in the hall and go to a hotel for two nights or else just move out for good. Even moving to a different apartment in the same building wouldn't do the trick, "Too long for the paint to dry, new tenants are scheduled to come in the day after the former tenants leave." So much for modern property management that tries for "zero" downtime.

Considering the mileage that everyone got out of Smokey's burnt duck, Smokey did not feel at all embarrassed by getting for free a new stove and the wall repainted by the apartment house management. It was maybe five year's later when Smokey and Harriet moved away from the apartment that Smokey had occasion to take some large items to the basement where they could be put in storage for sale or use by the tenants. In the basement he happened to see the ruined stove, still there for some reason, but even more remarkable, with bits of cooked duck still clinging to the oven shelves.

The story of the duck has a lively place in the family's dredged up history, good for a holiday chuckle. It has been used to indicate that Smokey is really not much of a cook, and, yes, by those very people who benefit most from his culinary skills. Harriet has expressly forbidden Smokey to cook another duck. His protests of having learned a lesson and his promises to use the first method are unavailing. Harriet makes threats and considers alternative lives, unspecific but nevertheless scary. Smokey has considered defying her and cooking another duck but it has been some twelve years and he has not asserted himself. Oh well, life is unfair, more to the point, women are unfair. What else is new?

THE ENCHANTED MESA—
How to Obtain a View

from the Enchanted Mesa, R. Climbed It to the Top and Down Again, and Later Managed to Conduct a Sheep Tally, Survive a Threat to Have his Throat Cut, Helped to Put Out a Fire in a Desert Cabin just as the Well Ran Dry, Observed the Arsonist from a Secret Vantage Point, Listened on the Radio to the Beginning of World War II—all in One Day, September 1, 1939. This Story would have been a Deal Longer if It had Continued to the Time that R. Testified, at a much Later Date, in the Arson Trial in Sante Fe that the Main Defense Witness was Perjuring Himself because R. Knew that the Line of Sight was Blocked from the Enchanted Mesa to the Cabin of Range Rider Humphrey, R. Failing to Convince the Jury because of the Indian Interpreter's Too Lengthy Translation of the Monosyllabic Words of Two Indian boys who could Speak English but instead Chose to Testify in their Native Indian Tongue and how a Second Trial Convinced the Prosecuting Attorney that the Case was Hopeless.

The Enchanted Mesa is in New Mexico, one of the first states to make a claim on its automobile license plates, "New Mexico— Land of Enchantment." The Enchanted Mesa, the postcard says, is a 600-foot butte rising from the desert floor on the Acoma Indian Reservation, its vertical sides all around preventing ascent to the top. In Indian lore the Mesa is the secret dwelling place of the Gods and is enchanted and unassailable.

The Mesa is about thirty miles off old Route 66, the highway the Okies, Iowans, and other Midwesterners took to California to escape the Dust Bowl, leaving their farms in ruins and bidding the sheriff and banks to do as they wished with their homesteads. The trek westward also opened up California as a good place to live.

The Enchanted Mesa cannot be seen from Route 66; it must be approached by car on a dusty unmarked road where one must concentrate to keep from losing the roadway and becoming disoriented and lost on the trackless range. R. was intrigued by the Mesa even before he had seen it. R. had hoped to take his car to the summit. R. knew the road would be narrow but R. was excited by the opportunity to show off his newly-acquired driving skills.

The man called "R." by the Indians, his parents, siblings, friends, almost everybody, was christened Ralston Murtaugh. His baby sister, Frances, could not pronounce his name, mustering only a growl, "Gr-r-r." She settled on "R." which his parents thought was cute and began calling him "R." So did others in his life and "R." stuck like glue.

R., fresh out of college and newly-appointed trainee in the Department of Interior, Federal Government, had been assigned as a Field Aide to the United Pueblos Indian Agency in Albuquerque. He arrived in Washington, D.C. by train for a week's indoctrination by the Bureau of Indian Affairs in the Interior Department, thence by invitation of Larry Stevens, another Field Aide from Harvard, and his wife, Steffie, to Albuquerque in their convertible.

They left D.C. at dawn and drove through Maryland on U.S. 50 on a sparkling June day. On to Ohio, they rolled across the wrinkled underbelly of the lower Midwest, snaked through ramshackle Missouri, picking up the famous Route 66, then through the poverty-stricken but eerily beautiful Ozarks of Arkansas, and broke out serenely on the baking plains of Oklahoma. Next, as they crossed the Texas Panhandle, R.'s first evening in the West, the sun put on a display—a gold-plated sky slowly turning to a scarlet smudge in the crystal clear air. They glided through Texas towns with only one street like a movie set, neon lights slightly more garish than the yellows, reds, and greens of the outcroppings of rock on the broken plain. The land was bare, placid, and strange to R. with its buttes, mesas, twists, and jagged edges. He would have felt more at home if he had been whisked clear to Los Angeles and the movie capital, Hollywood. The range became drier and the cattle scarcer as the travelers entered New Mexico and arrived in Albuquerque on the third day of their journey.

The Harvard Aides joined their fellows who had preceded them by train, seven Field Aides in the present class, two from California. They were the second class in the nascent program to improve administration in the Federal bureaucracy by on-the-job training. Most of the first class of last year was still in Albuquerque.

Albuquerque was the size of R.'s hometown, New Albany, Indiana, 30,000 plus. It lay along the Rio Grande River, which was no larger than New Albany's Silver Creek in a spring freshet, yet it was the most important river in New Mexico, its irrigation the lifeline of the farming industry. Route 66 ran straight through the heart of downtown Albuquerque, was named Central Avenue and, with a swerve, went over the Rio Grande bridge and up a long ten-mile grade to the rim of the tableland overlooking the Rio Grande Valley.

After learning to drive a car which R. had neglected to do in the first twenty-two years of his life, mainly because his family was without one, R.'s first assignment was to go to the Acoma Reservation and live about a month with Range Rider Humphrey, and his wife, in a cabin on the reservation. The Humphrey cabin was a mile or two from the Acoma Pueblo that was on top of a mesa overlooking the broad, dry plain. As a Range Rider, Humphrey's job was to assist the Indians in management of their cattle and sheep. Currently, it meant supervision of a program to reduce overgrazing and to permit the recovery of the arid, barren plain. At the time of the original pioneers it was a lush grassy field supporting thousands of buffalo.

R. was assigned a car and could return to Albuquerque on weekends but otherwise was to stay with and observe Humphrey go about his work with and assistance to the impoverished Indians. At the Agency garage in Albuquerque the Supervisor assigned R. what he knew to be the oldest car in the fleet, a Ford sedan with over 200,000 miles on it. R. knew it was oldest because he had worked at the garage while he was learning to drive.

R. drove to Acoma early on Sunday to be ready for work on Monday. The Humphrey cabin was about twenty miles off Route 66 on a dirt road on the way to Acoma Village. A fork in the road led to a rather secluded spot where Humphrey and his wife lived. R. found the fork and turned off on tire tracks that served for a road. The tracks wound among little hillocks at the foot of the Enchanted Mesa which rose vertically from the plain, some six hundred feet of brown-yellow-reddish rock straight up, like a gigantic sandstone sugar cube tossed nonchalantly on the Earth at the Beginning of Time. The Mesa was a stark unyielding wall. The rock wall made R. realize that his hoped for drive by automobile to the summit was ridiculous, and so was any intention to climb it on foot. R. strained to view the Mesa as he drove by it, excited at his first view of the Mesa, swiveling his head around and looking back to see the top rim of the Mesa out the car window.

(It is necessary at this point that the flow of the narrative be interrupted to set the record straight concerning the base canard which gained currency from an incident occurring as R. approached the Humphrey cabin. A tissue of falsehoods was concocted about R. and his driving that became a veritable mythology of lies and misinterpretations.

First, the MYTHOLOGY:

>R. hit the only surviving tree in New Mexico.
>
>There is a stone with a bronze plaque on the Acoma Indian Reservation marking the spot where the tree is or was.
>
>R. hit the tree because he was driving carelessly, cockily, looking backward at the Enchanted Mesa when he should have been looking forward.
>
>R. destroyed a government car because it was not his own property and R. didn't give a damn about the expense to the Federal Government.

After the confusing events in the afternoon of the same day there was the weirdest of additions to the MYTHOLOGY:

> It was expanded to say that R. was living in an "evil spirit world", he sees phantoms which make it impossible for him to function, caused him to bungle the sheep count and then, when a young Indian man had asked him if he thought his throat should be cut because of the wrong number of sheep that he had reported, R. refused to change the count. R. also said, in pure spite, that Indian food was no good and probably rotten.

The Indian youths maintained that for an Anglo, the man they call R. spoke very poor English or silly English, probably as a result of the phantoms he sees. He says the Sacred Mesa is "gleaming" when he must mean "shining", he says the Sacred Mesa is itself a "phantom" and calls it a "she"; he says this delights him, meaning what? Further he says he wants to eat the Mesa for daily food.

The two Indian boys said they overheard all this as R. talked on the telephone to his friends in Albuquerque and the boys reported it to the Chief of the Acoma tribe. Now everyone has heard it. The Chief said if R. was an Indian making these insane remarks he would be committed to an institution. The Chief is fearful that R.'s lies will cost the Acoma tribe thousands of sheep. Dr. Aberle, the Indian Agent in Albuquerque, will believe her own employee. It shows that Washington's effort to give the tribes greater independence, a New Deal for the Indian, as promised by President Franklin Delano Roosevelt, is being destroyed by their agents in Albuquerque and that the only good white man is a dead white man.

Now back to reality and away with the MYTHOLOGY. What actually happened? The FACTS are as follows:

> R. *did* hit a small tree in a government car. It was a car fully depreciated and in service beyond its normal life. It

would have been no great loss if the car had been totally
demolished which it was not. The small tree suffered
only a slight gash. Actually the so-called tree was not a
tree but just an overgrown bush.

R. was driving on a road that no one could be expected to
drive without, sooner or later, such an incident as R.'s.
The road was an accident waiting to happen. It is a
miracle that Humphrey had not hit that tree, or maybe
he had, the tree looked battered.

Specifically, the "road" was only a tire track across the open
range. Further, it had *two deep ruts* baked in the sun until hard as
iron. Another "road" with similar *deep ruts* intersected the first
road at a 90' angle. The "tree" was growing right at the corner of
the intersection, one branch overhanging both "roads." With car
wheels in the hard as iron *deep ruts* as it arrived at the intersection,
R. may just as descriptively be said to have *bounced* into the tree
rather than have *hit* it.

On such a "road" was R. on that day as he tried to see the
summit of the Enchanted Mesa. Further, it is emphatically *not
true* that it was the only tree for miles in any direction. Clearly
visible to the west of the tree that R. *bounced* into was a larger tree
of at least six-inch diameter. To the south there was substantial
timber growth just over the next butte. The tree in question was
not a lone tree. It was perhaps an *isolated tree*, a tree longing for
closer company, but nevertheless one tree among several of like
independence on what *could be described* as a *barren range*. And
surprisingly, New Mexico has many forested areas. If one were to
be dropped blindfolded on the Mescalero Apache Indian
Reservation in southeast New Mexico, upon removing the blindfold,
he/she might think he/she was in the Appalachian Mountains in
Pennsylvania.

The concluding part of the MYTHOLOGICAL story about
R.'s supposed "insanity" was a mangled interpretation by the two
Indian young men who overheard R. talking on the telephone in a
bar on Route 66 to his friends back in Albuquerque. It was the day

after the sheep count and the arson fire in the Humphrey cabin. The Indian youths were proud of their new mastery of "English," learned in the mission school, but wrong as to its meaning.

R. was particularly upset with this charge that he was mentally incompetent, was "insane." R. was not concerned about the allegations regarding the tree. Those wild accusations could be disposed of by a site inspection. The charge of insanity was insidious: it could be taken seriously by some people, perhaps R.'s superiors. Dr. Aberle might hear of it and wonder what kind of Field Aide had been assigned to her.

R. thought about his telephone call. He had told of the sheep count and the fire. Then his memory lit up like a happy light bulb; he had described for his friends how he had felt upon first seeing the Enchanted Mesa. He had quoted a poem by William Wordsworth, paraphrasing freely:

> "She was a phantom of delight,
> When first she gleamed upon my sight,
> A lovely apparition sent, to be a desert ornament.
> A jewel so bright and good,
> For enchanted gazers daily food."

Yes, pieces fell into place, "gleamed," "phantom," "good for daily food." By "food," R. clearly meant a sight that he could feast his eyes on every day.

R. smiled ruefully. The boys' fractured misinterpretation of "English" reminded him of a couplet by Alexander Pope:

> "A little learning is a dangerous thing,
> Drink deep or taste not of the Pierian spring."

This digression has been somewhat lengthy but it is vitally important to understand R.'s and Hump's difficulties with the Indians, newly empowered by Roosevelt's New Deal. Later on, Hump and R. got to know each other better and Hump decided that R. had not been sent to spy on how he was doing, at least R.

was not going to submit an unfavorable report. Then Hump confided that he did not really like the Indians. To R.'s chagrin Hump told him, "The damned Indians are lazy and no good. All they do is whore around and get pissy-eyed drunk, and try to get illegal whiskey. They can't handle liquor, you know, but if the G'ment wants to pay drunk Indians to do nothing, I'll help the G'ment do it. It's no skin off my ass," and he added, "election-wise I'm a Republican, you know, this whole New Deal is a No Deal to me."

To himself, R. reflected, "Too bad some people like Hump will forsake all principle for a job and a dollar." But he and Hump, politics aside, got along amiably on the business at hand. Apparently, Hump trusted R. not to abuse his, Hump's candor. Hump's view of the Indians would have been anathema to his superiors in Albuquerque, in fact, grounds for dismissal. The Indian Service was dedicated to the proposition that the Indian had been abused by the white man and often by the Government, more or less since Columbus had landed, an historical tragedy, a black mark on Thomas Jefferson's purported democracy. The New Deal of Franklin Roosevelt was now trying to make it up to the Indian by development funds and an extension of Indian tribal autonomy.

The explanation thoroughly aired, the story can be resumed.)

The car bumper had become inverted by the incident of the tree, and water was dripping from the front end. Subdued, R. drove on to Humphrey's cabin just around the bend, got out, and disconsolately listened to the water hiss out of the radiator.

No one was at home at the Humphrey cabin that resembled a summer cottage. There was another cabin on the other side of a well with a hand-cranked pump. No one was home in the second cabin either. There was a small barn in the rear, a truck, and a few chickens scratching in the dust. Off to the west beyond the road he had just traveled there was a flat reddish plain and every mile or so a few head of cattle. The land was parched, wind-swept, exhausted and poor. About two miles toward the right atop another mesa not as high as the Enchanted Mesa were Indian adobe dwellings, smoke, flat roofs—Acoma Pueblo. In the foreground about one hundred yards from R.'s spot was, of course, the so-called tree.

Rising in splendor behind him was the Enchanted Mesa. When R. looked at the base of the mesa, he could not believe what he was seeing. It was not a solid wall. Rocks long ago had fallen from the face at one point so that instead of a cliff there was a jagged pile of rocks, dirt, and green bushes almost to the top. Above the slope of rock R. couldn't really believe the sight of a long vertical crack in the wall of the Mesa, the work of ice or maybe earth tremors of distant ages.

R. wondered how far he could climb up the slope. It was quiet, eerie. There were none of the whirring insects of Kentucky fields on his grandfather's farm, no tractors in the distance, no singing birds, even the chickens around Humphrey's house scratched noiselessly, a beautiful silent void in a beautiful desert.

R. was to learn later that the two cabins had been built by a movie company on location for the filming of *The Vanishing American*, a silent film of the '20's with Richard Dix who had also thrilled R. with his portrayal of Red Grange in *One Minute To Play*. *The Vanishing American* had portrayed the noble redman doomed to extinction. The movie ended with Richard Dix, in the role of Indian, seated on his horse, naked except for loin cloth, gazing into the sunset, the horse hanging his head and as despondent as the vanishing American astride him. However, R. had just learned in his orientation that there were more Indians in 1930, counting the mixed bloods that had legal ward status, than there had been when Columbus landed.

The movie actors and crew had lived on location in the neat, trim cabin occupied by the Humphreys. R. also learned the second cabin was for the movie production equipment. It had a finished kitchen but the rest of the house was bare floor and walls. It housed Curry and his wife. Curry worked for the Soil Conservation Service, a part of the Department of Agriculture, not Interior. With Indian labor, Curry built check dams and contour earthworks to control water run-off and, therefore, erosion. It was a different and competing method of conserving the range and soil as opposed to

Interior's range management and reduction of herds. Inasmuch as Interior owned the land, Humphrey got the better cabin and Curry from Agriculture the unfinished shed. To R., it was ghostly to visualize the cabins full of actors and movie equipment, and now devoted to the prosaic business of range management by the government that had received the cabins as a gift. R. mused, "Life changes and we must let go of the past, no matter how pleasant it is to remember simpler days."

The picture postcard had said nothing about the slope of fallen rock. R. walked over to the base of the mesa and started up the slope of crumbled wall. Surprisingly, he found that he could climb to within a hundred feet or so of the top near the crack. He heard human chattering and saw two small Indian boys come scrambling down the ladder through the crevice from the top of the Mesa. They spotted R. and scurried down the slope. R. examined the crack. A ladder, that is, the rungs of a ladder had been improvised in the crack. By chipping the sandstone on both sides, hollows had been made so that rungs chopped from small tree limbs could be inserted from the rear, making a crude ladder leading up the fissure. R. started up the ladder and stopped to view the floor of the plain. It was a magnificent vista; he was higher than Acoma Village, one mesa away. He kept climbing and discovered that the series of rungs slanted backward around a bulge in the rock. The climb and view were exhilarating but a bit more than he had intended on his own. The rung he was standing on popped and he hastily scrambled upward. It occurred to him that he was more than twice the weight of the Indian boys. Then he discovered that the awkward thrust of a knee could loosen a rung. He experimented and found he could remove the rungs by pushing to the rear. They were secure only when pulled forward. He clambered to the top. The panorama was sensational, an unobstructed full circle. He looked down. It was a bit disconcerting to look from the top rung directly to the slope of rocks one hundred feet below. The rocks were near enough to break a fall but hardly enough to prevent a broken back or legs. A somersault on the head might be fatal.

R. determined not to let his qualms spoil his time on the

Mesa. He tried but found he could not see Humphrey's cabin or any part of the quarters. A rift in the Mesa top divided it into two parts and kept him from going to the side where the cabins could be seen. He was confined to the north end of the Mesa and the cabins were off to the southwest. It would have been reassuring if R. had been able to see the cabins and someone from the cabins could have seen R. The rift was a gigantic fissure and could not be spanned without rock climbing equipment, "Ha! Ha!" R. joked, "I didn't bring my Alpine equipment to New Mexico, thought it would be too hot."

R. enjoyed the enchanting view for more than an hour. The sun said eleven in the morning and Humphrey must be home and waiting for him. R. thought of the bent bumper and smashed radiator and wanted to talk to Hump about that as soon as possible.

R. then realized he was afraid to come down on that makeshift ladder. The ladder disappeared from his sight as it went backward under the bulging rock. No one knew he was up here. If a fall did not kill him he would still never be able to call loudly enough even if he were conscious. If he were to be spotted on top a light plane could not possibly land on the small mesa. R. waited an hour. If he were missing, the damaged Ford would be examined and someone might conjecture that R. was so upset that he had taken off or harmed himself. But who would suspect that he had committed suicide by starvation on top of the Enchanted Mesa? The vultures would pick him clean in a few days so that he would never be seen from the air. In the dry desert climate he would probably survive as a fossil to be discovered by an advanced civilization around 3,000 A.D.

R. considered that even if he stayed on the Mesa for the next few days, he would still be faced with climbing down the ladder, either that or wait for a Swiss Alpine team to be flown in and pass him down in some kind of basket and rope equipment. This unpromising conclusion and the noonday sun finally prevailed upon R. to come down. The return was uneventful. He did verify that each rung could be shoved out the rear by intent or carelessness. From the top of the rock slide he could not see if the Humphreys were at home, still could not see the cabins until he came around the side of the Mesa and was almost upon them.

He met the Humphreys. Humphrey had been with the Indians preparing for the sheep count. Mrs. Humphrey had waited for him in a bar on Route 66. The Indians apparently did not mind working on Sunday.

R.'s intuition told him not to admit that he had nearly been stranded on top of the Mesa. He didn't know the Humphreys and also was uncertain of the attitude of Agency Headquarters in Albuquerque. They just might think it was frivolous to get atop the mesa and be afraid to come down when he had been given a serious assignment. The damaged auto was confession enough upon first acquaintance with the Humphreys. R. told Humphrey that he had been out walking.

Humphrey stared at the bent bumper and, when R. explained, Humphrey gazed quizzically at the distant tree. Hump was a slight, lean man, balding with gray fringes and a weathered, lined face. He had skinny legs with just the suggestion of bowing, or it might have been the effect of his cowboy boots with high heels. Hump was dressed like a westerner, blue denim jeans, and black, turned-up Stetson, everything on him worn and expensive. Later when R. got to know the Humphreys better, Humphfrey reminded him of a villain in the cowboy movies—black hat, dour, and sinister. That is exactly what he had been with the Tom Mix Company in Hollywood for eight years. "I worked with Tom Mix," Humphrey told R., "although I generally worked agin' 'im," and added with a wicked leer, "if you know what I mean." Humphrey claimed that he had drunk a fifth of liquor every day of his employment with the Mix Company. That was during Prohibition, too. He had quit drinking except for a rare beer now and then.

When the talkies came in, Tom Mix was done because of a squeaky voice. Cowboy pictures dropped out of public favor and Hump was out of work. He had caught on with the Indian Service after a few attempts at door-to-door selling, and office work in Los

Angeles. Humphrey had been a real cowboy. He could rope, tie, and ride broncs. Hollywood, when forming Tom Mix's Company, had gone to Wyoming and recruited Hump from a ranch.

Humphrey stated briskly that there was no time for bent bumpers or anything else. Despite its being Sunday, it was the day for the sheep count which would soon begin in the afternoon. Humphrey had come home just to meet R. He must go back to the count. This was the day to determine if the Acoma Indians had met their reduction goal. In the days R. spent with Humphrey, he learned that as a cowboy Hump was the real article. He could still rope and tie calves but didn't ride broncos anymore at his age of maybe fifty. He was called Hump and his wife was Mrs. Hump.

Hump, Mrs. Hump and R. set out that afternoon for Route 66. They left Mrs. Hump at her favorite bar where she would wait for their return. The men went on to the Acoma sheep pens just off the highway. There was an adobe hut for business. The flocks had arrived, an awesome plain of some 13,000 bleating sheep. The tally had to proceed quickly. Sheep required water and subsistence and would have to return next morning to their widely scattered grazing tracts.

As with many kinds of work, the Indians had made the conclave into a social festival. Families from Acoma were camped out. Sheep had been slaughtered and were being eaten, entrails and all but hooves and hide. The all-inclusive menu discouraged R. from participating in the feast as invited. Hump enjoyed a deference from the Indians and R., by association, participated in the special status.

The tally was simple; the herds would be called up one at a time, penned, run through a narrow chute wide enough for one sheep at a time and counted as they came through. R. was placed in charge of the tally. He had two Indian boys as fellow counters. The flocks were sent through in lots of about fifty to make the tally manageable. R. and his two helpers agreed remarkably on the count of a lot, most often obtaining the same count. Almost always at least two of them agreed and then that was the official number. Only on rare occasion did they come up with three different counts

and then R. calculated the average to the nearest whole number. It
was long and fatiguing to count some 15,000 sheep but R. and
his Indian companions hurried and had a sense of accomplishment
after the count had been completed and tallied. When the last
flock cleared the chute by late afternoon, R. felt that the tally
could not have been in error by more than four or five and that was
a liberal estimate.

The result was a disappointment to Hump and the Indians.
The total was over 15,000. The Indians had not reached the agreed
goal of 13,000. More sheep must go. At stake was a family's living
since the sheep were not a common tribal resource but were owned
by individual herdsmen who were allotted a quota and a fixed
large area on an overgrazed range. In the hut the results were
reviewed, flock-by-flock, by Hump and Indian tribal officers. There
was milling about and, as the interested herders crowded around
questioning, R. watched impassively this example of Indian
self-government, thanks to the Roosevelt New Deal a new thing in
American relations with the Indians.

Finally, a young herder arose and made an impassioned speech
using the Acoma language that was translated for Hump. Although
English and Spanish-speaking for the most part, the Pueblos used
their own languages for official meetings and were paid for the
work of the Indian interpreter, thus adding to tribal funds.

The herder was angry and, as R. listened to the interpreter, he
realized with amazement that the sheepherder was mad at him—
R. The sheep count was wrong. "The man they call R." had botched
the tally. R. smiled knowingly at Hump who was sitting at the
official table up front. R. was not angry with the herder. He could
understand the man's attempt to hold on to his sheep. R. glanced
at his Indian helpers with the count but they, curiously, were
looking at the ground, not offering a defense of the count in the
Acoma tongue that the accuser would understand and accept. The
herder turned to R. and shaking his finger he obviously excoriated
R. in Indian. The interpreter related in English, "He say, 'if the
man they call R. would step outside, he, Black Bear, will cut R.'s
throat'."

R. looked to Hump for instructions and Hump advised blandly, "Better step outside." R. did not seriously believe that in the year 1939 he was going to get his throat cut by an Acoma Indian who questioned his sheep tally. Nevertheless, when he and the brave went outside accompanied by grown men, and small boys stopped their play and gathered round, R. kept his eyes open for a sucker punch. R. was a wrestler not a fighter and who knows what the Indian conception of fair play might be. The young Indian glowered for a moment, then burst out laughing and the others followed. He stuck out his hand and said in perfect English, "R., you OK, shake!"

Hump had not even bothered to come to the door and watch R.'s discomfiture. The group filed back inside and the small boys resumed pummeling each other in the dirt.

The tribal elders and Hump pored long and hard over the sheets with the tally that R. had turned in and could find nothing wrong. But the Acoma tribe officially rejected the count. In a subsequent appeal to Dr. Aberle, R. learned later, she acquiesced in the Indian complaint to the extent of agreeing on the current inventory, whatever it was, as substantial compliance. The Indian ward as well as the government guardian could play the bureaucratic game.

Hump and R.'s big day was over. They picked up Mrs. Hump at the highway lounge and drove toward home. Almost there as they forked off the Acoma road onto the side road to the cabins, they noted a plume of smoke above the hillocks hiding the cabins from view, a thin vertical wisp of blue. Hump hit the gas pedal and came hood to hood with Curry in his truck rounding the bend. Curry seemed agitated. He did not call out a greeting, He pulled off into the brush and around Hump's car, bumping and clattering on his way. Hump continued forward and as they came in sight of their cabin they saw flames about five feet high at one corner of the flat roof.

In seconds they jumped from the car and formed a bucket brigade with two Indian boys from somewhere joining and furnishing critical manpower. Mrs. Hump spun the handle of the pump, R. and an Indian boy carried buckets of water to Hump on a ladder to the roof. The second Indian boy inside the house pulled flaming clothes from the bedroom closet where the fire was concentrated. Mrs. Hump screamed for the safety of her parrot and R. ran into the kitchen and found the bird toes up in the bottom of his cage, overcome by smoke or fear. R. scrambled out with the cage and was himself choking from the smoke. After a dozen pails of water and the tossing outside of the burning clothing, the flames died in a sizzle of steam and smoking embers just as Mrs. Hump announced that the well was dry.

The fire had been quenched with relative ease and could not have been burning for more than a minute or two before their arrival. There was a smoldering closet and a small hole in the roof above. They strewed burning clothing about the yard. The closet was on the corner of the Humphrey bedroom beside an outside door. They cleaned out the closet and it became evident that the damage to the house was superficial. The closet floor was lightly charred but only in spots. The walls of the closet were hardly burned. The vertical flames from the clothes had eaten through the closet ceiling and onto the roof that was of lightest wood construction covered by tarpaper. The fire had not spread to the bedroom.

Mrs. Hump was almost hysterical over the fate of the parrot but the bird rapidly recovered in the open air and climbed onto its perch in the cage. R. was kissed and hugged for his dash into the kitchen and "thrilling" rescue. The Indian boys were thanked profusely by the Humps, grunted, and took off in their truck. It seemed that they had been traveling on the main road to Acoma, had seen the flames from about a half-mile away over a clear expanse of plain, and had come to the scene. They told Hump that they had seen a truck leaving the yard at the same time they had seen the flames and they, too, had met Curry's truck after he had pulled around the Humphrey's.

"Curry must have been drunk," Hump surmised, "he wouldn't have done it if he hadn't been drunk." Mrs. Hump was not so charitable. The acrid smell of the fire saturated the cabin and Mrs.

Hump was too upset to stay. It was getting dark. Hump would take his wife with parrot to a friendly neighbor's on the highway. R. persuaded Hump that R. should stay in case the fire should by some chance rekindle. R. had another reason for staying. The Humphreys left. R. filled three buckets with water from the replenished well, retreated to the interior of the small barn about forty feet away and in sight of the burned out closet, and waited. He relaxed from the day's excitement and almost dozed off.

He was alerted by the chug of a truck coming to a stop between the cabins. It was completely dark by now, almost nine o'clock, two hours after the discovery of the fire. A figure got out of the truck and R. recognized Curry. He walked carefully about the well and his own cabin. He smoked a cigarette, then another, making no move to enter his house, just looking around. After maybe a half-hour he walked around to the closet side of Hump's house. Peeking between the barn slats, R. could identify Curry with certainty. Curry stepped inside the door of the bedroom and stayed for a minute or two. He backed out and stared at the roof. He walked among the charred garments scattered over the yard. Then, he got back into his truck and drove away.

The case against Curry was complete and incontrovertible. R. felt like a veritable Sherlock Holmes. R. drove his own car to the highway and the friends of the Humps who invited him to spend the night. As their late night meal was ending the host said to his wife, "Turn on the radio, Emma, some guy at the gas station said that Germany has invaded Poland." The radio confirmed the grisly fact and R. sat up late listening to the news of the German "blitzkrieg." From a continent and an ocean away R. could thrill at the adventure of war, this time a living spectacle of his own age. Realistically, it was good to be a distant and uninvolved American and not a Polish or French youth who actually had to go up against the German Wehrmacht. From his quiet bed in New Mexico R. had no trouble visualizing the Von Richten sneers of the pilots of the German Stukas that the commentators were calling dive bombers, nor the arrogant stare of the German tank commanders atop their land cruisers in what the radio reporters called Panzer Divisions.

As a twelve-year old in New Albany, R. had read a five-volume history of the World War. Imaginary wars were fought in his fantasies as an adolescent. He played war with his younger cousin, Glenden, on Grandpa's farm.

R. felt just a quiver of relief that the inevitable had happened. Poor blood-stained Europe had gone to war again in another of history's deplorable but exciting wars. September 1, 1939. What a day!

Hump had dutifully reported the fire by phone to the Agency that evening. Next morning the Treasury man, Turner, joined Hump and R. at the scene and took pictures. The Treasury Department provided security services for the Indians. The spotty charring clearly showed the use of a flammable liquid, Turner said. A closer inspection of the clothing showed the same random charring and even a residual kerosene-type odor. Turner was also interested in R.'s account of Curry's return and the story of the Indian boys. Turner began to puff up like a pigeon at the thought of a criminal prosecution and its resulting publicity. Turner was known as a blowhard, full of stories of violent police action, but engaged in nothing more serious than having drunken Indians locked up overnight in Albuquerque.

The fire ended R.'s "home on the range," the title of a new song hit. Mrs. Hump needed time to recuperate on a vacation away from the cabin. Curry was easily apprehended and was charged with arson. Turner interviewed the two Indian boys and said their disinterested testimony made the case airtight. R. would be called to testify at the trial, set for the following spring.

Shortly thereafter R. drove to Albuquerque, his field assignment of a month was over. Hump helped R. try to hide the damage to the car. There were not many tools. They took off the bumper and inserted one end between two rails in the cattle guard at the entrance to the cabin compound. The cattle guard, in lieu of a gate in the fence surrounding the cabins, consisted of parallel links of iron rails about ten inches apart that spanned a ditch cut into the road. The spaces between the rails were a sure deterrent to a wandering steer but no hazard for a wheeled vehicle. The leverage of Hump and R. swinging on one end of the bumper bent it back into a semblance of shape.

The radiator was damaged in just one corner. By judicious pinching with pliers they managed to squeeze together a number of the tiny cells so that the radiator leaked only slowly. R. carried three cans of water in the car to insure the arrival of the car in Albuquerque.

R. liked to drive in the desert night, preferably without a moon. He started for Albuquerque after dark. The sparkling stars seemed to be loosely pinned to a blue-black desert ceiling. On Route 66 it was a short drive to the rim of the arid range overlooking the green irrigated Rio Grande Valley. Ghostly lights of Albuquerque suddenly appeared below like a pile of unsorted stars tossed in a heap. The town was still ten miles downgrade on the highway that pointed straight to Central Avenue, Route 66, the only street running the length of Albuquerque. But it was too far to see more than shining lights. R. cut off the motor and glided. Coasting down to the valley, R. could not, at first, distinguish streets and buildings. Ten miles is a long way for the human eye. But at about five miles, Central Avenue began to form into a lighted corridor of globes and signs, just enough neon reds and blues to affirm its human environment. On the long silent glide R. did not meet a single car. Then, closer, Central Avenue stood out, a continuation of his flight path. Buildings took shape, car headlights flashed. R. passed the gates of Kirkland Air Force Base out on the mesa and was soon on the bridge over the Rio Grande. He did not hit a traffic light in the first several blocks and went to Third and Central without the engine. He was on the way to living rooms, handshakes, laughter, drinks, fun, and exchanges with other Aides of wild tales of the Agency and Indians. Larry Stevens and his wife Steffie were his favorite couple.

R. continued to like his life and work as a Field Aide. If anything, he enjoyed his social life too much. He did not put in the extra hours in the evenings and on weekends that some Aides did. He preferred the nightlife of Albuquerque and weekend jaunts with the Stevens—to the Carlsbad Caverns and Organ Mountains in southern New Mexico, the rodeo in Soccorro, climbing Mt. Taylor and looking at the ruins of the plane crash in which Carole Lombard and Senator Cutting had died, to the Grand Canyon and the Petrified Forest, scene of the Humphrey Bogart movie, trips to Sante Fe to see the Indian jewelry and crafted items on display and for sale around the Square.

Field Aides were supposed to take exams for Civil Service registers in order to qualify for permanent positions in the Federal government. Most of the Aides did. It was R.'s intent in becoming a trainee. Now R. realized, his naiveté about the Federal bureaucracy and his brashness about being a Harvard graduate both gone, he needed political science credits for Civil Service eligibility. Messenger, File Clerk, and the like were all he could qualify for. Clerk-Typist wasn't a bad entry position but R. in his academic haste had learned to type only with two fingers on his father's typewriter. And interviewers for these positions were certain to tell him that as a Harvard Phi Beta Kappa he was overqualified and would be a poor risk as an employee. R. had no alternative, he decided, but to return east to school for Political Science credits.

R. was unhappy at leaving his friends in Albuquerque, the other Field Aides, the Pueblo Indians whose culture was so different from that of acquisitive Americans. They were called Communists by the Un-American Activities Committee of the House of Representatives chaired by Martin Dies. During World War II the appropriations for the New Deal for the American Indians were quietly phased out.

R. would miss the beautiful buttes, mesas, and mountains of the Southwest, Coronado's Cities of Gold. R. took the train, the sleek new diesel Sante Fe Chief to St. Louis, and the crack train from L.A. to Chicago. It was late afternoon and R. looked back at the last great sunset of the Southwest that he was to see, turquoise skies streaked with brilliant reds and oranges. R. sighed.

The sun was gone and the train slid over the plain. R. looked out the dark window a long time. "The world moves." had declaimed William Borah, the great orator and prosecutor at the Scopes Monkey Trial in Tennessee, "and the Republican Party moves with it." Or did Daniel Webster say that? Anyway, R. resolved to move with the world. He was young with a full life ahead of him. Nostalgia can be heavy baggage.

Arriving in the suburbs of St. Louis at dawn, R. got up early from his Pullman bed and scurried to the diner. He looked out eagerly at the green grass, green trees, and gardens, the little white houses and tree-lined streets. This, too, was intoxicating, the fresh, green countryside of the East as compared to the bare, dry Southwest range.

In St Louis he had to get off of the sleek diesel and board the smoky coal burner chugging slowly to New Albany. In a day or two, he found his Midwest bearings like a sailor once again on land. He accommodated to his mother's nasal, Kentucky drawl, and his father's clipped and sarcastic remarks. Soon he was talking with high school friends about the chances of the New Albany Bulldogs in the coming football season. Only a year ago he had visited New Albany. R. resumed his "singing" in the choir of the First Presbyterian Church. At least he could read music. He met some new girls at Newby's, the soda fountain where high school teens and returning college grads hung out.

Immersed in the familiar hurly-burly of his midwestern origins, R. would suddenly feel a lingering doubt about his sojourn in New Mexico. Was his three hours on the Enchanted Mesa just a dream? Or had it really happened?

*   *   *

Much, much later in his life R. saw the Enchanted Mesa again. It was part of a trip to the Southwest with his wife, Henrietta. They hired a rental car in Vegas and toured the Grand Canyon, Sedona of the red rocks, Flagstaff and on around a wide circle ending at Vegas again. On the leg of the trip from Gallup, New Mexico to Albuquerque they passed the Acoma Indian Reservation but the sign said they were entering the land of the Acoma Nation. R. thought it would be interesting to visit Acoma and see the Enchanted Mesa once more. After all his wife was skeptical of the "cock-and-bull" story he had told about climbing to the top of a sheer wall of rock six hundred feet above the plain. At least he admitted he had been afraid to come down. For Henrietta this was a charming modification of his constant bragging about what he had done as a youth. At least, he did not claim that he had climbed Everest.

R. noted that everything had changed in the Southwest since he had been there. For one thing, Las Vegas was then only an unnamed patch of desert. The arid lands had recovered from overgrazing and other harmful range practices and the range was restored to its pristine lushness and could have accommodated buffalo herds. Route 66 was gone, only a few yards remaining here and there, and they had to be sought out in the underbrush, replaced by 1-40, the legacy of President Eisenhower's Interstate Highway Program. Gallup was a thriving little city, not a dirty cow town full of whorehouses for the cowboys. So things have changed. "Don't beat a dead horse," R. told himself, "at least the hole in Window Rock is still there."

R. excitedly drove off 1-40 onto another paved road to find the Enchanted Mesa. Suddenly, it loomed up, it was still there, a million tons of solid rock cannot be bulldozed. R. looked up and saw the fissure, also still there. R. pointed it out to his skeptical companion. The road sign said they were on the way to Acoma. But they were alongside the Mesa. Another road branched off toward the Mesa. It said "Keep Out" but R. drove on anyway as far as he could. The approaches to the Mesa were covered with small and some larger trees in an abundant sea of grass. Maybe one of the large trees was R.'s tree that had survived his crash into it. Fifty years is a long time to recover and grow.

R. drove as far as he could before the ground began a steep slope up. There was a fence and another sign that said "No Trespassing." R. opened a gate in the fence and scrambled on foot. The terrain became rocky and Henrietta fell behind. R. began to climb over small rocks. His wife called after him, "Stop climbing the rocks, you silly man, before you break your neck." In a few more yards R. did have to stop. The big boulders piled on top of each other were too much for older legs and body. His wife caught up with him. He pointed out to her the fissure at the top. He knew the crude ladder would be gone. The slide of rocks became steeper as he continued. Bushes and small saplings grew out of the rocks. R. tried climbing a boulder or two. His cautious wife yelled at him, "Come back down—carefully—I didn't bring a body bag this trip!"

R. was licked; he could get no closer to the base of the Mesa. The two of them stared. R. again was thrilled by the Mesa. Henrietta admitted it was a natural wonder. "Of course, on this trip I have seen other mesas in the Southwest," she reminded him. R. drank his fill of the sight, but not as long as he had once stayed on top of the Mesa. Then they returned to their car. They had to make Albuquerque before night. He had proved to his wife that the fissure was there and she was beginning to doubt her disbelief that he had climbed up it.

R. hoped that she would tell their friends back east and maybe they would forget the ridiculous story of his hitting the only surviving tree in New Mexico. The forests they had driven through would dispose of that. R. wondered how the wild stories of his encounter with the tree had been circulated back in Cambridge and New York. R. suspects, but cannot prove, that the unflattering account was sent in letters to Harvard classmates by an archaeologist friend, David, whom R. had been shocked to see unexpectedly at a tribal dance on the Acoma Indian Reservation and who had stayed in New Mexico for his work in Indian archaeology.

R. and Henrietta got in the car and heard a siren. A pickup truck pulled alongside. R. looked up into the face of a young man. His truck was marked "Security-Acoma Nation." The Security Guard looked at R. with that pure, calm, impassive gaze that R. associated with Indians. The Guard smiled almost indulgently, but not unkindly, at the old man before him who earnestly insisted that he had climbed to the top of the Enchanted Mesa. First, it was impossible to climb the sheer walls unless one were equipped like a Swiss professional, next, no native American, let alone a white man, would be permitted to violate the home of the Sacred Spirit who lived there. The old man and his old wife were just making up a story to explain why they were violating the "No Trespassing" sign that clearly warned all stray tourists not to go beyond the approved boundary.

"I see you are senior citizens," the young man said, "I'm not going to arrest you. You probably do not know the rules." R. tried to thank him in the only word he knew that an Indian also knew, "Bueno very much." The Indian scowled, "I don't speak that old Indian dialect, my parents speak it some, but English is good enough for me." R. had to admit that his English was perfect.

Barred from the Mesa area, R. thought they would drive to see an Indian Pueblo at Acoma. They were stopped at the bottom of the mesa. R. could see the ascent up a sloping path that he had climbed easily in 1939.

"Off limits to tourists," the friendly woman Guard stated, "The mesa is used only for ceremonies of the Acoma religion. We don't live there anymore. We live in those trailers and houses you see there. She pointed them out on the plain.

R. who always confides too much to strangers said, "Too bad, I once saw an Indian dance up there."

Thinking these tourists will say anything to go into forbidden areas, the Guard replied, "We don't dance up there for tourists. We dance every Saturday at a hall on 1-40 and you have to have an advance reservation to get in."

"Well," fumed R., "I guess we are stymied again."

"If you really want to see a dance," she advised, "there is a Parent Teacher Association at an elementary school which is having a Parent Day at the school. The children will dance."

R. eagerly obtained directions for finding the school which fortunately was only a mile or two off 1-40. As they prepared to leave for the school, the Security Guard admonished. "By the way, don't call anybody at the school an Indian. Don't make the same mistake Columbus made. This is not India. The world is round but not that round."

As they drove away, R. pondered that last remark: "not that round" was not good geography, it was not even good physics. But he thought he knew what she meant. They drove up to the school parking lot that had been cleared for the dancing and parked outside. R. and his fellow traveler arrived and took seats on benches just as the dancing was beginning. They were the only Caucasians there.

Children of all ages danced or tried to, from kindergarten to high school. Parents took the pre-school class to the performing area and held their toddlers' hands and tried to lead them step-by-step. It had never occurred to R. that Native American kids had to learn their dances just like white people learned to dance, but not in kindergarten. Grades One and Three were announced. They knew a few steps, but at a slow tempo, and still were led by their parents. The dancing improved with the high school teen-agers performing quite well. The drums at one side began to play for the high school dancers. That completed the school dancing.

R. had a lump in his throat. This was becoming an unexpectedly emotional trip to the Southwest. R. did not know what had caused his reaction. Was it the sight of the little Indian tykes learning the steps of the tribal dance? And the patience of their smiling parents? Or was it R. lamenting his lost innocence, nostalgic for New Mexico? A youth who could climb an Enchanted Mesa? A body that was beautifully functional. Was he wistful that he had wasted his opportunity to learn more about the Indians as an example of how to enable minorities to assume their place in American life? Was it simply too great a contrast between the potential of his youthful years versus the actualities of a life that had included sorrow and wrong turns in marriage, career, and personal accomplishment? R.'s heavy thoughts were provoked by a beautiful afternoon and sweet Indian children. Since he was an old man and could afford it, he wiped away the tear that had strayed over his eyelid.

Then the parents took over and R. and Henrietta saw some dancing that curdled his blood, men with all the wonderful rhythms and intricate steps that R. had seen in '39 atop the Acoma mesa.

R. and Henrietta were urged to stay for the dinner which was to be served indoors. They had to refuse because they must get to Albuquerque soon to find lodgings. They had heard that there was to be the annual balloon race tomorrow at dawn and hotel rooms were at a premium.

R. looked forward to coasting down the approach to Albuquerque and showing his companion what a beautiful sight it was. But long before they got to the rim they were surrounded by houses and with the cuts in the hills for roadways there was no rim. They paid an exorbitant price for a motel and got up before dawn to see the balloons. In the pre-dawn night they ate their special breakfast of buffalo burgers and watched the balloons being inflated with hot air blowers, one by one as they reached the lift-off platforms. Soon the sky was filled with hundreds of balloons, R. looked at his program and the list of sponsors. There were several hundred all right, maybe five hundred.

After watching the balloons drift toward the Rio Grande River, many of them disappearing over the rim of the mesa (there was a rim after all), R. and his wife prowled around Albuquerque by car. Central Avenue was hard to locate but they found it. It used to be the main street, Route 66, entering from the east past the Sandia Mountains and leaving for the West up to the plains and on to Gallup. R. persevered and found the old orange Federal Building, six floors, the tallest building in town in 1939. It was surrounded now by high-rise office towers. R. insisted that they take a picture of him in front of the former Federal building. Henrietta was grumpy but finally got all six floors in the sight of her camera and almost got run over by a car because she was standing in the middle of the street.

The top two floors had housed the United Pueblos Agency but now housed the overflow files of a Federal Court, the signs said. No one in downtown Albuquerque had ever heard of United Pueblos Indian Agency. R. and Henrietta drove to the other side of the Sandia Mountains and took an aerial tram to the top, overlooking Albuquerque. On the tram R. asked the passenger next to him where he was from. It turned out he was a "native" of Albuquerque and lived on Indian School Road. R. asked him if the

Indian School was still there. The "native" had never heard of the Indian School and didn't know how the road had got its name. This nostalgia game, R. concluded, can go on forever and can be boring even for R. who had known the people and places. They headed for Sante Fe and the rest of their journey around the Southwest. The plane at Las Vegas took them to New York. After a few days at home and the big metropolis, the whine of police and fire sirens, and the nightly sound of gunfire, R. had both feet on the ground again. But he had this recurring doubt that he could not resolve. Did he really spend an hour seeing the Enchanted Mesa a second time? Or was it just a fancy of his imagination?

Perhaps R.'s two journeys into a land of enchantment are best remembered as fantasies, brief interludes in the logical flow of his life, unlikely visits to a fairyland where Indian folk inhabit a magical kingdom of unbelievable adventures and illusions.

AN ELECTRIFYING PROPOSAL

Smokey Maggart was a grass widower living in an efficiency apartment in Philadelphia. He had learned to cook, using only fire and water and, understandably, made no sauces, cakes, pies, or other dishes requiring a lot of mixing. Smokey's housekeeping was midway between bachelor slovenly and adequate. Smokey played tennis. He frequented the neighborhood bars, found many winners there as well as losers. He thought bars provided necessary companionship while he was waiting for a more desirable future, a rather vague image of another house and wife. Often in bars with similar men without wives he exchanged recipes rather than sports or women talk. He thought of himself as a man who did better with a wife but was in no particular hurry to get one. He had been elated at his new freedom when he left his wife but he also was bruised by the failure of his human relationship after years of marriage and felt he needed time for healing.

At 53 Smokey had a considerable past but looked forward to a still considerable future. He was rather Spartan in attitude except for, like many Irish, a taste for the bubbly. He thought he held his drink quite well. Withal, he was an optimist, almost a futurist, who came to be known as a typical man about the neighborhood. Oh yes, he worked at a nearby hospital in Administration, not hands-on patient care. He insisted that administration was rather harder, and more misunderstood, than direct professional care of patients.

In his apartment house Smokey knew quite well the security guards and clerks behind the desk. It was a spacious busy lobby, with mail, services and information to tenants from Desk Clerks, and questions and rent payments from tenants to Desk Clerks. Tenants included graduate students at the nearby university, foreign students—some just off the boat and a formidable challenge to the Desk Clerks who spoke only English assisted by their hands, grimaces and diagrams—also elderly pensioners, young marrieds, the variety you would expect in a university neighborhood. The area was called "University City."

The apartment house had been converted from a hotel. Smokey knew Bert who ran the commercial activities on the former hotel's first floor—ballrooms for rent, bar, offices for an experimental theater, a room for a bridge club, physical therapy space, etc. Bert was required to be alert and innovative in finding tenants for the commercial space that was unsuitable for apartments. The lobby had a mezzanine and a high ceiling with a beautiful chandelier worth many thousands. It was an elegant setting for just an apartment building.

The Philadelphia Eagles football team used to bring the visiting team to the hotel for a party after the game. That was in the days when visiting teams did not just hop on their charter planes as fast as they could and take off. The Eagles invited them to a party where they exchanged game stories, laughed, drank a few brews, and shook hands, staying in the hotel until morning and then making a leisurely plane departure.

When Smokey lived there those days were gone, of course, but some visiting players out of nostalgia, perhaps, came to a bar down the street, sat and talked to the rabid, as in mad dog, Eagle fans. The Cowboys were completely approachable. Smokey made the acquaintance of Don Meredith and Bob Lilly, icons of the Cowboys.

Smokey told them of his playing days in high school and how a severe injury had ruined his chances at college ball and from there, who knows, maybe pro ball like his listeners. Smokey gave details on his injury, it was a torn cruciate ligament which in his day they had no treatment for, let alone knowing about the operation which would have permitted him to return for the next season. The Cowboys were quite sympathetic. Only on occasion did Smokey see eyes glazed over as he related his woeful story but no listener ever fell asleep and off his bar stool.

Bert had a bright idea. He established the Matchbox, a small grocery store selling a few staples and household items. Regular markets were several blocks away and the large apartment house did have some five hundred residents who could forget anything from orange juice to toothpaste. The feature of the Match Box was that it was fitted into a rather deep closet along the entrance hallway. All residents had to pass it coming and going. There was room for only the stock on the shelves and the Clerk. Customers did not come into the store. They were served at the entrance, a Dutch door doubling as counter and barrier.

Smokey noticed the intriguing new facility and the youngish lady at the counter. Hereby hangs the tale of this story—the youngish lady, very chic with beautiful red hair. On the way home from work at the hospital, Smokey would stop at the Matchbox and buy an item he already had. The young lady was personable and willing to converse. Perhaps it was Smokey's Irish nature, he delighted in schmoosing with clerks, waiters, and other service people who would exchange stories with him; he loved the sound of his own voice and tried to make people laugh at his jokes. The young lady was no exception. She must have laughed occasionally because Smokey kept dropping by and telling jokes. She had the most gorgeous head of auburn hair that Smokey had ever seen. It was an unusual color verging on pink. Soon Smokey was lingering at the window and asked the young lady her name. "Harriet," she replied.

"Were you parents very strict?" he inquired benignly, hoping to get a clue as to her religion without actually asking. Smokey was nominally a Unitarian but he was not fond of the downtown Philadelphia church. Instead he was having a flirtation with the Ethical Society. He distrusted and openly opposed the Evangelical Right of Billy Graham and the televangelists.

"My folks were not really strict" she replied, "we're just ordinary Lutherans, not Missouri Synod."

"What does Missouri have to do with it?" he wanted to know, "You live in Pennsylvania."

She explained, "The Lutheran Church is funny that way. The Missouri Synod is much more conservative, I really mean more hide-bound than the rest of Lutherans. The Missouri Synod has churches everywhere."

After their acquaintanceship turned into friendship, Smokey learned of the idiosyncrasies of the Lutheran faith and its famous Missouri Synod that had churches all over the country. He also learned that Harriet had been called "Honey" or "Honey Baby" when she was a youngster. In view of her maturity, when Smokey used her nickname it was just "Honey" or "Hon."

Smokey, wondered, "Did families try to influence behavior by the names and nicknames they gave their children? Was "Honey" supposed to encourage sweetness, a happy-go-lucky temperament? Were girls named Lily supposed "to spin not nor reap" like their Biblical namesakes? Not being concerned where her clothes and food came from made a Lily sound like a kept woman. Was a Chastity never supposed to get married? Even the most innocent of names sometimes has loaded political implications. For instance, Virginia, a girl's name had also been given to a Commonwealth of the United States. It was coined as a tribute to the first Queen Elizabeth. The road to Hell is correctly paved here because good Queen Bess, for all of her undeniable accomplishments, was not a virgin.

Not to be supercilious, more names refer not to a virtue but to a personage. Thus Mary is a direct assumption of the name of Jesus' mother; Ralph, Raoul, Rafer, Rolfe, and all the other ethnic variations mean "the Lion-Hearted." So, Paul is for St. Paul; James, John, Peter, John, Simon are namesakes of the other apostles, except Judas. Maybe Jude is a circumlocution for Judas. Are Christophers and Christians supposed to be Christ-like. Enough already." Smokey told himself! "Just call her Harriet."

Smokey's contacts with Harriet were becoming more and more enjoyable. As he walked home from the hospital, he hurried in anticipation. He now felt confident enough to order toilet paper as Harriet's "finest Irish linen," and to read her his mother's letters from his adjacent mailbox. He amused her by saying after he had read a letter that he was going to his apartment and figure out what his mother had really said—between the lines.

One evening when Smokey was late getting home he was disappointed to find the Matchbox closed. Eight was its scheduled closing time and it was only five-thirty. Maybe Harriet was sick, or something had happened to her. His heart skipped a beat.

He dropped into the bar across the hall. Two girls were there sipping a drink. He sat down by one of them, an attractive blonde much younger than he. It turned out that she was a nursing student at his hospital. Her name was Brenda. She remembered Smokey because he had spoken to the incoming class of student nurses. He, of course, hadn't noticed her among the many. His job was to speak each year to the incoming class. He was old enough to be their father. He had used that gap in their ages to flatter them, saying something like this; "I'm always a little nervous to be speaking to so many attractive young ladies in the same room with me. I must appear to you to be antiquated and I try not to be. But your generation is so much superior to mine. In all the ways we can measure you are better—you make better grades in high school, you are smarter, you are better informed, you are skilled earlier in the social graces, you are taller, you can run faster, you have bigger feet." The remark about bigger feet always got a laugh, even from the instructors present.

In the bar, Smokey peered around Brenda to take a look at her silent companion. It was dark, he couldn't see very clearly. She appeared to be a somewhat older girl, maybe a woman going back to Nursing School for a refresher and return to nursing.

"Is that your roommate?" he asked.

Brenda laughed, "It's my mom."

"Your mom?" Smokey was dumbfounded, it couldn't be.

The two girls giggled. Smokey kept looking. The other girl certainly looked young. Then, her laugh gave her away. It couldn't be but it was, unmistakably—Harriet, Harriet of The Matchbox.

Smokey was a little embarrassed; the other two seemed elated, laughing. Smokey, too, thought it might be a good joke on him. As a mom Harriet must certainly be older than she looked. That was probably a good thing; he could not be accused of robbing the cradle, not quite.

The Matchbox eventually went out of business. Bert had an unusual way of replenishing the inventory. Harriet tried to persuade him to buy the fast-moving items for their limited space. Bert demurred, "I don't have enough money for those, they're too expensive." Maybe Harriet didn't know about taking a loss for tax purposes. Bert kept on stocking small amounts of the slow items but eventually they took up most of the shelves. When the cash flow practically ceased Bert closed The Matchbox. Harriet, who had run the little store for eighteen months, sold off the stock at a discount, wept a little and closed the Dutch door. However, she had made good friends with the Manager of the apartment house and went to work for her as Desk Clerk and later, Rental Agent.

After work Harriet began to meet with Smokey in the bar across the hall, the Beer Mug, for the pinball machine, the jukebox, and, of course, good conversation. He found out she was an early widow and had raised two children on her own, Brenda and an older brother, Jamie to his friends, but James to his mother.

Within a month or so of these meetings, Smokey invited Harriet to the movies and although the word "date" was never spoken, they went to the movies and he drove her to her home in the suburbs when she missed her train. Smokey realized she was quite poor but, thanks to Social Security, she had stayed at home for years to bring up her children. She believed that she should stay home with young children, participating in PTA's, Cub Scouts, Brownies, cooking, disciplining, consoling, laughing, maybe trying a little to be both mother and father.

Smokey described his hopes for Harriet by telling her, "You have spent your life taking care of your children, now it's time for *you* to have some fun. Brenda is graduating from Nursing School and Jamie has been away on his own for several years now, Chicago being his current landing place. How about you?"

Harriet seemed to be in step with that. In effect, when she became Rental Agent she was Smokey's landlady. The two of them continued to see each other and were indeed accepted as an item by her friends and by his friends.

In due course, Smokey took Harriet to the amusement park at

Great Adventure in New Jersey, a Six Flags enterprise. He bought tickets for unlimited rides. Harriet was venturesome, she loved roller coasters. That was one reason that Smokey liked her. At this stage of their romance, if it could be called that, Smokey thought that Harriet preferred an element of risk in her life, so they rode the roller coaster.

Harriet often talked about famous roller coasters she had been privileged to ride. She liked the old-fashioned wooden coasters and wouldn't ride the newer metal ones on a single track that spun you on your head, that is, until they visited Busch Gardens in Virginia and Smokey demonstrated that he could ride the Loch Lomond Monster and survive. She then tried it, liked it moderately, but still preferred to go right side up.

On this date they rode the coaster at Great Adventure and Harriet pronounced it exciting. So Smokey immediately took them on a second ride. He, too, thought it pretty good fun. The spring air was crisp and cool, quite stimulating as they whizzed down the big drops. Harriet did not holler, though, as they dived down the hills. As mature people and not teenagers they both believed in just having an enjoyable, satisfying ride, not squealing as if this were an orgiasticc-losng-your-virginity-once-in-a-lifetime-thrill.

To fully understand what happened next, certain facts must be known. Smokey, over the years, how many years is not anyone's business, had felt the time had come to acknowledge their feelings, his at any rate, so he had proposed marriage. She laughed and turned him down. He proposed again—and again—maybe the word is periodically. Harriet treated it lightly usually, with a jesting, "Why?" or "I'm not the marrying kind," More soberly, "Why should we get married, we're through having children. You'd be a grandpa when any children of ours got out of high school." Smokey was reluctant but determined to be gracious about the rebuff. So, to the evening at Great Adventure.

On the second ride as they started the plunge down the final and steepest hill, the power suddenly failed and they found themselves straining forward, noses pointing straight down, firmly stuck on the highest and climatic final plunge of the Great

Adventure roller coaster. It was not a simple malfunction; lights all over the park were out. They were not only pointed straight down, they were looking into a frightful abyss of darkness. Smokey's Marine Corps training taught that when the situation was hopeless to do nothing at all, wait and the situation might resolve itself.

Harriet was calmly patient for a few minutes but then began to moan. Smokey did think of the eventuality that a cherry-picker might have to rescue them. He tried unsuccessfully to reassure Harriet. Harriet had not been to church in the past year except on Easter morning and Christmas Eve. Nevertheless, she decided to trust her standing with the Almighty, "Please God, get me out of this . . . if you just would get me down, I promise . . ." Smokey thought she was going to promise to go to church more often. Instead she finished the sentence with a most remarkable concession, "I promise, God, . . . I'll . . . I'll . . . I'll . . . MARRY SMOKEY!!"

In a remarkable coincidence, either the emergency generator kicked in, the regular power was restored, or God answered Harriet's prayer, maybe two out of three of those things happened. Anyway, the lights came on all over the park and the coaster went on down the incline. None of the teen-age girls in the car squealed or made a peep. The car rolled to a stop and all stumbled out, somewhat subdued, even shaky.

Smokey embraced Harriet, kissed her, she hardly protested. But Harriet is durable. In a few moments as they weaved toward the midway she had recovered completely and was even thinking of the outage as a lark.

Smokey reminded her, "You know, Harriet, you promised to marry me if you got down alive from the roller coaster." The closest Harriet comes to a scowl crossed her pretty face and she shrank away, and spat out testily, "0h, you're not going to try to hold me to that, are you? I swear, aren't you something?" Immediately occurred one of those rare coincidences, which are hardly believable, but which shape so much of our lives, whom we marry, our choice of occupations, whether we serve time in prison on trumped up charges. Why even the fact of our individual existences is an incalculable miracle.

Harriet just got the words out of her mouth when a shattering thunderbolt struck the ground, it seemed like fifty feet away. Smokey swears he saw sparks flying and little tiny bolts snaking along the midway concourse. Smokey might have been reminded of the ancient Greek stories of Zeus hurling his lightning bolts at unfortunate mortals, but Smokey didn't have time for such memories. He was busy enfolding Harriet in both arms and trying to calm her. Harriet was afraid of lightning. Smokey glanced at the nape of her neck and saw the hairs standing straight up. He thought how nice it was to have her clinging to him this way. She was soft and curvy and helpless, in a more sincere way than had ever happened before. However, Smokey kept his head and he coolly but firmly rem1nded her, "Look who I got on my side."

Harriet did not go back on her word. She married Smokey, but they did have a long engagement. She made him wait ten months until Feb. 14, Valentines Day, of the next year. She said that was because it was the anniversary of their first date and she wanted everything nice to happen on Valentine's Day. For a tough babe who had resisted marriage so long she proved to be an incurable romantic. Smokey didn't mind, Valentine's Day was easy to remember and he could celebrate two holidays for the price of one.

Harriet remembered that on their first date when Smokey thought that everything was going rather well, for a first date that is, they had gone to see the movie, *One Flew Over the Cuckoo's Nest*, a picture that was the first big hit of Jack Nicholson's fabulous career. Harriet also told Smokey rather sternly that only one of them had flown over the cuckoo's nest. Harriet's remark was illogical, a non sequitur, but Smokey had no doubt as to which one of them she meant.

Alternative Ending

(Editor's Note: It has been suggested that the lightning bolt was unnecessary and that it strained credulity. The author's wife was one of those critics. She was a feminist type and identified strongly with Harriet. She maintained, "Three miracles in one evening are too much for the story, particularly one that is supposed to be believable." She admonished her husband, "You can never quit when you are ahead, can you?"

"How do you figure three miracles?" the writer inquired.

His wife sighed. "One was when Harriet's prayer was answered and the roller coaster got down safely, the second was when she promised to marry Smokey, and the third was that ridiculous addition of the lightning bolt. At that point your readers are going to shrug and curl their lips. It ruins what up to that point had been a believable story."

In fairness to all, this editor proposes that the reader be given the choice of endings and hopes that everyone will be satisfied.)

HOW TO WIN AT TENNIS WITHOUT ACTUALLY CHEATING

This is about playing winning amateur, all-in-fun tennis among friends who must see each other frequently—at work, at church, in each other's homes, with or without spouses or other companions. It's tennis for people who want to remain friends and frequent doubles partners. It is *not*, repeat *not* tennis the way the pros play it, the McEnroes, the Agassis the Hewitts. They play in large stadiums with crowds cheering them, perhaps betting on them, with umpires and beaucoup linesmen to follow with eagle eyes each ball, and who meet around the umpire's chair with the players arguing a call.

Friendly tennis has no officials, usually no spectators, no prizes. Betting is frowned upon because it might decrease the purity of conscience with which the players must officiate their own games, being strictly truthful about the ball that lands inside by an inch on their side of the court and noncommittal when their own shot to an opponent seems to be in by two feet and the opponent for some reason calls it out. In case of doubt, the etiquette of tennis requires that one's doubt be resolved in favor of one's opponent, unless by common agreement a let is played.

Professional tennis, on the other hand, is played without etiquette, or one might say, without any requirement for civilized behavior. That is, civility by the players is not required; witness Natasse, McEnroe, Connors, Hingis, and that Rumanian girl, the nasty Irina Spirlea. She has been fined for swearing on the court in her own language (the officials can recognize bad language even in a foreign tongue they don't understand).

But civil, even perfect, behavior is required of the crowd that must be silent during the rallies, applaud good play with polite clapping, and never cheer or jeer for an error on the court. A player can even have a fan ejected from the stands for talking, saying something the player does not like, or even looking in a way that upsets the player. After a match is over, clapping for the winner is OK but never boos for the loser. (As a contrast, witness football in Philadelphia where they throw snowballs at the visiting team and at Santa Claus; even their mayor has done it.)

The friendly game of backyard tennis, however, must be governed strictly by the rules, perhaps what one might call "etiquette" as well as rules. One must always call the point lost if he/she so much as touches the net inadvertently and unobtrusively. It cannot be regarded as a slip of the foot that the opponent did not see. One must call a foot fault on oneself if he/she looks down and sees that he/she has indeed stepped on the back line as he or she serves.

There is only one exception to this rule. That is when the opponent has never apparently been taught what a foot fault is, or who ignores it by stepping onto the court even before his/her serve is hit. In that case, one should also ignore the foot fault, preferably stepping further into the court than the opposing server. It might cure the latter of his habit if you start creeping toward the serving box before serving the ball.

Three is the ideal number of opponents to play friendly tennis with, one who is better than you whom you play to improve your game, another player who is not as good as you are in order to return the favor for the tennis community, and the third is one who is roughly equal to you and with him you play ding-dong, sweat-pouring battles. It is still enjoyable, and at least acceptable, when you lose. It's all right to get hot under the collar when you lose a tight match but by the time you get home and sit down with your good friend, hopefully your best friend, and either replay the game—permissible, talk about girls who are sexy baggages,—

permissible, seriously complain about your wife,—not permissible. If you try to have more than three opponents, called partners in friendly tennis, someone is going to feel slighted and will drop out of his own accord.

Once there was a young man playing in a pick-up game of mixed doubles. No one knew the others very well, beyond the forgettable names they used to introduce themselves before starting the set. The young man was playing opposite a sweet young thing that unfortunately hit him with a batted ball right in the eye. Both players were close to the net and the young girl seemed to fire directly at the young man. That was perilously close to a breech of etiquette. At close range one is not supposed to aim right at the opponent, man or woman. One takes precautions not to do so, contorting if necessary to find an angle from which one can hit the ball *away* from the opponent and yet win the point.

The young man who was hit was suspicious of the girl's intentions. His eye puffed up and would be black in the morning. They continued to play. A game or so later the young man was playing close to the net and so was the girl who had hit him, *except she was playing over on the opposite side of the court. In tennis lingo she was playing the add court while he was playing in the deuce court, twenty-five feet from her.* The young man got a "pigeon", that is a ball came floating up to the net so softly and well positioned that he could have smashed it, not letting it drop for an easier shot, but simply driving it back and down for a sure winner. Then, an unbelievable accident happened. It couldn't have happened in a hundred years if a player had tried to do it. The ball ordinarily cannot come off the rim of the racquet at an odd angle if the racquet is going forward. Apparently, by a miscalculation the young man swung and did not hit the ball squarely forward. He must have stroked the ball with the outside rim of his racquet. The ball went off at a 90-degree angle. Any tennis player will tell you that hitting a ball at a 90-degree angle is likely in one in fifty thousand swings. The player was left-handed and lefties can come up with some quirky shots that no right-hander can make. In this instance, the left-hander's ball did squirt away at the impossible angle of 90 degrees and with considerable speed, called "pace" in pro tennis, and hit the young lady twenty-five feet away upside the cheekbone. It was a glancing blow but the young lady bellowed in "pain." Another fact one must know—girls/women on the court exaggerate the "pain" of being hit by a mere tennis ball. For Chrissake, how hard can a tennis ball hit you? It's not a baseball thrown by Randy Johnson, or a football spiraled into the noggin by a Donavan McNabb, or even a Jim McMahon floater who usually can't break an egg with his fluttery pass. Golf and hockey are different matters. (Editor's note. In the interest of fairness, when Jim McMahon was younger and had Buddy Ryan's line protecting him at both the Chicago Bears and the Philadelphia Eagles, Jim may not have thrown a tight spiral or a picture pass but he did break quite a few eggs, and made omelets of opposing secondaries.)

The young lady dried her "tears" and looked reproachfully at the young man. Ordinarily, he would have been flattered at the thought he could control a tennis ball that way. In this case, he was made to feel guilty. But he dismissed it as a bad racquet day for him and a bad cheek day for her. He also dismissed the idea of ever getting on the same court with her again.

Those who find it onerous to live by the rules should take up golf where everyone occasionally neglects to record an extra stroke. Or play miniature golf where there are no rules at all. So, living by the rules does not necessarily limit one's ability to win.

However, one may select poor players as partners. It really is no sweat to beat worse players. Bang away and wait for the opponent's errors to hand you the game, that is, unless it is your boss or someone else who holds you in thrall. One other caution: the inferior player may resent his losing and take to cheating, principally on line calls. There are two answers—one may refuse to play with him or her, or one may start cheating in response. The latter option makes for a crazy game, certainly the end of a friendship.

It's a real downer when the cheater is one's wife or significant other and you are doubles partners. Correcting a wife's mistakes can lead to fighting, divorce, or worse. Why am I telling you how to play with your wife when I don't believe you should be playing with her, or any woman, for that matter, regardless of whether they cheat or not? The fact of cheating is simply a red herring.

As I review the last few paragraphs, I feel there have been too many digressions, perhaps necessary, but nevertheless, distractions. Although occasionally they may even be diverting, such distractions are time-consuming and eventually frustrating. They are hindering us from getting to the meat of the topic, "How to Win, etc."

These rules are not for those who are playing a superior opponent, a near-pro. There is no way one can beat a superior opponent without cheating. One should not play a pro-type player; he might do something drastic if he catches you cheating, like having you barred from the club, or take the lead in ostracizing you at the Saturday night dance. No, this advice is for individuals who are rather evenly matched, at whatever level that might be, but still amateur, of course. So here goes:

The first rule is that living by the rules does not prevent one from taking full advantage of the rules, or better yet of situations where there are no rules. Take advantage of what the rules do not cover, such as:

(1)   Use the clock on the wall if you are playing indoors. It is the official time that tells you when your time on the court is up. Leave the court promptly if you are in the lead or if you are two points down in the final game of a set. Women are especially dilatory about leaving the court. I believe you are justified in belting a ball right into the young lady's butt when she is leaning over at the net as you come on the court and need to assert your playing time. That usually produces a vacancy on the court that you are entitled to. If you are being beaten, particularly, if you have won the first set and are behind in the second, remind your opponent that you cannot play longer than an hour or whatever is the agreed upon time. If time expires and you haven't completed the second set, clearly you are the winner. Walk off the court.

If there is too much time left and you are being beaten, or are about to be beaten by an opponent who has rallied and will soon overtake you, the rules say nothing about suddenly remembering that you promised your spouse/significant other to be home by such and such time and that you are very sorry that you forgot to tell him. Walk off a winner.

(2) The rules say nothing about how many times you can toss the ball up for a serve, and find it unsatisfactory and catch it. This can be used to kill time or to unnerve an opponent when you do it six times consecutively and on the sixth suddenly hit it. Even the pros catch a lot of bad tosses.

(3) When your opponent has run you ragged on a succession of shots and you are on the brink of a collapse or a heart attack, you can walk around behind the back line. You can retrieve a ball four courts away, you can drop the ball, you can hit yourself on the knee with the racket. Nothing of these things is forbidden in the amateur rules. In the pros there is a clock (in the umpire's head) which limits the time between serves but there is nothing like that in a friendly game.

(4) If you are gasping for breath, you can towel off unlimited times, you can dry and clean your glasses, you can discuss whether the time should be controlled by your watches or the time on the court clock.

(5) The above permissible strategies may seem to be aimed at delaying the game when losing, and might be questioned as not promoting winning. That is not true. One may indeed win if permitted to recover briefly. And the above actions, slightly modified, may indeed be positive factors for winning, testing the patience and concentration of a friendly opponent. One must use intuition in applying these remedies. You don't want your partner to leave the court, or even not play with you again. The more likely result is that, exasperated, he will do anything to get the

match over with and begin to serve badly and hit wild shots, but he will play you again next week, thinking your previous behavior will not be repeated. This is the ideal result.

(6)   To an opponent with a penchant for double-faulting, say something like "Charlie said you had such a hard serve. I'm really surprised, it doesn't seem very hard, once you get used to it."

(7)   If your opponent stops to tie a shoe lace or for any other reason, occupy the void by batting the ball into the back stop or side wall, taking your time to resume play, "Oh, you all ready, already? Oops, I made a funny. Was it a pun, strictly speaking, or just word play? There is a difference, you know. Sometime when we are not playing I will explain it to you. What do you think? Was it a pun, perhaps a puny pun? Huh I say huh?" There is nothing against talking to an opponent between points in a friendly game.

(8)   Vary the bounce of the ball before serving. Some players get into a predictable, unchanging rhythm in serving. There is Ivan Lendl feeling the sawdust in his pocket in order to dry his tossing hand. There is Steffi Graf doing just the opposite, spitting on her hands to moisten them. There is John McEnroe rocking back and forth. A consistent rhythmic movement or action is a mistake for an amateur in a friendly match. Instead, bounce the ball once and hit it, next time bounce it six times and serve, occasionally bounce it three times, stop and glare at the sun, bounce it four more times, look again at the sun, put on your sun glasses, look up, take them off, don't bounce the ball, just serve it. You might find the guy on the other side of the net "out to lunch," so to speak But don't overdo this "stalling." Your frenzied opponent might hit you with his racquet at the next interchange at the net.

(9)   Some players are hardened old timers who may be affected very little by these distractions. They may bellow, "Hit it,

knucklehead," or maybe, "I'm going home." However, this is not a great worry. Number one, they are not going home unless they are way behind, in which case, quickly run out the match. Number two; they are not going home if they are ahead. In this case, shout back, "This is supposed to be a friendly game, don't get your shit hot!"

(10) If all else fails there is a sure-fire ploy, perfectly legal, since friends are supposed to inquire about one's personal life. If you are really getting beaten up, the next time you change ends and meet at the net, say quietly to your friend, "It was awfully nice of your brother to take your wife dancing the other night." He might scowl and say, "I don't have a brother or my brother lives in New York," or possibly, "I don't speak to my brother." Then you are flustered and stammer, "Oh, I guess that wasn't her." At the next changeover where hopefully you have turned the game in your favor he might growl, "What makes you think it was Janice," and you reply, being as blithe as you can, "Oh, I'm sure it wasn't Janice, I wasn't that close to her, made a mistake I guess." Man, if that doesn't have your friend spraying balls wildly over the court and foaming at the mouth, you'd better get another partner.

For women tennis players, that strategy will not work, I repeat, do not attempt this with a female opponent. Remember that the woman across the net from you has a heart of gold and the instincts of a wild animal, which, biologically speaking, she is, just like the seemingly tame animals in Yellowstone Park who can rend you with tooth and claw if you violate their vital space—about four feet in most cases. In women this vital space is also about four feet. If two women are life-long friends, however, as soon as they meet and like each other, there is no vital space, they will kiss each other with abandon, although not with the tongue in the French way.

In the case of their husbands who are being approached by another woman, the explosion line is at eight feet, maybe ten feet.

Don't gamble; know your woman. If it's a sitting situation and the aggressive female sits on your lap in your wife's presence, for you and the giggling young lady twisting a strand of her hair, or perhaps yours, both of your geese are cooked. It's all over! You are road kill! (Editor's Note: Relative to the writer's remark about the animals in Yellowstone Park, or any animals for that matter, with the right handling and training any animal can be trained to be a pet. To run the gamut of animals—tigers, bears, horses, snakes, skunks, Aussie dingoes, monkeys, the Great Primates [no, that does not include the Archbishop of Canterbury], and llamas—all animals can make good pets. So can the wildest of all animals, a woman, but don't try petting her on the tennis court.)

Farm kids are adept at making pets of chickens, lambs, and pigs, with or without the concurrence of their fathers. The kids also learn of the heartbreak that can ensue from a too close attachment to an animal pet. There must be a clear understanding with one's parents on the fate of the animal as it grows. Otherwise, a father may insist on the final rights of ownership, in the case of a calf, for instance, the father may insist on full cooking rights when the calf grows into a steak.

Violating a woman's vital space, or her husband's space in the aggressive approach of another woman, provokes violence in return. She might murder her husband or inflict bodily harm on the other woman, or kill herself in an accident going 110 mph. It is highly preferable that a woman satisfy her animal instincts by acquiring things, going on a shopping binge, or eating, like slurping down double milkshakes with ice cream, thus fulfilling her "other" instinct as a food gatherer or the making of fine garments. But her response to over-the-net calls of mistaken identity or wiping-with-towels dirty gossip involving husbands/boy friends, this is too chancy for women to do.

So far as men are concerned, *just don't play with women at all.* Particularly, don't play mixed doubles. That compounds the error. I don't care if Billy Jean King does still hold the women's record for most mixed doubles at Wimbledon and hopes to add to it. For an amateur like you, why multiply your difficulties with that added risk? Billy Jean King is a pro, not only still good at the game, a veteran of many emotional mixed double matches with men, all kinds of men—single, married and men secretly unsure of their gender. Billy Jean is older now and hardened. Her scars are not only physical, she has been ravaged by mental conflicts, both from the games and the insulting advances of her male partners.

John McEnroe, the has-been, proposed in a recent Wimbledon to Steffi Graf that the two of them play mixed doubles in the regular tournament with the youngsters. Steffi does not play doubles of any kind but McEnroe was either unaware of this or else thought that for an opportunity to play with him she would make an exception. He claims that she accepted his offer but she probably just spit on her hands to indicate the idea was cock-a-mamie. Wisely or because she thought it was a joke, Steffi did not show up. McEnroe would not let go of the "rebuff." He complained about it on TV for which he is a paid, objective commentator. My advice to John is: stick with being a legend, McEnroe, in those dull over-promoted tournaments of bleary-eyed nostalgia which the network TV is trying to pawn off on the public as tennis.

(11) There is one last rule to remember: don't *be afraid* to win. Believe it or not, there are times when a player is clearly on the way to winning, or before play starts, and he is afraid of winning. There are all kinds of reasons for this reluctance. The opposing player maybe complains of feeling bad and is pleading for sympathy. This may be a ploy or real. Disregard it in either case. If he is trying to con you by feigning illness drub him unmercifully for his bad sportsmanship. If he is really sick, he should not be on the court, send him back to bed as quickly as possible. There are other extraneous "reasons" for failing to win. An opponent might hurt himself, with the racquet or otherwise, in the middle of the match. Allow him the required time to walk it off, but do not prolong the time-out indefinitely. Insist that he play despite a sore hand, blister on the finger, heel or toe, or else forfeit. You are not running a first-aid station. All other phony reasons, a relative asking to be humored, a Medicare fart pleading age, stiffness or both, treat these people the same way they would treat you if the roles

were reversed. Enough of this, fearing to win is as bad as not knowing how to win, worse actually, because it is throwing away a victory.

One of the nice features of tennis and tennis players is the camaraderie that exists among players, even greatest rivals. Players love to sit in the clubhouse, tavern, or on a hard bench and talk over old battles, the legendary heroes of the game, and yes, the gossipy stories which have become legendary themselves. One of the best, but little known, storytellers was a young man, Reginald Malone, who was a tennis player who went to the University of Cincinnati. As Irish as they come, the young man was naturally called Reggie by all. Reggie came from Marietta, Ohio. He hadn't played much tennis in Marietta which was all about football and basketball, with a little baseball thrown in. At U. of Cincinnati, Reggie developed a passion for tennis and spent a great deal of time on the court, learning, getting beaten, then becoming a passable player, enthusiastic, brash and mouthy, but a genial and conscientious singles opponent and a good doubles partner.

Most of the students were co-opting and worked in the afternoons that limited their tennis to week-ends. Reggie's family was well off, on his mother's side, so he haunted the courts. Apparently he did enough studying to stay in school but was far from an intellectual. An ideal life for Reggie would have been to be good enough for the tennis circuit, amateur in those days. It included the women players who were reputed to be accessible.

Reggie's tennis was observed by Professor Lowery who was head of the Political Science Department. He invited Reggie to join him in a friendly game at the home of an alumnus who had a court that the Professor was welcome to use at any time. Reggie was flattered, or complimented, he hardly knew which, that the old gentleman wanted to play with him. Dr. Lowery had white hair. Reggie was in his prime of youth. Thus, his confusion over "flattery" or "compliment." Reggie was also somewhat afraid of being seen as a brown-noser, but Lowery was in his fifties or sixties and Reggie didn't much care what others might think. Besides the court was out of town.

It was a long drive out of Cincinnati to the tennis court on an estate overlooking the Ohio River. It was the domain of the Wurlitzers, the organ and jukebox people, and lately more jukebox than organ. They were filthy rich from the looks of the mansion high above the Ohio. The steep slope down to the river seemed to be about three-quarters of a mile, Reggie observed.

It turned out that the professor was a society-conscious individual who bragged about whom he knew. Reggie learned later that he had gone to the Chairman of the University Trustees and wangled an invitation to play on the Wurlitzer court. He could have been fired for that, Reggie said with a chuckle. Reggie, himself, admired the "creative solution." No wonder that Lowery and Reggie did not stop at the house but went directly down the slope to the court, about half-way to the river. The Wurlitzers wouldn't have known them from a pair of Adameses.

The court was all that had been promised, truly the best court Reggie had ever played on or hoped to play on. It was cut out of the hillside years ago. Trees that were now very tall had been planted on all four sides, pines, keeping the sun off the court except when it was directly overhead. So one could be assured of playing in the shade if it was afternoon or morning, the times people play tennis.

As for the tennis, Reggie found the white-haired Professor pitty-patted the ball. Reggie's forehand was on and he almost knocked the ball down the Professor's throat with his hard drives. Alas, the game does not always go to the stronger player when playing an inferior opponent. There occurs what is called "playing down to your opponent's level." One has a tendency to overhit, make foolish errors, etc. That is what happened on the Wurlitzer court, Reggie swears. He began shanking his shots, missing simple overheads, knocking others over the line and off to the side. The latter shots were what did Reggie in. The beautifully manicured court, it was grass, of course, had a fatal flaw for Reggie's game. The Wurlitzers had thoughtlessly, neglected to build a wire netting around the court. This made no difference on the uphill side where spectators, if any, sat on sculptured grass, i.e., the hillside was cut into at each twelve inches of rising slope, and the seats were sodded. So, not only was the court grass the spectators sat on grass.

On the downhill side of the court, lack of chicken wire made a big difference. Errant balls hit off to this side went under the trees and a considerable distance down the slope, maybe even a hundred yards. Since Reggie was so much younger than Lowery, and also accounted for most of the bounding balls, he felt obligated to go after both his own balls and those of the ancient one. It wasn't much of a tennis game. Reggie didn't bother to keep score. He was glad when they went back to town. Thereafter, he found excuses for not accepting the Professor's kind Invitations.

Having nothing better to do after graduation Reggie went on to Graduate School and enrolled in Fine Arts, not that Reggie was interested in art but he had heard that the course wasn't too hard and the professors lenient. Reggie, consciously or unconsciously, looked forward to abundant time for tennis.

He began to notice on weekends a gangling tall blonde kid with a good serve and volley and what appeared to be a strong forehand and weak backhand. Since he hadn't seen the guy before he surmised that he was a freshman. He spoke to him and found that his surmise was correct. The kid's name was Winifred Larson. He was of Swedish extraction and looked the part. He came from Van Wert, Ohio. Reggie heard his classmates calling him Winny, so for Reggie it was Winny and nothing else from the start.

Reggie found out that Winny played a passable game of tennis, had potential but would never be on the circuit and was unlikely to make the college varsity. Of course, he was only a freshman. At the moment Reggie and Winny were evenly matched and they soon were enjoying ding-dong, knock 'em out, blood-on-the-court tennis.

Reggie introduced Winny to his favorite bar after tennis. It seems Winny wasn't used to beer after a game, in fact not used to beer at all, but he demonstrated that he was willing to acquire the taste. It seems that the two of them had in common a strict Protestant rearing back home. They exchanged stories of their hometowns and their youthful years.

Reggie learned that Winny was a scholar as well as tennis player, a scholar-athlete that made Reggie a bit envious and admiring in spite of himself. Valedictorian of his high school class, Winny won a scholarship to Oberlin but nonetheless, it had been a financial stretch for his family. Winny had chosen the graduate school at the University of Cincinnati because it was co-op and Winny had exhausted his own and his parent's funds as an Oberlin undergraduate. Co-op students would go to class in the mornings and work at a University-sponsored job in the afternoons. Winny took a course called Training for the Public Service and hoped to land a job in government. It was the 1930's and the Depression and New Deal led many idealistic young people into government service. For Winny the Federal Government would have been his strong preference. Franklin Roosevelt was elevating the economic status of the common man and bringing a new relationship between government and business.

In Marietta, Reggie's father was a Methodist minister, his grandfather was Superintendent of Schools for the county, and an uncle was President of Marietta College. Reggie wanted to go far enough away from Marietta so that he would not be under surveillance by his father, nor his mother, nor his grandfather and uncle, for that matter, but close enough to go home when he wanted to. His family were all strong Methodists, and Reggie, while not exactly the proverbial "minister's son-devil's grandson," had real reservations about the strict moral standards of the Methodists who disapproved of smoking, drinking, and petting girls before marriage, all of which Reggie enjoyed and practiced in private.

Reggie's parents were well-off on his mother's side. She was a stiff Presbyterian who knew what was good for Reggie and always would. Reggie did not co-op and had time for lots of tennis on the University Courts, picking up a game with whomever he could who was in his league, like Winny.

Winny played tennis when he could, usually on weekends when he was free from his co-op job at Traffic Court in downtown Cincinnati. The University was located on one of the hills surrounding downtown Cincinnati. Downtown was referred to as "the Basin" which was all that the name implies. The University site was called Clifton Heights. It had a Clifton Ave. running like a spine across the broad side of the high ground overlooking the Basin. Clifton Ave. had retail, amusement, bar and grill, and services establishments supporting the University which spread out to the other side away from the Basin.

In their favorite watering hole after tennis Winny was often amused by Reggie's stock of tennis stories. Reggie's stories were not just about the private lives of the top national players but gossip about the players they both knew and saw on the University courts. Reggie made no exceptions; he would just as soon become the butt of his own stories. Winny discovered that Reggie was a good guy but he had a serious flaw. Reggie was long-winded and at times irrelevant. But Winny found that Reggie's stories were like peanuts, addictive, that once Reggie started Winny couldn't stop listening. However, the long-windedness *could* become frustrating and sometimes even—well, boring.

Reggie was chuckling. "Some of the things that have happened to me in Cincinnati! Sometimes the tales after the game are more interesting than anything that has happened on the court. I know that's true with me."

Reggie probably heard Winny sigh, but Winny didn't care, he knew what he was in for, "I'd really like to get back to the tennis talk if you don't mind."

"There's more to life than tennis," Reggie barked, "you told me that yourself."

Drinking beer in their favorite bar, Winny was looking forward to this Saturday afternoon's tennis game. Winny laid his head on the table, closing his eyes but keeping his ears open. Winny admitted that Reggie did have some amusing stories in his repertoire, although he exaggerated so badly that you never knew when he was outright lying or maybe just shading the truth a bit. However, he did like Reggie, they were buddies and what if Reggie did have to be indulged occasionally thought Winny. This afternoon Winny resolved to make no remonstrance.

"Well to begin at the beginning . . ." began Reggie.

Winny immediately forgot his resolution and exploded. "Oh, my God," wailed Winny and swallowed the shriek that welled up in his throat. Reggie often became so absorbed by what he was saying, or laughing so hard, that he didn't hear anyone else. Winny hoped that this was one of those times that Reggie didn't hear. He really didn't want to sound critical of Reggie. Reggie was a good guy and always upbeat.

"I was born in Marietta, Ohio," intoned Reggie rather mournfully Winny thought.

"Jesus Christ," Winny yelled, again forgetting his vow to be nice to Reggie. But he did suppress the desire to ask, "Was it a breech delivery or a Caesarean?"

However, it wasn't mattering to Reggie at this time if Winny was even there, which in a way he wasn't. With a groan or two, Winny settled in for a long afternoon.

Reggie spoke without animation, "My father was a Methodist minister."

"How many times have I heard that?" Winny wheezed as Reggie continued, "My father and I, in fact the whole congregation and I had a disagreement over religion. And so did my mother and I but from a different direction, she was a dignified, uncompromising Presbyterian, I don't care what the church rolls said."

"Yes, YES!!" Winny tried to hurry him along.

Reggie continued, "Father told me not to worry that I would learn more as I grew up. I never did, learn more I mean. Father and I dropped our argument and to this day have not resumed it. My mother, however, worried about my 'apostasy', as she called it, and still reproaches me at frequent intervals. She blames atheistic professors at the University of Cincinnati for my irreligion."

Winny interrupted, "Would have made more sense if she has blamed your tennis racquet."

Reggie didn't even pause, " . . . and she wasn't even a Methodist, she was a Presbyterian by birth who had been incompletely converted by my father. "Methodists are too emotional," she said, "there should be some emotion when we praise the Lord, perhaps a *little* like the Methodists but certainly not so excessive as the shouting Baptists. I strongly prefer the dignity of a Presbyterian service, it seems more respectful of God."

Despite Winny's resolve, he broke his silence again, softly, "Holy shit, spare me from your mother, please." He was trying his best to keep Reggie from hearing him but Reggie had ears for what he wanted to hear.

Reggie glared at him, "I think she is just like all mothers, even yours, crudhead."

"Leave my mother out of it, she's my mother, not yours, not ours, just mine," commanded Winny sharply. Reggie hesitated angrily. Winny relented and added gently, "Seriously, old man, do I have to know all this to appreciate your story?"

Reggie solemnly assured him that it was all relevant, even necessary. Winny moaned so audibly that it's a wonder the bartender didn't come down the bar to see if he had had a heart attack. Winny resumed his former position, elbows on the bar and head hung, with his hands cupped under his chin, W1nny used his hands on head as axles, permitting him to rotate his head downward toward the table, now all ears and no mouth.

Winny must have dozed off because the next thing he knew the bartender was flicking his finger hard on Winny's noggin. It resounded through his skull like a bell in a belfry.

"You can't sleep at the bar, buddy," the bartender said and cited the Ohio law. Winny had grown up in Van Wert where they didn't pay much attention to those things.

"I'm not sleeping," Winny protested, "I am just resting my eyes." He really meant his ears because Reggie was assaulting them. He persuaded Reggie to leave the bar and sit at a nearby table.

The bartender barked, "Don't be a smart ass, or I'll throw you both out. The law applies to every part of the bar, wise guy." Winny looked straight-ahead and slept with his eyes open.

Reggie droned on, "To make a long story short . . . . you know until I was thirteen, I was very much a Methodist, like an Assistant Minister to my father but that is a long story, one I'll not bother you with, oh, impatient one," Reggie laughed at Winny's discomfiture. Reggie continued, "Now I will tell you something that is the result of all I have told you about myself. All this has been background for my story. In fact, it wouldn't have happened without it, the story without the background, that is."

There was a long pause and Winny showed a flicker of interest. "Although I have given up Methodism, I confess," Reggie confided, perhaps a bit sheepishly, "I still like churches, the church without the religion you might say . . . . call it a hangover if you like . . . . from the warm feeling of a happy childhood . . . . in snuggling up to my mother in church while father preached hellfire and brimstone from the pulpit . . ."

"When I was in Europe after graduation," Reggie looked wistful, "I was awed by the cathedrals . . . . Chartre, Rheims, Mont St. Michel, many others, works of art . . . . medieval history in stone and mural painting . . . . medieval longings . . . . in the twentieth century . . . . but I also like 'the little brown church in the wildwood' of my grandfather's farm in West Virginia."

Winny was touched by this unexpected softer side of Reggie, his near eloquence, maybe sadness on the departed bliss of his youth. He remembered that Reggie was taking Fine Arts. Now Winny was listening.

Reggie shifted gears and resumed briskly, "With time on my hands here in Clifton Heights, I got into trouble once, as an undergraduate before I met you. I hadn't been to church in a while but nostalgia for a church's smell and feel got to me. I decided to look for a Methodist Church to visit for just one Sunday. I couldn't find any in the neighborhood and I didn't have a car. There was a Baptist Church about six blocks away so I went one Sunday, shaved, wore a tie and good clothes. I do own a white shirt and tie, Winny."

"I am not sure that what I might have thought had happened did actually happen. Well, I guess the first confession is that I am a patsy for a pretty face. This girl I met at the church that Sunday was sitting in the pew behind me and when I looked around I would have sworn she was giving me the eye."

"Now I know what you are thinking," Reggie said as he confronted me, "you think I am a sucker for any good-looking babe who comes on to me. Well, you couldn't be more wrong. I run like Hell whenever I suspect a woman is after me. I'm the type that wants to pick his own girl friend, the old-fashioned type that wants to do the chasing, be the man and she the woman."

Winny assured him, "I would never accuse you of not being the man and her of not being the woman."

"Well," Reggie huffed, "however it was, this girl touched my arm as soon as benediction had died on our tongues and said 'Hello'. I had no choice except to shake her hand and say. 'Hello, yourself'."

She said, "My name's Adele."

Reggie said, "My name is Reggie."

"What kind of a name is that?" she inquired, "Reggie-veggie, veggie, Reggie?" She laughed or snickered, Reggie couldn't tell which.

"It's a perfectly good name, 'nickname'," Reggie told her.

"What's your real name?" she shot back.

"Everybody calls me Reggie," he said, "and if you really want to know me you would do the same."

She was persistent, trying to worm his last name out of him, "What is the name on your birth certificate?"

He tried to devastate her, "I'm not in the habit of discussing birth certificates with someone I don't know."

"I told you *my* name," she said coyly.

He had forgotten her first name. "What is your last name?" he asked her. Reggie thought, "I have her trapped which ever way she wants to go."

She wriggled free, "I'll tell you my last name if you tell me yours."

Reggie punted, "Enough of this," he replied firmly, "We sound like two five-year olds in a sandbox." That gave her pause, alright.

Reggie had had enough. "What are you trying to get out of me," he tried to sound sophisticated and weary at the same time. Reggie turned to Winny with a self-appreciative laugh, "Guess that's true sophistication, huh, weary and sophisticated?"

Winny tried to be truthful with Reggie, "You don't sound sophisticated at all. You sound like a guy squirming because a broad has her hooks into him."

Reggie then looked actually weary. After a pause he told Winny. "I don't want to keep arguing with you. You are a nice guy; good tennis partner and I don't want to make you mad . . . . whatever it was, it did the trick."

"What trick?" Winny was puzzled.

"Why I found out what she wanted."

"What was that?"

"She wanted to invite me to the Baptist version of Christian Endeavor, that's Presbyterian, Epworth League is Methodist. That's a young people's group that meets on Sunday evenings before the eight o'clock church service."

"Did you go?"

"I had no choice."

"Why not?"

"Well, I had taken up so much of her time and I had led her on, you know how that is." Reggie drew a blank from Winny. Then Reggie exploded, "Or, maybe you think you know damn little how that is . . . . or, maybe I mean you do know damned little about how that is."

Winny protested, "Reggie, stop spitting on me. Good buddy, we are quarreling again, just tell me calmly what happened."

"OK, all r1ght," Reggie conceded, "I went to the young people's meeting but there was no meeting."

"Why not?"

"She said the meeting and the evening church service had been called off. She couldn't call me because I hadn't given her my telephone number. My telephone number? I was a student, I didn't have a telephone, I used pay phones."

"What did you do?"

"Oh, the evening was not a total loss." She said she had a key to the church that was deserted and very dark, of course. She suggested that we go into the church and see how it looked when deserted. The empty pews and all. You know, eerie.

"Didn't that make you suspicious?" asked Winny.

"I didn't think much about it at the time. We went in, the big church door creaked like a castle lowering the drawbridge. We sat

down in an upholstered pew and she told me that she had been a
Jew and was now a Baptist. She was very sincere about this."

"A Jew? A J-E-W Jew?" Winny asked.

"Yes, a real Jew. I didn't know much about Jews except they
were people in the Bible. I had hardly seen a modern Jew and
didn't know how I was supposed to behave."

"What was she doing sitting in an upholstered pew in a Baptist
Church?" Winny wanted to know.

"She's one of those people you read about in the papers, a real
live Jew who has converted or should I say reconverted to
Christianity. 'JEWS FOR JESUS' they call themselves."

"And she told you all this while sitting in an upholstered pew
in a Baptist Church when the lights were out and she had a key
BUT THERE WAS NO SERVICE?"

"The upholstered pew has nothing to do with it" Reggie
insisted.

"I'm not so sure," said Winny candidly.

"Well," Reggie admitted, "She did keep looking up at me with
dreamy eyes as big as saucers."

"In the dark?" Winny was skeptical.

"Some women have eyes like a cat's," Reggie informed him,
"and she was one of those women."

"In a dark pew?" Winny sounded sarcastic.

"Of course in a pew," snorted Reggie.

"What happened next?" Winny was annoyed at Reggie's drawn
out and unforthcoming narrative.

"We found ourselves face to face."

"Beside her?"

"No"

"Where then?"

"I swear to God," Reggie blustered, "I didn't plan it."

Winny gave Reggie a long, unblinking look and Reggie looked
out in space. Finally, Winny stated in a voice that indicated that
he had come to a conclusion, "Were you on top of her?"

"You might say that."

"Are you claiming that she drew you to her?"

"No."

"Well, how did you get there?"

"I fell on her . . . . actually, I fell to sort of one side of her."

"Was anyone hurt, mouth or teeth or head, anywhere?"

"Apparently not."

"What do you mean apparently?"

Reggie did not answer. The two sat at the bar, each with his own thoughts that seemed to be completely different. Finally, Reggie rose to go. "Let's get out to the tennis court. Times a'wastin'."

Winny remained seated, "I don't want to play tennis—not yet."

"You were so hot to play tennis, old man," Reggie gave a nervous but good natured chuckle, "Why, you're practically begging me to stay here and not play tennis. That's a switch."

Winny was petulant, "You can't leave me dangling like this," and silently asked himself, "Was I actually begging? My God, what a dirty old man I am at such a young age!"

"Oh well," Reggie relented, sat down again and Winny waited.

"If you are expecting a lot of lurid details . . . . ," Reggie stopped short.

"I don't mind lurid details!!" Winny fairly screamed at him.

Reggie fairly snapped back, "There aren't any details worth telling."

Reggie paused and in a carefully modulated voice said calmly, calmly but firmly, "If anything had happened it would have meant a Methodist father and a nagging Presbyterian mother would have given their wayward son a guilty conscience for succumbing to the wiles, or worse, of a Jewish Christian in a Baptist Church. Now that's damned unlikely to happen, it's possible, but the odds are against it."

"Yes," Winny agreed, "no matter how unlikely it was, if it had happened it would have happened, would it not, in a church in Cincinnati where the better class of people who go there even at night have higher standards than the hill they live on, not like down in the Basin where one could expect that sort of thing to happen, is that correct? Is that what you are saying?"

"Good God you are acting like a prosecuting attorney except that you are inwardly laughing and looking down your nose."

Winny went on with the interrogation, "Is or is that not what you are saying."

"Approximately," Reggie said, "Let's play tennis."

"And if it had happened it likely would have happened in an upholstered pew?" Winny persisted firmly.

"Very likely," Reggie admitted.

Winny never gives up, "Just one more question?"

"Yes?"

"Did you ever see that girl again?"

Reggie scowled, "Are you nuts?" he replied.

They had a good game of tennis but neither that day nor any day thereafter could either of them remember the score of the tennis game.

To summarize this essay on the rules of winning tennis without cheating it may be noted that Reggie generally followed these rules as presented and they served him well. But he had a lapse once and it was a humbling experience. In a friendly game that got too exuberant he was doing things like throwing his racquet as high in the air as he could after a missed shot. That was really high because of his youth and the leverage applied. Then he tried to catch it before it hit the ground. He was still losing. When he lost the set point he batted a ball into the wire backstop as hard as he could, except he hit it a little too high. It cleared the backstop and landed on the asphalt road paralleling the court. It bounded down the road like a baseball headed for center field at the Polo grounds, the longest center field in baseball, the field where Willie Mays had run forever and caught the ball over his shoulder, and Willie still had not reached the center field bleachers.

Etiquette required, of course, that Reggie retrieve the ball. He had a long walk and long return to the court. His friend was nowhere in sight. Neither was the car. They had come in the friend's car to a distant court. Reggie had to walk the two miles home. Neither one of them said anything about it and never has since. When they played tennis after that, Reggie managed to keep his temper and never again threw a racquet or hit one into the backstop.

ONLY THE WEATHER WAS FINE IN ANNAPOLIS

The blame cannot be shifted. Bob can't do it now any more than he could have shifted the blame in 1963, the year that it occurred. Bob McDonald was completely responsible for the Great Books fiasco in Annapolis on a beautiful Maryland day in May.

Great Books discussion groups were started throughout the country after World War II. Great Books became a popular, even phenomenally popular, form of out-of-school adult education in the fifties. The non-directive "leader" was perhaps the unique contribution of Great Books to adult discussion. Newcomers often reacted with a fervor akin to a religious conversion and with the same desire to proselytize others.

In Baltimore Bob McDonald joined in 1956 a first-year group led by Howard Wilhelm. Bob took Leader Training that same year and the next year was leading a first-year group and also continuing in Howard Wilhelm's second-year group. Bob welcomed the opportunity to read some of the classics that he had missed in college and he thrived on the question-and-answer format with a leader who did not summarize the discussion and who was forbidden by Great Book rules to express his or her own opinions.

Bob also immensely enjoyed meeting the varied personalities in a group and their different reasons for being there, ranging from getting out of the house, meeting a prospective spouse, or, as in Bob's case, to continue his learning. Many groups followed their evening meetings with a visit to a tavern, where they could pursue opposing views to the point of drunken confusion, or maybe find out what the leader thought, permissible after the formal discussion was over. Or, just learn more about the lives of group members. It was a way of associating with people on a more intimate basis than contact with their every day social personas.

Bob and many of his group joined Great Books at a time of life when they were at the height of their powers, enjoying success in their occupations, having children, active in community affairs like church activities. They were far enough beyond high school and college to have considerable confidence in themselves as human beings and, in their minds, to have learned a score or two. Ah, the Greek sin of hubris, the pride that tempts Fate that they were reading about in Great Books. In close human association their minds were being stimulated by intellectual striving and their bodies being warmed by shared confidences. Bob, usually not very sensitive to unexpressed subterranean emotions, nevertheless detected attractions between certain members within his group, some so obvious as to require little intuitive awareness. With sufficient examples, sometimes affective emotions will lead others to succumb to them.

Bob cannot plead that others were responsible for his behavior. As leader of the group Bob should have set a better example of concentrating on the readings and toeing all of them to the line. However, in their second year a young new member joined the group. She was blonde, soft-spoken, doe-eyed with a silky skin, also had married young, and had two children. Her name was Pamela Brenner that soon became Pam in their tavern bull sessions but, according to the fashion, was Mrs. Brenner in formal group discussions. She seldom answered Bob's questions unless called upon directly but her answers demonstrated a maturity that all could recognize. Although extremely young, about nineteen years younger than Bob, he found out she had a good grasp of Great Book fundamentals. She belonged. It did not take Bob long to realize that he was falling for her and before the first half of the year was over he was convinced that Pam was his soul mate.

Eventually, Bob was not able to conceal his feelings from all of the group. Mrs. Miller, an avid Great Bookie, asked Bob several pointed questions that Bob tossed off as frivolous and demeaning. Mrs. Miller, Mildred when in the tavern, invited the entire group to a Christmas party at her house and most of the group attended.

Mildred's husband, Charlie, who was not in the group, was immediately attracted to Pam, and flirted with her, paid her extravagant, sexy compliments as he placed an arm around her. Pam accepted his attentions, perhaps flattered that two men in the same room admired her. Mildred didn't seem to mind Charlie's arm around Pam. Mildred twittered waspishly at Bob. "Look," she said for all to hear, "Charlie is making more time with Pam at one party than Bob has made all year."

Bob looked sharply at Mildred. Was it possible that Mildred was jealous of Pam, that she desired Bob himself? He had had inklings that he had ignored. No one seemed to be in love with the right person. Pam seemed to love nobody but was thoroughly enjoying herself. Bob was mad at Mildred and was wretched within himself, "Oh hormones, where is thy victory, where is thy sting?"

For some reason in his second year, Bob was asked by the Baltimore Area Great Books Council to be coordinator of a joint one-day conference of all the groups in the Baltimore and Washington areas. For some reason Bob accepted. "Conference" was the early name for "Institute", a full day of discussion by all groups of readings not in the regular courses. It took both Washington and Baltimore to produce a worthwhile number of participants, perhaps a hundred and fifty to be divided into smaller groups for discussions. One could see different faces and hear new ways of expression and argument.

Bob had ideas about how the one-day meeting should be organized and planned. WITH HIS ADMINISTRATIVE EXPERIENCE, perhaps the reason he was made coordinator, he believed in delegating all tasks. In the planning meeting Bob delegated the tasks to individuals and subcommittees who then became the overall committee. A subcommittee chose the group leaders for the conference, with help from a Washington representative, of course. Another subcommittee picked and provided the books. A key individual working alone, a young Johns Hopkins physician, was responsible for the arrangements for the mid-day meal.

Bob's only input to any of the sub-committees was to the one selecting the readings. The theme was "What is a Practical Education in the Modern World?" The morning reading was from Henry Adams who wrote a book about his nineteenth century education in England and America. As a personal favor, Bob requested that the afternoon reading be from one of his favorite philosophers, Alfred North Whitehead, *The Aims of Education*. The committee accepted Bob's suggestion.

The committee organization worked well. Facilities at St. John's College in Annapolis, Capital of Maryland, were obtained. St. John's was the inspirational model for the concept of Great Books, believing that all education could be obtained by reading the classics, mainly the neglected classics of the ancient Mediterranean world. Mortimer Adler was the guru of the Great Books idea.

The Conference was on a Saturday. Participants would have the day off from work and St. John's classrooms would be free of students. The physician in charge of dining arrangements reported a veritable coup. He had come up with an offer of a local, Annapolis church to prepare and serve the meal. Mouth-watering recollections of church socials with groaning tables, laughing women parishioners, and a substantial cost savings over restaurant fare prompted the committee to accept at once. The church was just a few blocks from St. John's.

When conference day dawned bright and seventy degrees Fahrenheit, Bob couldn't believe their good fortune. The ladies in particular, dressing in hats and gloves, looked forward to these outings as festive occasions as well as intellectually stimulating. Bob arrived early in Annapolis to check on any last minute hitches. Bob found arrangements in order at St. John's and nothing amiss anywhere. Bob didn't think about the reading in the morning sessions, as he visited each group for a few moments to check if the discussions were lively and the leaders able. Principally, Bob glowed in his euphoria with the turnout, the weather, and the fact that they had reached noon sailing smoothly.

Bob's nervousness began with the mid-day meal, more accurately, a few minutes after the break for lunch. Bob's physician committee member in charge of lunch whispered to him that there had been a change in plans. They were not going to eat at the church two blocks away but in a hall across and down town by the waterfront and its marina. When the crowd came out of the building after the morning session they warmed themselves in the gorgeous sunshine, enjoying the slight May heat after a winter of snow and ice. Bob duly shouted to all within earshot and trusted that the others would fall into the line of march. "FOLLOW US TO LUNCH!!"

The physician and Bob led the procession, the physician to show the way and Bob to take responsibility that at first Bob did very loudly. They marched through town, stopping traffic at red lights. Annapolis was used to these files of marchers ignoring red lights, often bound for the State House and protests to the legislature, or citizens expressing themselves in front of the Governor's Mansion.

Great Books went on past the Maryland State House, explaining to several curious onlookers who they were, past the many good restaurants uptown that were sought out by visitors to this charming Colonial town of Annapolis.

Bob's file of expectant diners trekked down a side street to the waterfront. Bob had frequently visited the Annapolis marina and had enjoyed the seafood and also sailing on the Chesapeake with friends who owned boats. But as the line of march approached the waterfront, a feeling of unease crept into Bob's consciousness. The waterfront wasn't nearly the upscale marina that the ladies wished for and expected. For them it was decidedly blue-collar, a working area for shipping and ship's chandlers. Bob knew vaguely that some of the ladies were hobbling on the cobblestones that they hadn't thought of when they had dressed in the early morning in hats, gloves and high heels.

They marched across the cobblestones to a long brick building and into it. The building's light and air were two modest windows in front for light and the open front door that provided the only air. It was a warm spring day and sweat had broken out on the ladies' forelips and God knows where else as they marched the three-quarter mile in the hot sun through Annapolis.

Bob realized in desperation that a lot of heated bodies would have to be accommodated inside that small barn of a building. When they finally arrived he found that the open front door was completely ineffectual in admitting a whiff of cool air. The air was stagnant, moist and hot. The interior looked as though the last use of the building was by a ship's chandler in the nineteenth century and it was now empty except for the long wooden tables that had been set up to seat the Great Books luncheon. Bob knew that physical comfort was going to get worse and never better throughout lunch.

The one hundred and fifty or so people shuffled and squirmed into the dark recesses within. The long tables were close to the next row. Bob mumbled apologies in a low voice for stepped-on toes and squeezed matronly fannies. The light from the two front windows penetrated only about fifteen feet. From the long tables where they took their seats the diners stared at solid brick on both sides and the back.

Bob began feeling small as soon as they entered and as the meal was served felt smaller and smaller. As the eyes of the ladies sought him out, he wished he could disappear in the really large pot from which the church ladies were ladling baked beans with tomato sauce added. Dinner was served on paper plates with plastic spoons—baked beans, frankfurter pieces, applesauce without cinnamon and, on a side plate, cold slaw. Bob believed that iced tea was to be the drink because of the stifling heat. It was hot coffee. There was no dessert, either not planned or forgotten. The church ladies offered all the hot coffee one could drink.

Bob slumped down at the table and tried to be invisible, also deaf because some of the ladies from Washington were muttering in his direction. On the way back to St. John's Bob mingled with the crowd without identifying himself. He heard the ladies complaining that they had looked forward to a pleasant, chatty meal and really wouldn't have minded paying a little extra for some ambience and air-conditioning.

The afternoon session was a blur. Whether the meal had dampened all spirits Bob can't say, but Whitehead's *The Aims of*

Education laid an egg. At the closing evaluation in the auditorium with all participants attending, the Whitehead book was pronounced, "good reading but undiscussable," the ultimate kiss-off of an unsatisfactory discussion.

"Sly" Kingman, overall paid coordinator for the Baltimore area, didn't criticize Bob, to his face at least, for the poor conference. In fact, "Sly" never spoke to Bob again, except perhaps for a "hello" or "good-bye" when they happened to meet on Great Books business back in Baltimore.

At the next meeting of Bob's regular group that he was leading, Bob was relieved to find that only two or three members of the group had attended the conference. In his remaining years in Baltimore, Bob was never asked to do anything more than lead his group. The experience taught him valuable lessons: never trust volunteer help; when you delegate, stick your nose into each subcommittee's business, be skeptical of all their recommendations, relentlessly nag everybody to stay on the ball, and try your snooping best to find out how things are going.

Bob continued to long for Pamela. She continued to cause that aching feeling in the pit of the stomach. Now his love had been exposed to all and they both were embarrassed. He left for another city soon after. Frankly, he had suffered job disappointments in Baltimore and wanted a new start in a new city. He also remembered that he had a wife and children.

Unexpectedly, he did see Pam outside of the group on an August-hot parking lot and accosted her. They met, he explained that he was leaving on August 15 as they shook hands and said goodbye. He prolonged their meeting, then impulsively seized her. She did not object to his sweating brow and beaded forelip while they embraced in the only kiss of their years of each other's company. He mumbled something and walked away quickly.

From a distant city Bob poured his soul into a poem he sent to Pam lamenting his lost love for her. He thought it was his best poem ever.

RESOLVE

I must go back, untrack the years
Of dusty tears,
Resume old pleasures, dig for treasure,
Neglected fact.

There was a time when
A single star was sufficient by far.
A simple meaning, caught unweening
Was joy then.

From the ground unbound,
Swift rise to the skies,
A Body resplendent, earth independent,
A heaven found.

Those days were lost
Tossed in a thunder of worlds asunder,
Unscheduled collision for the gods' derision
At lovers swept under.

Oh celestial fire,
Retire, as you must, in flickering dusk,
Not without knowing, you have left glowing
Every spire.

Bob obviously preferred rhyming to lazy, modern, free verse, showing his enthusiasm for the Elizabethan poets' lyric cadences.

He never heard from Pam, then or ever.

EARLY ROMANCES AND UNREQUITED LOVES

One day R. was ruminating. When he ruminates he is certain to come up with a lengthy anecdote or tale. This day he was thinking about being a late bloomer when it came to women. He attributed this to the fact that as a teenager he had been busy with books and had spent a lot of time in libraries. He didn't learn to dance until he got to be a junior in high school and was under duress to go to proms and club banquets. And he was never a good dancer, faulty rhythm, lead-footed. Or, was it that he just wasn't attractive to women in the first place. R. wasn't ugly but he wasn't handsome either. He took an occasional gamble in life but he wasn't a daredevil. There was nothing about him to make a woman's heart skip a beat.

R. thought of Abraham Lincoln who was ugly but he had a red-hot romance with Ann Rutledge who died and later a marriage to Mary Todd. She was no prize. Lincoln became a melancholy, often depressed man. We can only speculate if history might have been different if he had married his true love. Would it have changed the outcome of the Civil War? Would soldiers have died for him if he were a smiling extrovert with a satisfying and beautiful First Lady and had not insisted upon unconditional surrender by a gallant Confederacy?

Then there was George Washington. Good looks and fighting for one's country do make a difference with the ladies. They can even overcome wooden dentures as George did. He interested Martha who was an older widow and she married him. He had a way with the colonial dames.

George Washington was the Father of his country. He slept many places on his frequent travels and obviously he didn't always sleep alone. He was a father in more ways than one and it didn't hurt his reputation either, then or now. Women don't look down on roués they just don't want their husbands to be one. Suppose Martha, instead of being an experienced women, wise in the ways of the world and, therefore, tolerant, suppose she had been a much younger girl who nagged her husband about his dalliance with waitresses and maids in taverns, a wife who engaged in crying jags. Would George have had the peace of mind to calmly lead his ragtail army and inspire men to do more than they thought they could? We'll never know how the country would have reacted to a hen-pecked George Washington. Then look at Thomas Jefferson— better not, the point has been made.

R. ruminated on the girl friends he had had and on other female encounters that had had mixed results. At a very, very early age, R. perceived that boys and girls had a special attraction for each other, almost as though they were meant to be paired throughout their lives.

He does not remember a romantic fantasy before the age of six—thoughts of a girl to go to sleep by. Before he was six, girls were different human beings to like or not like or maybe to contend with. As soon as his sister, Frances, was no longer a baby, R.'s mother put her in bed with him. Frances made his bed comfortable. She was a real heater, like a warm brick in bed, better than a warm brick because she never lost her warmth throughout the night.

The next experience R. had with a girl was not pleasant. It probably happened at a Kentucky Wesleyan football game in Winchester, Kentucky, long before the college moved to Paducah. R. was aware that his father was a minister in the church next door and that it was called Presbyterian to distinguish it from the Methodists which he later learned his mother was before she had met his father. But he did not know that his father had been a former coach of Kentucky Wesleyan football, also men's and women's basketball; these were normal extracurricular activities in addition to his faculty appointment as professor of Greek and Latin.

On the sides of the football field at Kentucky Wesleyan there were no bleachers, just grass. People sat or lolled on the grass. R. was probably tussling with this girl when she sat on his face. That made a lasting impression because she smelled bad, it was a surprise, puzzling, upsetting and hard to explain. That's all he remembered of her but the memory lasted a long time.

The next encounter that R. remembers with a girl had a pleasant smell associated with it. The family of the girl next door had a bakery on Main Street in Winchester a half-block from his house. She got to know R. and invited him upstairs in the bakery where the ovens were. He sniffed the wonderful aroma of the warm bread as it came out of the oven and often he was given a piece to eat.

When R. was four his family moved to St. Joe, Missouri, where his father was minister of Hope Presbyterian Church and where the Pony Express had originated on the way to San Francisco. R. met Junior Thompson who lived several doors down the street. They had their fifth birthdays just five days apart, R. being the older, and, therefore, the leader. They each got a knife for their birthdays. In a few days they wanted something to cut with their knives, besides whittling, and were feeling venturesome.

There were two girls going down the street to the grocery store. One of the girls was young, maybe four, her sister was six or seven and must have started to school already. R. and Junior Thompson hid between the houses and jumped out at the girls, knives upraised and yelling, "We're going to cut your ears off." The girls ran screaming down the street. R. and Junior chased them all the way to the grocery store where the girls went inside.

R. hid in the breadbox outside on the sidewalk and pulled down the lid. The grocery lady saw him, came out, pulled R. out by the ear, but he didn't squeal. The lady gave him a swat on the behind and told the two boys to be off. "Leave those nice little girls alone," she called after them. R. and Junior went down the back alley where they couldn't be seen from the street, then sneaked in between two houses, and waited for the two girls to come by. They came walking down the street holding hands, fearful, eyes darting at every bush. R. and Junior dashed out at them, brandishing their knives again and threatening again to cut off their ears. The girls screamed, dropping the loaf of bread and ran, the older girl pulling her little sister behind her. The big girl was fast and R. was not gaining on her while she kept hollering. R. glanced around alarmed as he felt eyes upon him from neighboring houses.

He was caught but he did not feel guilty. He ran and hid under the back porch of his own house, his favorite place to go when he thought his father and mother were going to blame him for something. He didn't know what Junior Thompson did. All was quiet for a long time. He had no lunch. He could hear his family eating with sister Frances slurping her milk and getting spoken to. Then all was quiet for a long time.

R. finally heard another man's voice upstairs, gruff and loud. His father was replying and then got angry and shouted back. R. put two and two together and decided it was the father of the two girls who was insisting that the boys be punished and R. heard something about watching or even giving the punishment himself. Apparently, that was what made his father mad. The man left and father still talked mad to R.'s mother.

R. stayed quiet under the porch a lot longer, until he could smell supper cooking and his mother called him. He came out and crept up the steps and into the house. He said not a word and kept his eyes on his plate. Mother tried to talk but got no help from R. or his father. Frances rattled on as if she had no gumption. Father said nothing until he had put R. to bed without a bath, then demanded, "Give me the knife." He didn't kiss R. as he usually did. R. meekly surrendered his knife. He was disappointed at losing it but reflected that his punishment could have been worse.

R. remembers nothing else of importance about girls until he started in the first grade in Jeffersonville, Indiana, where his father was minister of the First Presbyterian Church. His family moved a lot because his father was a minister.

At the Fourth Street Elementary School on Spring Street where R. started to school, they had a nice practice in the lower grades of pairing off boys and girls in line when they marched out of the building at recess, or to get a drink of water at the fountain, or to come in from the schoolyard in the morning. The first three grades on the ground floor simply marched out quietly holding hands, but upstairs in the fourth, fifth and sixth grades they separated the boys and girls. The big boys from upstairs came marching down the steps like soldiers, tramp, tramp, tramp, as a phonograph record played music. One record was the hymn that R. thought was the most popular one in church, and certainly was his favorite. "Onward Christian sold-a-gers, marching as to war, With the cross of Jesus, going on before."

Because R. was the smartest boy and Martha Jane Frank was the smartest girl in first grade they sat across the aisle from each other in the front row, were first in line and held hands. R. discovered that the attraction between boys and girls could be mutual when Martha Jane was quoted by her mother as saying that R. had "the cutest, fat, little hands." The remark was repeated by other mothers and R. heard about it. Martha Jane was also supposed to have said she wanted to marry R. He thought that was absurd. The way his preacher's family moved around, no telling where he would be when he grew up and was old enough to marry. R. discovered that boys could be nasty in their rivalries for attention of girls. They teased R. in the schoolyard, calling him, "Fat hands! Fat little hands!" R. took it right, he ignored them. After all, he had the girl!

In the first grade his teacher was Miss Dunn who reminded him of a little gray mouse. Maybe her name and the color "dun" had something to do with it. But her face was mousy also. She sent him often into the hall to read the clock, come back and report the time because she didn't have a watch. R. was the only one in the first grade who could tell time.

R. soon was aware of his own fickle nature. The affection between him and Martha Jane cooled. They still held hands because they both stayed number one in class. When he skipped the second half of the third grade, however, he left Martha Jane behind and seldom thought of her again.

In the second and third grades R.'s teachers were Miss Liston and Mrs. Thixton. R. thought that the two names spoken together were remarkably melodious. Miss Liston had blue eyes, stood up straight and enforced strict discipline, but was fair. Mrs. Thixton was squat and fat and grumpy. It was said that she didn't like children. R. laid low in her class. Unlike his usual self, he did not put up his hand and volunteer answers. R. was rid of Mrs. Thixton by skipping the last half of her grade and going upstairs to the fourth grade.

Miss Brooks was the fourth grade teacher, fair but she didn't take any nonsense. R. learned that the hard way and also that girls could get him into trouble. He noticed Jeanette Dodson. Jeanette was a tall blonde, snooty and demanding. R. admitted to himself that he was sweet on her but didn't like her attitude. She refused to acknowledge that R. was the smartest boy in class, even after he had won the spelling bee for the fourth grade and had gone to the school finals that were held in the principal's office. A girl from the sixth grade won and a boy from the fifth grade was second. R. missed first, spelling "mayor" with a "j," "m-a-j-o-r." When he was given the second chance, he thought maybe the principal had not heard him so he again spelled it "m-a-j-o-r." The boy snickered and curled his lip. It was pretty dumb to spell it the same way the second time, R. conceded. After he was spelled down R. went to the boys restroom and cried. Wilbur, who was in R.'s class and who had been excused to go to the rest room came in and saw R. crying. R. begged him not to tell anyone that he had cried and Wilbur didn't. R. and Wilbur became fast friends. R. got a quarter from the principal for finishing third.

It was the mail system that R. had invented which got him in trouble in the fourth grade. He had the pupils around him make mail boxes out of paper, attach them to the sides of their desks with chewing gum which had to be chewed without moving your jaws or else the teacher would make you spit it out or even stay after school. In their mail system, they wrote each other notes and R. acted as mailman.

R. got into trouble with certain things he did or tried. Sometimes he wondered why he did such things. His mother told him to ask his father. He as a minister was in charge of sins, big and small, and things that were bad but not bad enough to be called sins. His father seemed to be amused at the question and said, "Simply call it the 'Imp of Perversity'." The Imp sometimes gave R. a good time; at other times it caused lots of trouble.

R. didn't invite Jeanette to join their mail system and she seethed. Worse, R. sent gossipy letters to Cletus Higgins and others about Jeanette. He wrote Cletus about something that Jeanette was supposed to have done. "It was so shocking," he wrote, "that Jeanette lost her pants." Cletus laughed when she read it. Jeanette knew, without seeing it, that it was about her. She told Miss Brooks about the secret mail system. Miss Brooks promptly came down the aisle and took out all the mailboxes. She didn't know whom to punish so she didn't punish anybody. You can see that she was fair. Some teachers would have punished all of them, or try to get someone to tattle.

At the time R. thought he liked Cletus Higgins. But once when she recited her reading lesson in front of the class she pee'd and the urine ran down her stocking, making a puddle on the floor. While students stared at the puddle, she recited until she finished the assignment and went back to her desk. R. was disgusted and didn't give Cletus another thought.

It all ended when R.'s family moved to New Albany Indiana, in the middle of the second semester of the fourth grade, a town down the Ohio River but still across from Louisville, Kentucky. Father was again pastor of a First Presbyterian Church.

R. entered the fourth grade in New Albany and found it much easier and different from the Jeffersonville school system. That was mainly because the river rats came to R.'s school. They were children who lived down by the river. The area was lower than the rest of town. New Albany did not have a levee as many river towns did. The river flooded every two or three years and the river rats' houses filled with water. If the flood was bad enough they had to be taken out by boat and put up in schools and gymnasiums. Their houses, one room wide and running from front door to kitchen door, were swaybacked from the constant flooding.

The river rat children were snotty-nosed because of bad or little food sometimes. They ate lard on bread and had lots of colds. They were dirty because they wore their clothes a long time without washing. Some people uptown thought the river rat parents had brought their troubles on themselves by drinking bootleg liquor and not trying to get steady jobs. Some river rat women drank liquor which was forbidden by Prohibition and which respectable ladies did not do. R.'s father believed that river rats lived in sin because they had not been converted to Jesus Christ. Father's mission school was attempting to bring them to the Lord. R. learned that this opportunity for Home Missions was the reason they had moved from Jeffersonville.

The river rat children came to R.'s Market Street School. They were nice to R., because he was "the Revener's son." They liked R.'s father because he had started the home mission Sunday school in their dilapidated slum neighborhood.

However, the river rats caused R. trouble with a girl, Lenore, and her friend, Hazel. The girls at school would cut switches and chase the river rat boys at recess. It was their defense against the river rat boys who would hit girls, sometimes with their fists. The girls tried to switch R. but usually he would skip nimbly away. They seldom touched him except when he daringly taunted them.

The river rats did not like for the girls to switch R. because he was "the Revener's son." They told R. that he must get even with Lenore and Hazel for switching him. R. was not sure he should do that. His mother would disapprove of his hitting a girl but when R. hesitated the river rats called him "yellow," about the worst name you could be called.

Finally, R. did chase Lenore and Hazel down the street but he couldn't catch them. The river rats suggested that the next day he should go down the street and hide, and catch the girls when they came by. R. did and when they came abreast he ran out and hit Lenore in the stomach. She doubled over gasping for breath and crying. R. felt bad immediately and ran away with Hazel chasing him and trying to hit him with her pocketbook. R. did not hit her, he had already done enough damage, and he felt bad because

Lenore was crying. Thus, R. learned you should not hit a girl unless you thought she needed it, but if you were a real man you would let her beat on you unless it got too painful. You definitely should not let someone talk you into hitting a girl as the river rats had done. But after all they were river rats and what could you expect?

The school principal in New Albany was different from the principal in Jeffersonville. Mr. Snodgrass, the principal in Jeffersonville had ruled with an iron hand and a paddle. In New Albany the principal, Mr. Shoemaker, was nervous and afraid of his own shadow. He also taught R.'s class because the school was small, having only four grades.

Once when he tried to paddle a river rat the kid took the paddle away from him and tried to hit Mr. Shoemaker with it. Mr. Shoemaker managed to get the paddle back. The boy went home and brought his brother back with him. Mr. Shoemaker sent the brother sprawling. Next morning the river rat's father came to school. The pupils knew what was happening. They listened as Mr. Shoemaker met the man in the hall. R. was told that the father was a really big guy who worked in the foundry. He knocked Mr. Shoemaker down with a right hand and then a left. Mr. Shoemaker staggered back into the fourth grade room and swallowed the blood on his lips instead of wiping it with a handkerchief in front of his students. R.'s father would sometimes shake his head over the river rats' behavior. He wondered if Sunday school was doing them any good.

In the sixth grade, another school that R. attended, he met a girl who had R. carry her books home for her once in a while. When Christmas was approaching she confided archly to R., "I've got your Christmas present, have you bought mine yet?" R. nearly panicked. He thought that they had not known each other that well. He had spent all his Christmas money. He robbed his piggy bank without telling his parents and dashed to the department store downtown. He spent seventy-five cents for a bottle of perfume. It was good-sized, however. He wrapped it and gave it to her when they walked home the day before Christmas vacation.

Christmas came and went and no sign of her present. When school resumed after New Year's Day R. asked the girl if she had really sent him a present. "Oh," she assured him blithely, "it was lost in the mail." R. knew then that a woman's treachery knows no bounds. She can completely knock the wind out of a man and laugh about it. Oh, if he could only apply these lessons for the rest of his life.

When R. was twelve or so Mother hired a colored girl to iron once or twice a week after school. Her name was Naomi Love. What an unusual name R. thought. R. would watch her iron and would admire her coffee cream complexion. He began to tease her and she, in turn, would tease him. After she was through ironing they used to wrestle on the floor, seeing who could pin the other. She was fourteen and stronger than R. One day she not only put R. down with his face pushed hard against the floor, she got his arm behind his back and pushed it toward his shoulders. You can get your arm broken that way and she wouldn't let go.

No one was at home, not even R.'s sisters. Hurting and desperate R. called her a name, a name he knew she wouldn't like, and one he was forbidden to use. "Let go of me, you nigger!" That was a mistake. She let him go but then she really beat him up with her fists, no wrestling. When Mother got home Naomi told her. Mother made R. cut a green switch and she whipped him until she drew blood. Mother told Father when he came home and he whipped R. with his belt which he had never done before. Father took his religion very seriously. Mother dismissed Naomi whom R. never saw again. Nor did he use that word again in an angry way—or in any way at all.

R.'s thoughts about girls took a definite new turn when he entered the seventh grade. Actually, it was his first romance, one that was intense, and whose memory lingered and lingered, surviving his dating of other girls in high school.

Students from all the elementary schools in the city came to Main Street Junior High for the seventh and eighth grades, just a block from R.'s Market Street School and even nearer his home. He was in the smartest class based upon scores in the sixth grade.

The kids from uptown were different, they had more money than R., they weren't ashamed of their houses, and their mother's housekeeping the way R. was. R. never, never let any of his uptown friends visit him at home.

The uptown kids were much better dressed than the river rats. By the seventh grade most of the river rats had dropped out. R. knew their dropping out would hurt their chances for good jobs but they had no choice. R. sympathized with river rats but he didn't miss them and stopped thinking about them. The seventh grade was too much fun.

In his homeroom R. was taught English in the first period. R. noticed two girls right away. One was Bonnie Parsons who sat behind him and the other her closest friend, Rosalyn Reston. R. found himself competing with Bonnie who had been first in her class at Silver Street School. In the first semester R. clearly showed that he was smarter than Bonnie. Rosalyn, who sat across and up the aisle near the front, spent a lot of time turning around in her seat and looking back at her friend, Bonnie. They kind of giggled at each other from twenty feet away and through the students between them. R. was right in their line of sight. It took only a few days for R. to fall in love with Rosalyn. She was a gangling dirty blonde but R. liked everything about her. He thought even her name was beautiful. Her laugh did something to his insides.

This was different from all his other near "romances." It was real. He thought of her all day long when they changed classrooms and teachers for each subject. Different classrooms and teachers were a new feature of Junior High. At night Rosalyn was on his mind so that it was hard to go to sleep. The romance was painful because he lost sleep and he was tired the next day. He did not speak to her, of course. After all they were together all day listening to the other reciting in class.

Perhaps out of self-defense, R. told somebody that Rosalyn was making goo-goo eyes at him and that person told Rosalyn. She was indignant and informed him that she was looking only at Bonnie and that "he could keep his eyes on his own self." Her friend, Bonnie, did not like R., mainly because he was the smartest one in class and she knew it. She was used to being first at Silver Street School and she also seemed to be threatened by R.'s remark about Rosalyn's goo-goo eyes.

Bonnie took charge of Rosalyn to keep her out of trouble. Rosalyn was a heedless tomboy. Once when Rosalyn was leaning over the banister on the second floor, R. was looking up and could see right up to her panties. Bonnie made Rosalyn step away from the railing.

Bonnie wasn't always so successful. Rosalyn was an innocent creature who didn't know how to take care of herself. At the class picnic in Glenwood Park at the end of the term, Rosalyn fell into Silver Creek. She sputtered and climbed out, then took off her panties and wrung them out. She went to the bonfire to dry her dress and while she was waiting she roasted marshmallows with the other kids. She did not know or care that R. was gazing at her naked silhouette through her wet dress. Bonnie tried to steer her away from the fire but she refused to budge. She was beginning to make her own decisions even if Bonnie was smarter.

In the ninth grade and a new school R. experienced a disturbing fact of life, which he had known about since he was quite young and which he knew would affect him in time. Even so, the actual event was a surprise in many ways. He discovered SEX and its twin, LUST, coloring all his relations with girls from then on. He didn't lust for Rosalyn or any girls his own age. He lusted particularly for his Latin teacher who had red hair and a mature woman's body. He had visions of his Latin teacher keeping him after school so she could do it with him. R. tried hard in class to imagine it and stared at her with mouth agape and a piercing lustful stare which he hoped she would recognize for what it was. She never kept him after school.

When sophomores R.'s class moved to the new Senior High School a mile uptown, already too small for the freshman class. R. and Rosalyn saw each other every day but R. cast his lustful stares at Mrs. Pritz, another Latin teacher but black-haired. She had a daughter in R.'s class and he knew that that would prevent her from even thinking of keeping him after school.

Rosalyn and R. became more like friends. He heard that the junior and senior boys were after Rosalyn; he paid no attention to that. He never saw anything between Rosalyn and the older boys, but like most things in this new world of sexual attraction it was a secret and a mystery.

In high school a lot of students became more interested in dating than in school work. R. kept his grades up without working very hard. He found time to go out for football and made the team his junior year. R. was tougher than he looked as a scholar. He went out for basketball but he was cut because he couldn't make lay-ups, called crip shots in R.'s day, or hook shots with either hand. He was also short and slow. This *was* Indiana, not Ohio or Illinois.

R. did not lust for girls his own age until he met Jane Giles in the Senior Class Play. She was a Jean Harlow type. In the play, *Skidding*, Jane was the daughter coming home from college and R. was the father, Judge Stone. They were rehearsing the opening scene where June comes home, runs into her father's arms, and kisses him. It was not just a kiss; as Jane did it, it was more of a moist osculation. R. had never been kissed like that before. He embraced her awkwardly. Miss Watson, the teacher who was the play director, made R. and Jane practice the scene again and again. Metaphorically speaking, R. was all thumbs. His boyhood chum, Strickland, who played Andy Hardy, began to count aloud the times they tried for an acceptable kiss—four, five, six times. R. lost all interest in getting it right. Jane was warm and plump in his arms and seemed to enjoy the kissing as much as he did. Whereupon, Miss Watson called a halt, seeing that they were abusing her good nature.

On the night of the play R. looked forward to the moist kiss before the audience of students and parents. R. would be showing the guys that he was not just a scholarly grind, that he could kiss like any other football player. At the crucial moment he puckered up his lips but Jane barely grazed them, making R. look like a frustrated, lustful dummy. It turned out that Jane's boyfriend, Tony, home from Purdue, was in the audience and Jane did not want him to get the wrong impression. There was something Jane did not know. Before the opening curtain R. had been given a greasepaint mustache by the make-up artist and as Jane grazed his lips a long black smudge of greasepaint was left across her cheek. What did Tony think of that? Jane wore the greasepaint until the curtain went down at the end of Act I and she looked in the mirror. R. was glad that she saw how she looked. In the rush between acts the greasepaint was quickly swiped, but a gray circular shadow remained for the second and final act.

In the play R.'s character, Judge Hardy, said as the plot reached a crisis, "This family is really skidding," and that gave the play its name, *Skidding*. Of course, a senior high school play has a happy ending so the family righted itself and no longer skid but danced at the final curtain.

Before the summer was out the cast of the play saw their high school comedy picked up by Hollywood and brought out as the first of the Andy Hardy series. Strickland's part of Andy Hardy was played by Andy Rooney who had outgrown his part in the Our Gang Comedies. R.'s Judge Hardy was Lewis Stone. Margaret Rutherford was the daughter, Jane Gile's character. As they watched it at the Grande movie theatre, the cast felt somehow honored that their play had "gone Hollywood."

R. was off to Harvard College in the fall and was plunged into a school without girls for the first time. As a freshman he had nothing to do with girls, the freshman dances were huge affairs in cavernous Memorial Hall, costing a great deal and R. knew no one to date. His fantasies were confined to waitresses at the Freshman Union dining room and other working girls around Harvard Square who had no inclination to meet a Harvard freshman.

When sophomores, students moved into the new college Houses, patterned somewhat like the separate colleges of Oxford and Cambridge. There were about three hundred men to a House that had its own dining hall, library, athletics, and social affairs. The Houses were much better equipped for a wide range of activities than college fraternities and R. was proud of their superiority.

All sophomores who were inclined and accepted moved into

the Houses. Some did not have the grades and had to live in the Cambridge jungles. Others, mainly the blue bloods and wouldbes of "old Harvard" lived in the private rat houses abutting the College Houses, what remained of the slums of Cambridge after the Houses had been built in the early 1930's.

R. was admitted to Lowell House. His social life took an upward bound. R. went to Lowell House dances. The Houses hired bands like Tommy Dorsey, Benny Goodman, and "Les Brown the Band of Renown." R. took girls to the dances from Wellesley, Smith, and in a pinch, even Radcliffe next door. The girls would come by train. Their Harvard dates would meet then at the Boston train station and after the dance would accompany them to the station and see them onto the train home. Fortunately, the girls would stand the expense of getting there.

While in college R. once visited Indiana University to see Sherman Minton and other friends at I.U. before the Harvard term had started in late September, later than midwestern colleges. He looked up Rosalyn, his seventh grade flame and high school rival, for old times sake, and maybe to brag a little and bask in the reflected glow of Harvard. He took her to a dance. She was a lot better dancer than R. but he enjoyed the evening. He walked her to her sorority and said good night. It was a pro forma kiss. That was the only intimacy ever between them.

R. seldom dated the same girl twice and, frankly, none of them inspired the passion R. was feeling for "the girl he had left behind" in New Albany. This was a younger girl, June Gohman, whom R. had put on hold until she grew up.

When he was in high school June was still in the eighth grade. She and R. sang in the choir of the First Presbyterian Church. She was bright, gay, giggling, and pretty and accomplished on the piano. But June at fourteen was much too young for R. even when he was a high school senior. He had dated appropriately other high school girls, almost all seniors he had gone to school with since the seventh grade. Most were members of the Speakers Club for girls. They exchanged dates with R.'s Wranglers Club for their respective annual banquets. He didn't feel quite equal to dating

Rosalyn, a Speaker, whose interests seemed to be elsewhere and who would have shown him up as a dancer. However, she was always at the banquets with someone and R. danced with her. Nothing happened.

R. kept in the unthinking part of his mind that June Gohman would someday be old enough to date. Meanwhile they were the best of choir friends, giggling and trading quips. In his sophomore year and on the bus ride home for the Christmas holidays, R. dreamily indulged in thoughts of the warmth of his family's celebration and then seeing June on a date. June had been much on his mind since he had seen her so tan and vivacious in September after summer vacation. "She walked in beauty like the night, when first she gleamed upon his sight." He knew it was time to pursue June in earnest. At fifteen or sixteen and a sophomore in high school, June was quite old enough for him and had undoubtedly grown in maturity and social behavior.

He arrived in New Albany after the tiring forty-four hour bus ride, saving money at Christmas rather than going by rail as he did in the fall. He eagerly awaited choir practice; the choir was going to present *The Messiah*. He hurried to the church on Friday night for practice. June was there and the sight of her immediately hit him in the pit of the stomach. She was radiant and giddy with girlhood. She had been worth waiting for. She had grown taller but was still gangly, legs not quite sure of themselves, but that just emphasized how natural and unaffected she was.

Christmas vacation was all too short for a real romance. At choir practice, R. managed to blurt out that he wanted a date with her and would call her after Christmas. She turned her demure gaze on him and gave a teasing Mona Lisa half-smile. On Christmas Eve the First Church rang with the triumph of The *Messiah*. R. outdid himself, a booming bass, not his usual timid, uncertain quaver.

R. pondered the possibilities for their first date, whether it would be a double date and what they would do. Maybe he could line up someone for a double date who had use of a car that R.'s family did not have. They could go dancing at the Lavender Cottage.

June was probably not a great dancer and would tolerate his lack of polish, actually his deficient rhythm. R. had found out he could get along on the dance floor if his partner didn't expect too much and liked him. His clever and intelligent conversation could overcome mistakes in footwork. At Harvard in those days, Noel Coward's wit was the model, sharpened by Harvard peers, for talk on the dance floor. Harvard, so to speak, had prepared him for his date with June.

R. decided that for a first date he would like to see June alone, perhaps take her to a movie. Double dating could wait until they knew each other better. He called her and asked for a date. Hearing her throaty voice, R. knew that he was already in love with her.

R. was not naive, he understood the connection between romance and desire, also the differences. June was not overtly sexually exciting to him. She did not have the animal sexiness called glamour. R.'s passion was filtered through a screen of hoped for warm understandings, potential exchanges of confidences, a meeting of like minds, in other words, mutual respect. The thought of June in his arms also gave R. this knotting of the stomach and the glow up and down his spine, but it did not lead to a dream of sexual embrace as seeing a movie star might. Toward June, R. felt a mixture of tenderness, nurture, excitement and even a bit of a desire to teach her and show off his new college learning.

June lived out on Charleston Road beyond the city limits, farther than the end of the streetcar line. It was an area of large, middle class houses, private clubs, tennis courts and pools— symbols of affluence beyond the city and socially above the crowded city dwellers. R. took the streetcar and then walked to June's. The street became a country road, no sidewalks, dark, with ditches and culverts. R. had no trouble bumbling along feeling for footing. Nights on grandfather's farm had taught him. His heart was light and his tread was feathery.

Mrs. Gohman, June's mother, met R. at the door. June's seclusion upstairs conformed to social requirements. From watching his sister, Frances, prepare for a date, R. knew the etiquette. Mrs. Gohman and R. eyed each other as they sat in the living room. R.

had had only a glimpse of her previously. The Gohmans went to an uptown church befitting their circumstances. Only June's friendship with Ruth Kirk, her best friend known as "Precious," whose father belonged to R.'s church, brought her to First Presbyterian.

Mrs. Gohman was an outspoken woman of substantial build and a face bordering on the attractive. Mrs. Gohman asked truly inquisitive questions about Harvard, one of the few people in New Albany who had bothered. R. was determined to like Mrs. Gohman. Other than her approval of him as a Harvard man, R. thought that he had detected a certain coolness toward the rest of him and his family. She did not inquire about his parents and his sisters. She must have known something about his family, Dad, in particular. As minister of a large church, R.'s father was a public figure. R. had expected inquiries from Mrs. Gohman.

She looked out the window and confirmed that R. had not arrived in a friend's car. June made her entrance down the stairway, more made up than R. had ever seen her. The vermilion lips made her look ravishing and sexy. June required no eyebrow pencil, nor eye shadow. Her dark brown brows were quite heavy and she had hollows under her eyes similar to R.'s. It gave her a serious, soulful look.

R. was telling Mrs. Gohman as June was coming downstairs where they were going—to the movies on Vincennes Street. That involved, as she knew, catching the streetcar three-fourths of a mile from the Gohman house. The streetcar stopped at the end of the paved street, the city line.

R. found himself standing there exposed for what he really was, the son of a poor minister of one of the less prosperous churches in town, whose family did not own a car and who was proposing to walk the daughter of an upper class family to and from a Toonerville Trolley to go a couple of miles to a small business area that was on the verge of folding, to see a Grade B movie that R. had not had the courtesy to consult June about, and with whom he would return at an uncertain hour if they did indeed catch the last street car of the evening, leaving R. to get home as best he could in the wee hours.

R. saw clearly what an unattractive date he was for Mrs. Gohman's daughter. Somehow he managed to clear the house with June, surviving the mistrustful look upon Mrs. Gohman's face. June did have trouble walking on the shoulder of the road in the loose gravel. A long wait for the streetcar was not relieved by conversational gems from either of them. Without much thought, R. had planned to go to the Vincennes Theatre. It was the least desirable of New Albany's three theatres, getting pictures long after the Elks and Grande downtown, or else booking pictures that would never make it to a first-run house. R. considered momentarily the possibility of staying on the car and going downtown to a good theatre. He realized instantly that then they would have no chance of catching the last street car to Charleston Road.

The streetcar banged along Charleston Road and then Vincennes Street, bumping noisily over a route that would have been comfortably and quickly covered by automobile. As they passed the high school June told him she seldom rode the streetcar. Her father took her to school on his way to work and her mother picked her up after school. June told R. that since she was now sixteen her father had promised to teach her to drive next summer and then she would not be dependent upon anyone for transportation.

The show was a gangster movie with Lloyd Bridges, King of the B's and actresses that no one had ever heard of. At the movie, June smiled wanly in the dark, neither shocked nor amused. Before the evening was over and they had had ice cream at the corner drugstore, it was clear that June was bored with R.'s company and inconvenienced with the dating arrangement.

As they walked back from the streetcar to the Gohman's R. began to describe his plans for the next date, to go dancing with another couple, maybe a group. He pointedly made clear that it would include door-to-door transportation. June assented without enthusiasm. Before they got to the door a few drops of rain were falling. Mrs. Gohman was waiting up for them, if it could be so described since it was not even midnight. She promptly opened the door, killing any possibility of a warm parting between June and R., a real breach of parental etiquette. Mrs. Gohman surveyed her daughter for damage. June was dry. Nevertheless, Mrs. Gohman said, "I should have driven you in the car as I thought about doing," June and R. assured her that the night had been fine for the little walking needed.

The goodbyes were swift and June went upstairs without a commitment on a future date. Her mother noticed the raindrops beginning to fall, "It's raining quite hard now. I'd be happy to drive you home. You live near the Presbyterian Church, don't you?" The offer to take him home was the crowning humiliation. R. wanted to say, "Hell no, you meddlesome old hag!" but instead he lied, "I have a tentative date to meet some guys at The Nook," a high school hang-out on the way down Vincennes Street, "and I won't have any trouble getting there."

"But the rain," Mrs. Gohman persisted.

"I'll run between the drops," R. promised airily.

The last street car had gone and it poured every minute of his five-mile walk home. R. was disappointed but at the same time was strangely exultant. He had broken the ice. June was just as stimulating as he had imagined and was a scintillating conversationalist when she wanted to be. Smart, attractive, unspoiled and a young thing who sent his senses soaring! What more could one ask of a girl? Perhaps a friendlier mother, he admitted.

R. got home soaked and bedraggled. His mother stirred and went to the bathroom as he undressed in his room. She had the good sense not to come into his room. His suit in the next few days shrank and was never the same even though it was sent to the cleaners. Mother stared at his suit and wondered aloud but he did not answer questions about the evening.

R. was sobered and embarrassed after his first date with June but not defeated. Silently, R. quoted, more or less, the old saying, "The course of true love never runs smoothly." As R. analyzed his fiasco, he told himself that it was alright for a guy with a car just to pick up a date and do something spontaneously, even if was only to park. But men without resources like R. must have a better plan. It was his own arrogance that had led him to cut such a poor figure. No wonder that June and her mother had been so offended. June was coming into a happy time in her life with dancing, dating, the sillies and romantic dalliance, and so deserved the best in transportation and entertainment. R. had to double date with a friend who had use of a car.

He made arrangements with Strickland, his chum, before calling June. They would have Strickland's father's car and go to a *good* movie in Louisville, an early show to leave plenty of time for dancing at the Lavender Cottage on the New Albany side of the river. Strickland had two or three girls on the string and, although sympathizing with R., he felt quite superior. However, he assented to all of R.'s requests.

In growing up in New Albany, R. had never really missed not having a family car. He liked to walk and did walk everywhere. His father was his model. He was a minister and had no car, saving his money, he said, for his children's college educations. He walked all over town to visit parishioners, shut-ins, to food shop and for all other business. Now as a suitor, R. saw that to go anywhere interesting, one had to have a car. The girls expected it. It was the Depression and some girls would date you without a car. But those girls were definitely blue-collar types; their boy friends had not gone beyond high school.

Having to depend on the generosity of friends to accept him, as a double date, was demeaning. Besides there were times when he wanted to be alone with a date, park on Silver Hills, overlooking the river and Louisville, pet a little in private, not have to share a moment with another couple, a friend who might be copping a feel in the front seat.

R. had difficulty getting June on the phone. She was either out or they thought she was in, nobody knew quite where. R. finally found June at home. She hemmed and hawed, giggling over R.'s suggestions as to why she might be hesitant. He was only joking, of course. R. reassured her that she would not get wet under any circumstances since Strickland was certain to have his father's car. He mentioned that they probably would go to Louisville. Finally, June assented.

On a cold, crisp Saturday night R. bounded up the steps to the Gohman's door in fine spirits and breathing clouds of steam. Mrs. Gohman again met him at the door and despite a baleful glance at the car in the driveway, she seemed pleasanter to R. From a back room, Mr. Gohman chirped, "I guess it's OK for you to date my daughter. You are going to Harvard and they say you are smart and have good prospects." Mentally, R. did not take umbrage but was comforted by the father's remark.

June took longer than usual before coming downstairs and when he saw her R. wondered what had taken so long. Her outfit was quite ordinary, a plaid skirt and sweater, suitable for school but nothing special for a big evening on the dance floor. To this ensemble June had added a beautiful, brown fur coat for warmth. It was her married sister, Henrietta's, who was home for the holidays.

They were going to Louisville to Loews, a new luxury movie theatre, featuring a blue sky overhead and twinkling stars, floating clouds made by steam, with a surrounding Spanish or Moroccan skyline, R. couldn't tell which even after History 1 in college. It was brand new, Louisville able to follow the lead of New York. Loews was the place to take your best girl when you wanted to really impress her and have a wonderful time together. R.'s mother who knew about expenses for a glamour girl had slipped five dollars into his palm.

June was not talkative on the way to Louisville, rather persistently gazing out the window. It was cold in the car. In the back seat R. put his arm around her, embracing more fur than girl. In June's mood he dare not slip a hand under the bulky fur coat even at the waist. His face was close to June's but she kept her face averted. As they sped across the river the side railing rattled on the old, condemned Kentucky and Indiana Bridge. June was in the dark except for the flashes of the small bridge lights on and off her face, as when the movie projector slows to one frame at a time. June's dark hair and luminous eyes were beautiful.

The movie had already started when they walked in. The movie was the latest Marx Brothers picture, *A Day at the Races*. The critics were beginning to accept the Marx Brothers buffoonery as truly a folk art that the intelligentsia could enjoy without apology.

June was not amused with Chico's cute piano playing. She was taking piano lessons at the Conservatory in Louisville along with her friend, Precious, on the violin. June did not laugh at Harpo's silent clowning nor was she amused at Groucho's lascivious eyebrows. Strickland was guffawing so hard that R. thought he would blow a tonsil, if he had had any, and his girlfriend was trying to shriek in unison. So June and R. were mostly silent. R. was not a hearty laugher. A noisy chuckle was his most demonstrative. R. saw Strickland's date eyeing them and arrogantly laughing in June's face. It augured poorly for their evening together at the Lavender Cottage.

At Strickland's insistence they stayed into the second show to see what they had missed, actually well into the show because Strickland wanted to see the horse race again. Then it was a wild ride back to New Albany to make up time. June sat looking out the car window, twisting her beautiful raven locks with one finger. R. saw the stare on her pale, cold face, felt the limp icy hands. She did not return his embrace when he tried to kiss her. They had lost even their juvenile ease and teasing with each other during choir rehearsal.

On the New Albany side of the river June made it immediately known that she had to go home. It was just a little before eleven and they could have buzzed up to the Lavender Cottage, had an hour of dancing, and delivered June by 12:30. R. had been around enough to know that a half-hour late on Saturday night was a trifle. When the wheels rolled to a stop in her driveway June got out and was up the steps before R. could come around to her side of the car. She disappeared into the house with only a slight glance that acknowledged R.'s presence and contribution to the evening. He retreated to the car precipitously and caught Strickland with his hand under his girl's skirt, a faux pas by R. that was definitely caused by June's abrupt dismissal of him. Strickland's girl glowered at R. When R. was let off at his door he knew that Strickland and

his date were headed on the long ride back across town to the
Lavender Cottage. R. heard the girl laughing at him as the car
pulled away.

For the rest of the vacation June's face swam continuously before
R.'s eyes, her voice sounded in his ears. His disillusionment with
June did not seem to relieve him of an obsession that was painful
and constant. He went over their conversation of the last date,
pinpointing where he might have said something more interesting,
funnier, or just less stupid. He thought of the girls he had impressed.
Why should June be immune to his charms? At least she could
have played the dating game graciously without serious intent as
everyone else did.

In the next few days he heard from his sister, Frances, that
June was back in high school. When R.'s longer vacation was over
and he climbed onto the bus for the exhausting ride back to Boston,
June's image was vivid all the way to Cambridge and hardly
dimmed in the ensuing weeks. The weather in January and February
was dull, raw and dirty, without the clean, crisp snow that made
New England winters so exhilarating for those from midwestern
snowless drought lands. R. took long walks, talking to June as a
silent companion, pouring out his affection and hopes for them as
a pair. He explored the recesses of Mt. Auburn cemetery and
followed the Charles River upstream until it was only a trickle. He
branched out on Cambridge streets beyond the shadows of the
University and into neighborhoods where "Harvard" was a word
like "hell" and "bastard." He walked day and night, discovering
new areas, and seeing by night how familiar places took on an eerie
cast. In class, going to sleep, playing basketball on the Lowell House
team, horsing around with his roommates, he was sad and had no
relief.

Gradually his image of June began to change into the real
person she was, the one with spaces between her teeth, the hollow
eyes that made her look unhealthy. The edges of her front teeth
were slightly serrated. The fuzz on her upper lip was as black as
her hair and resembled a mustache. Suddenly R. saw in the girl
that he had been so romantic about a rather sallow teenager,

contemptuous of his best efforts to please. His pursuit of her had been based on a false image that he had concocted in his head. She did not give a fig for him. Realistically, June was an ordinary, raw-boned, awkward young adolescent.

His unflattering image of her did not seem to help at first. Actually, the tactic turned against him because he now began to regard June as ungainly, almost gauche, and in need of special nurture. She was not a typical, mindless teenager. She was thoughtful and vulnerable. She needed R. as a protector if she would have just come to her senses.

June continued to prey on his mind until the passage of time produced its magic healing. The months dimmed even his realistic picture of her. Now his fading memory of how she really looked was beyond his recall. He could remember the broad outlines; she was tall and angular. He could not remember the details of what must have been her attractiveness, nor the giggling laughter that once had been music to his soul. Crowding out all others was the single picture left—her cold, dead, half-sneering face in the car back to New Albany. That helped him to forget.

In poetry class R. discovered John Donne, mordant necrophile, his imagery unforgettable, "Men have died and worms have eaten them, but not for love," but then, "Ask not for whom the bell tolls, it tolls for thee." R. decided it was much too early for the bell to toll for him.

He suddenly came to and realized he had not been concentrating on his studies. He could not afford the luxury of unrequited love. He could lose his scholarship. He resumed hard work in school. R. enjoyed Lowell House and his roommates. He went to House dances and met other girls imported from Vassar, Skidmore, and even Wellesley. He thrived, he became a mini-hero as a Junior and was a nostalgic Old Boy as a Senior. But, frankly, none of his dates sent his spirits soaring the way June had.

All good things, college, too, come to an end. R. was graduated and found himself facing the real world. Harvard had encouraged him not to be concerned as an undergraduate about a profession. That would be for graduate school. The only thing Harvard seemed to prepare one for was continuation in one's major field of study. R. was tired of English literature and besides desired a life of action, not research and study. He was not sure what he wanted to become in his life, the long road ahead.

R. was enamored of Franklin Roosevelt's New Deal and decided that he wanted to be a government bureaucrat and further the Roosevelt Revolution.

A recruiter from the Federal Department of the Interior came to Harvard and firmed up R.'s aspirations. He interviewed R. about a training position in the Interior Department and R. was accepted. Interior sounded right for him with its mission of conservation, running the National Park Service, protecting wild life and fishing, continuing the legacy of the first Roosevelt, Theodore Roosevelt. R. was assigned as a Field Aide in the Indian Service, Albuquerque, New Mexico, which R. had never heard of. He was assured that protecting what remained of the American Indians was an important part of Interior's mission.

In Albuquerque, a whole new vista opened up for R. He had never been west of St. Joe, Missouri, and that was before he had started school. Albuquerque and the Indians were the real West.

In Albuquerque R. met a nice dish, Cecily Taylor who pronounced her name "Sicily" and lived with her widowed mother, and had never been east of the Sandia Mountains just outside Albuquerque. R. believed that Western girls would be looser than Eastern girls. Then he had met Cecily. She permitted no petting, no kissing, no nothing. She had a pretty face and was curvy well-rounded. They had dates using R.'s government car to go to Old Town and take them to the best restaurants for authentic Mexican food, soft tortillas, pinto beans and rice, flavored with Mexican music.

Under Cecily's tutelage, R. learned the graceful Varsuvyana, "put your little foot, put your little foot right out" and the Raspa which was no more than a stomp. Cecily fit right in with R.'s Field Aide colleagues on multiple date nights. R. admired the courage of Cecily and her mother who coped without a man and asked no favors. Cecily was a student in Laboratory Technology at the University of New Mexico in Albuquerque.

After a week's work with the Indians, R. began to look forward to his weekend evenings with Cecily. The United Pueblos Agency knew that Aides used their assigned cars on non-government business besides driving to meals and home from downtown Albuquerque. How were Aides to have any social life without the use of cars? The Agency winked at the Aides' illegal use of cars and to hell with the Washington bureaucrats who wrote the regulations. The Agency didn't care where the Aides drove so long as it was in the Albuquerque area, but no midnight jaunts to Sante Fe or Gallup.

R. wooed Cecily by singing to her on the road to Sante Fe, "Come to me my melancholy bay-be, cuddle up and don't feel blu-ue." He got nowhere, not even a hand on her knee. Cecily was honest. R. thought his crooning was quite melodious, his narrow range expanding in the car's resonant interior. "If you think that sounds good, you are mistaken," she stated firmly but it was still said with a giggle that told him his efforts were appreciated. Cecily's mother was a voice and piano teacher and Cecily's judgment did not call for diplomacy.

Cecily did R. the honor of fearing his attractiveness, none of "don't touch me, you creep," no posture of the rejecting iceberg. Instead it was, "we don't know each other very well, I don't think I can trust myself with you" and "I get too emotional." So R. had to forego the goodnight kisses, almost a ritual of his midwestern dating. Somehow, they settled for a chaste pressure of R.'s lips on the back of Cecily's neck. Even then she shivered and R. sometimes let his hands from the rear slip to the front. Too bad R. was such a hip and thigh man, not too excited by mammary glands. He had been imprinted as a youngster by the frequent sight of nursing babies in church. There was a time at a revival meeting in the country where his grandparents lived that a young mother, overcome by the preacher's invitation, had impulsively marched up the aisle to accept Christ as her personal Savior while Junior was on her arm, still clinging to his supper. Generally, R. accepted Cecily's scruples.

As often happened among the Field Aides, R. was given an assignment that would take him away from Albuquerque and involve his staying overnights. R.'s assignment interrupted his courting of Cecily. It was to go to the Zuni Sub-agency way out toward the Arizona border, far from the other Pueblos along the Rio Grande River, more in Navajo country than Pueblo. R. was to spend a week or so evaluating the need for Zuni's eight-bed hospital. Closing it would save nursing funds and add to other budgets. R. drove out Route 66 to Gallup and took the road south to Zuni. He was forbidden to tell the Sub-Agency Superintendent of his mission. Of course, the poor fellow was already insecure about the future of the Sub-Agency, felt neglected by Headquarters in Albuquerque, and was generally disenchanted with the Indian Service. R. de-emphasized his visit as just a friendly trip for R. to learn more about United Pueblos in this distant outpost.

R. was assigned a room in the Visitors Quarters and prepared to goof off. The Zuni Indians were interesting; their pueblo was not far away from Agency buildings. This surveillance of a small idle hospital with a pre-determined answer beat work on a real project. It so happened that R. was there over Thanksgiving, a holiday for all personnel. After breakfast R. holed up with the Steinberg best seller, *The Grapes of Wrath* and with time out only for meals he read the book by evening.

Then, there was a turkey dinner in the guest dining room for a variety of visitors. A traveling construction crew from the telephone company was staying in the guest quarters. The crew was building an intercontinental telephone relay station on Zuni land, a project taking weeks. One of the telephone crew had a good voice and he was prevailed upon at the turkey dinner to sing a new hit that was sweeping the country, "South of the Border." The lyric tenor sang soulfully, a flaw being that he could not pronounce his "th's." The line became, "Souse of ze border, down Me-hi-co-way."

Another visitor slipping in from somewhere was the Director of Arts and Crafts from Albuquerque. She was there on business and seemed a bit embarrassed in R.'s presence. But he was just a harmless Field Aide. Another odd visitor was an airline hostess visiting a nurse at the tiny hospital. An impromptu party was arranged for the evening in the Nurses Quarters for all personnel stuck on the Zuni Reservation for Thanksgiving.

At the party good liquor appeared. The Director of Arts and Crafts was there. Because she was a full-time Civil servant and had been employed for an important New Deal program—to end the exploitation of Indian artists and to give them adequate financial rewards for their work—it is best that the Director's name not be divulged. She sat on the tenor's lap where she was surprisingly loquacious and limber but she was drinking less than most of the party. Liquor was illegal on Indian land, including the Agency. This perhaps explained the Director's seeming discomfiture at R.'s presence and imminent return to Albuquerque Headquarters. However, things are seldom what they seem. R. later learned she was less concerned about the liquor than the possibility that R. would say something to her boyfriend in Albuquerque about the tenor. The tenor was about her age.

Missing from the party was the middle-aged Nursing Supervisor who ran the residence, and in fact the hospital. The other nurses present said she ran both "like a prison or a convent." The Nursing Supervisor had accepted an invitation to spend Thanksgiving in Albuquerque.

R. drank his share of Old Crow and was feeling quite mellow when he had to go to the bathroom. On the way back there occurred one of those unfortunate coincidences that an innocent victim can never explain. R. could give his version of events ad infinitum, but no one would have the slightest desire to believe him. For those at the party, all drinking on an Indian reservation, the disbelief may have been affected by the undeniable fact that thirty minutes before the incident the airline hostess had plopped down on R.'s lap, or maybe he pulled her down, what difference does it make after a few drinks. He bussed her which is more thorough than just kissing but far short of copping a feel in a well-lighted living room of a Nurses Residence on an Indian reservation.

When R. went to the bathroom the airline hostess had left his lap and was then on a bed in the bedroom. She probably had had too much to drink and had wisely wandered in there for a short nap. On the way to the bathroom R. passed her by with bare notice and used the toilet. As R. groped his way back to the party in the dark he lurched heavily onto the bed and fell on top of the airline hostess. The triad went crashing to the floor—R., the hostess and the bed. Perhaps the bed had been carelessly assembled. The hostess had been asleep.

R., befuddled, did not arise immediately, not displeased with the position he found himself in. There was no movement, repeat, no movement, until those in the living room rushed into the bedroom and snapped on the light. Fearing the worst, they saw the best, R. on top of the hostess on a broken down bed.

Back in Albuquerque the Director of Arts and Crafts proved to have a poisonous tongue. R. was obliged to walk around the hall in the Agency offices enduring sneaky glances from secretaries, hearing titters, catching an occasional word or two "creaking springs until . . . . boom, drunken brawl, lonely nurses" and other uninformed surmises. The venom infected even R.'s fellow Field Aides who should have resisted the temptation to deal in third-hand fabrications since they hadn't been there. As often happens with R., the Director counted on his silence about the tenor at the same time as she was blackening his reputation concerning the airline hostess.

R. resumed the good life and wooing of Cecily in Albuquerque. Suddenly R. had a precipitous return east when Washington discovered he was not the man originally recommended for the job, a case of mistaken identity by someone in Washington who was consulted by R.'s recruiter. Also, R. had to admit to a checkered career in the Indian Service, beginning with his trying to drive a car when he didn't know how and continuing when his naiveté about government practice led him to challenge Dr. Aberle, head of United Pueblos. Her understandable rule was that all correspondence to Washington should be signed by her. R. didn't see the point of this, and really thought it unethical because section chiefs in Albuquerque corresponded "unofficially" but directly with their Washington counterparts.

R. had a last date with Cecily. She melted and let him put his arm around her, and when he said his final goodbye, to hell with her mother, she grabbed him and kissed him warmly and frontally, almost passionately. R. wondered if it was because he was leaving or that she would have eventually succumbed anyway. By "succumbed" R. meant would she have permitted just a normal expression of affection, nothing more.

On the train back to New Albany R. pondered his time in New Mexico. He did not feel guilty for necking with that airline hostess and putting himself into such a compromising position. Actually, he was rather proud of the escapade. Nor did he feel untrue to Cecily who offered only the nape of her neck . . . and yet, a small voice of his Puritanical upbringing tweaked his conscience despite himself. He had had too much to drink. That was bad. Did all his inhibitions dissolve when he drank too much? Could he only have fun in a life without inhibitions?

R. went home to his parents. He had no job and no choice. He had vowed never to look to his parents for financial support, once he had graduated from college with their help. But here he was, living at home, and not paying for board because he had no money. He caught up on the news and saw old friends again. He was depressed. The war in Europe cast a pall over the whole country. Life seemed to be on hold.

One evening in May when the German bombing of London was at its height and the newspapers and magazines were full of the suffering of the English civilians, R. was sitting on the swing on his front porch. He suddenly realized that the country would eventually go to war against Hitler, Roosevelt and Churchill's promises notwithstanding, and that he would be in it. No longer did he have the luxury of a comfortable non-interventionism. The years of opposing our involvement and letting the French and English take care of history were over.

Meanwhile and pro forma, he resumed his place in the choir. June was there. R. had not seen her for years. Many things had happened. She had gone to Wellesley. This was a surprise to R. but should not have been. Her family could afford it and June was bright. He thought she might have gone to Oberlin or some other college with a strong music department. She was now on summer vacation. At Wellesley June had met some of R.'s friends still at Harvard as graduate students, including Tobias. He had known of R.'s painful, attempted romance with June. Despite his intellectualism, Tobias seemed to take interest in R.'s girl friends and a whiff of scandal was not unwelcome. In fact, Tobias preferred to think of R. as a rake. "Ah, if only" thought R.

Maybe it was Wellesley, maybe it was Harvard, maybe it was Plato whom June had discovered, but she made it abundantly clear in the choir loft and after church that she had changed her mind completely about R. She wanted to hear all about Albuquerque and the Indians. R. *did* resume dating her for old times sake. Perhaps there was also a faint desire for revenge, but no, it was against R.'s grain to hold grudges. However, he was young and lusty. Cecily and others had rebuffed him. And yes, at Zuni, R. had really wanted the Director of Arts and Crafts to sit on his lap instead of the airline hostess. The Director had previously turned him down in Albuquerque when they were cold sober. She had as much as said he was too young for her. Well, she *was* in her thirties as her faded complexion and cat-like wrinkles on her upper lip showed all too well. Then, about this time R. surmised that he was probably the last remaining virgin in his college class.

Perhaps June appeared to his subconscious as ripe for the picking. Consciously, he thought of this resumption of dating as blowing on old coals that could not be rekindled. Or maybe R. was just weak enough to be led by the nose by any pretty face. Anyway, he began to "date" June as in the old days, old days that never were.

One evening he and June wound up in the home of Precious, still June's best friend. A prodigy on the violin, Precious was even more talented than June. On their dates June talked of her fondness for Plato. She told R. about his Soul, that is, R.'s Soul and its Beauties. R. replied that frankly he wasn't sure he had a "Soul" with a capital "S," his soul was spelled with a small "s." They began to disagree about Plato and for some reason took off all their clothes, including skivvies and panties and in June's case her bra and sat next to each other on the couch, not touching the other and using their hands only to argue with. Apparently it was to prove something about Platonic love. Precious didn't take off her clothes. R. didn't know where her father was. He was an early widower; he and Precious still lived in the family's large two-story house so that Precious had a great deal of privacy.

June asserted dogmatically that the Greeks had discovered the Real Beauty of the Human Body, that it had nothing to do with sex, only the pure Love of Body and Soul. She opined that modern morals would be improved if that Ideal had more True Believers. Platonic Love it was called. R. countered with all the reasons he didn't like Plato—his introduction of dualism into philosophy, his mystical theory of Real Ideas in the sky, his a priori assumptions, etc., etc.—resulting, according to R., in Plato's leading Western philosophy down a blind alley from which the world was just now recovering.

June was working up to her next remark and blurted out, "R., you don't have a damned Soul!" R. knew that she had learned to swear at Wellesley. Most prim girls do when they go to college. "If you don't *believe* you have a Soul," she hissed with faulty logic, "that means, that actually means you *really don't* have a Soul." She should have had a course in Logic 101.

June waited for him to deny that he didn't have a Soul. Instead he agreed that he didn't have a *Big "S" Soul*, just a *little "s" soul*. June didn't appreciate his attempt at humor. She stared coldly. It reminded him of a certain time in the long ago of her stare on the way to see the Marx Brothers. With a sigh, she declared vehemently, "I hate you, but I love you anyway!" June could talk this way in front of Precious because they were intimate friends. Precious was dumbfounded, of course, when R. and June had taken off all their clothes. However, Precious had never had a boyfriend, the violin took all of her time and energy.

Dawn was breaking when they redressed. R. thought Precious'

father either slept the sleep of the dead or he was out of town on business. R. called a cab and took June home. They did not kiss goodnight. When R.'s returning streetcar let him off near his house, his family was eating breakfast, his parents and three sisters. Suspicious eyes greeted him. His mother whispered loudly to him, "I shouldn't use this word, but your father says you have been out tomcatting around." R. was shocked by his Preacher Father's choice of words and his mother's willingness to use them. Ruth Ann, his youngest sister overheard mother's remark and asked, "What was Brother doing around a tomcat at night? You always told me that was dangerous." R. also thought it was dangerous but he didn't say anything.

June cooled off. R. acquiesced and they got together again. Before June went back to Wellesley they agreed that if anything happened to their affections, they would send the other a card with one word "Mame," and no other explanation. In the fall R. went to work at Wright Field in Dayton, Ohio, as a civilian for the Air Corps. He moved to Dayton. He was self-supporting again and didn't have to apologize to his mother for eating free.

He saw June several weekends when he came down to New Albany to visit parents and friends. She sent him passionate mid-week letters to Dayton about True Love and, my God, his Soul, which she was still confident, he really had. She complained that he didn't come back to New Albany every weekend. He reminded her that there was a war in Europe and Wright Field was working overtime-expediting materiel to the Allies.

In September it was time for June to go back to Wellesley. In a terribly romantic gesture, R. took a bus from Dayton to Cincinnati and met June's Pullman from New Albany. He climbed aboard and rode with her to Xenia, Ohio, not paying any fare, incidentally. On the train they really said their goodbyes.

R. climbed down from the Pullman in a downpour. He had hoped to hitch-hike the nine miles to Dayton but the drenching rainstorm in the blackness of night discouraged anyone from stopping to pick him up. He walked and got back to Dayton at dawn. The rain had stopped and he was almost dry when he sat down in the office at Wright Field with all the other Budget Analysts who stared at his wrinkled, damp clothes and wrinkled hands. Two months later he sent an overdue card to June, "Mame" it said.

As the school term went on Tobias reported that June had obtained a white rat from a Wellesley Lab. She called it "R." She kept it in a cage in her room and fed it leavings from the dining room. She showed the rat to Tobias on his visit to Wellesley and undoubtedly told him how the rat had got its name. R. chuckled. June was bright and had a good sense of humor. When they had looked at The *New Yorker* magazine together, June would seem to get the joke a few seconds before R. and would look at him impatiently, waiting to turn the page. He wished her well and hoped to hear someday that she was married and had four children, or maybe had stayed single and had become a concert pianist. His conscience *did* bother him about June and he mooned about it to his new girl friend. She finally told him to grow up, things like that happened all the time.

Many years have passed and to this day R. has never seen June again. He did *hear* from her once. He was with the Marine Corps in the South Pacific. She wrote him a V-mail, asking, "How are you? What are you doing these days?"

"Good God," R. thought, "I am fighting the Japanese and have been through three island blitzes, and she wants to know what I am doing! She is still living in Plato's Ideal World which has nothing to do with Okinawa or Iwo in 1945."

Eventually, World War II was over. Back home, the triumphant heroes, R. and his peers, after the combat glaze had faded from their eyes and they had recovered, they began to feel again like a part of the human race. They tried to relive their past happy lives but discovered it was a new world. They strove to fit in, to enjoy family and new friends, to buy houses with G.I. money. Like others their age, soon they were susceptible to the mating urge, to the prospect of having a wife who valued her children more than she did "romance." R. was thinking of what he would do for a living. Did he have enough education without the graduate degree that most of his college friends were getting? They were becoming doctors, lawyers and Ph.D.'s in their academic fields. Comparing their educational accomplishments with his own, R.'s naked A.B. stood out like a sore thumb.

FRANCES'S EIGHTIETH BIRTHDAY PARTY

APRIL 27, 2000

Dear Fellow Unitarian-Universalists,

I have been asked to send something for a memory book to be presented to my sister, Frances, at an occasion honoring her 80th birthday. There is no one more deserving of such a tribute than Sister Frances. I don't have pictures, that will be explained later. The next best thing might be word pictures, so I have described a few incidents in her varied and full life, some of which may be well-known, others not so well-known, and all from a brother's perspective. They say that siblings, the most closely related of all family members, have a unique bond giving them uncommon, but accurate, insights into each other's characters, emotions, virtues and the like. I hope this is true, so here are some recollections that stand out in memory:

Frances was born on April 30, 1920 in Winchester, Kentucky in a yellow brick house at the end of a yellow brick road. No, that's not true about a yellow brick road, but it was a yellow brick house on Washington St. beside a Presbyterian Church where her father was a Presbyterian minister. Her mother thought that Frances was an exceptional child. Others remember her as exceptionally bald, that is bald as a billiard ball, bald until the age of two, maybe longer. I had a picture to prove it but what happened to the picture will be explained later.

As a toddler Frances had a "blue," a swatch of blue blanket that she dragged behind her while sucking her thumb. Once she got too near the gas fireplace and the blue caught fire and threatened to burn down the yellow brick house and Frances with it. But her brother, helped by her father, stomped it out. The blue tasted scorched afterward, causing Frances much anguish, but she still sucked her thumb.

When Frances was two years old the family moved to St. Joseph, Missouri, where her father was minister of the Hope Presbyterian Church. Frances was burned again. One Saturday her father was giving her a bath out of a washtub in the kitchen. The kitchen had a small kerosene heater. In a careless moment, perhaps a misguided effort to stay warm, Frances sat on the heater. It made a red imprint on her behind, lasting for several weeks, and which she was obliged, against her will, to show in public.

When Frances was four, the family moved to Jeffersonville, Indiana, where her father was minister of the First Presbyterian Church. Frances, throughout her life an accomplished linguist, had her first job as interpreter. She had a boyfriend of her age, Junior Haas, a neighbor, who had a speech impediment. Frances was the only one who could understand him. Frequently, the Haas family had to summon Frances to come next door and tell them what Junior was saying. Frances and Junior entered first grade together and Frances performed the same function for Junior's teacher.

It was about this time that I discovered that Frances had robbed me of a first name. She called me simply "Brother" and so did my two other sisters when they came along. So did my mother and father, my grandparents and even outside friends. To this day, "Brother" has not fully recovered his first name. He has been known as Good Ole, Laughing Boy (sarcastically), Bumpkin, Bumpsie, but almost never by a first name, even by wives and assorted relatives.

In time our family moved to New Albany, Indiana, where father was minister of another First Presbyterian Church and Frances went to high school. In the Storm und Drang of adolescence, she suffered a bout of hysteria when the young man of her choice took another to the Junior Prom. To protect the innocent the young man's name will not be divulged. Suffice it to say, a nephew of his became a famous golfer called Fuzzy Zoeller, one of New Albany's most famous citizens.

Frances fared better in a later romantic episode with Tony Bennett, the singer. At least I think it was romantic. Tony came to Chicago in his early days to sing at the London House, a restaurant and nightclub in Chicago. Frances, who by then was a leading waitress in the London House, was assigned to entertain Mr. Bennett while he was visiting Chicago. With Frances's skill as a conversationalist, I am sure that Tony was not lonely while in Chicago. Tony left Chicago and went west to become famous for leaving his heart in San Francisco.

Brother moved around a good bit in early manhood. When he and his family lived in Baltimore, Frances visited with a new husband. Brother and family lived in a nice little house in the suburbs that did not yet have a sewer. The family lived modestly, sewage-wise, and there was no trouble. But Frances innocently stayed thirty minutes in the shower and the septic system was ruined. When she left Brother had the overflow tank pumped out but it was never satisfactory again. The county sewer came through a few years later.

Frances moved to New Brunswick, New Jersey, where she was a leading member and volunteer for the Presbyterian Church.

Frances moved to California where she was an active member of the Walnut Creek Presbyterian Church. She was so interested in church affairs and welfare that she became a staff member of the national Presbyterian organization. Working out of San Francisco, she traveled throughout the Western States, organizing women's groups and preaching fiery sermons to Presbyterians. Frances was offered a job at Presbyterian headquarters in New York but turned it down because she could not leave the marvelous California weather.

For recreation in those days, Frances took time off to lie down in front of bulldozers and other equipment at nuclear plants and military installations. She worked to better conditions for illegal farm workers from Mexico.

She retired promptly at age 65 after a lifetime of Presbyterian activism and was given a large going away party. The Sunday after her retirement she renounced Presbyterianism, saying that she had been converted to Unitarian-Universalism, and turned up at the

Mt. Diablo Church where I believe she is this very Sunday. Thus, the falling away of siblings from Presbyterianism is complete. Brother is also a Unitarian-Universalist; one other sister was an atheist and the other a stage actress.

Brother expressed himself as somewhat aghast at Frances's sudden leaving of the Presbyterians after spending her working lifetime on their payroll and is still collecting her Presbyterian pension. Brother was particularly puzzled as to how she quickly became a wheel in her new church as a Unitarian-Universalist. "You hardly skipped a beat," is the way he put it. Frances dismissed his chiding remonstrance out of hand with the observation that "Churchmanship is churchmanship in any denomination." As for continuing to draw her pension from the Presbyterians, Frances said that she had always believed retirement credit should be transferable between employers and she was happy to see that Presbyterians were fair employers. Before asking, Brother knew what Frances's answer would be to the going away party and the lavish presents her Presbyterian colleagues had given her, "Those are personal gifts from friends and have nothing to do with theology."

Frances has renounced her mistreatment of Brother over the years (there is no other explanation), and has made it up to him gloriously with wonderful gifts, messages, visits, tapes of her activities, and countless tokens of affection, including laughing very hard at his jokes. This is impressive for if you have heard Frances laugh you know it's like a sudden explosion or the twanging discharge of a coiled spring. For Brother's 80th birthday she showed up in Philadelphia with a collage of snapshots and other pictures of his life from birth to his later years. For the occasion today, he would like to have done the same for her, Frances's life in pictures, except that Frances has purloined (is that a nice enough word?) all the family pictures which are now safe in her hands.

Oh well, just as there is with Mary, "There's 'something about Frances'!" Almost everybody loves Frances, including her fascinated—

Brother

SNAKES AND A BRIDGE
NAMED SHERMAN

(Author's note) To this point all the stories in this book have been fictional. The next two accounts are non-fiction. Sherman Minton is very much a historical person as is his distinguished father and the others in this account. The story is true and non-fictional to the extent that any biographical writing can be. Nostalgia is the thief of memory, as biographers know. Also, in the interest of telling the story, I have taken the liberty of quoting conversations that, of course, are seldom recalled verbatim. The second account of certain high jinks at Harvard is likewise non-fiction. It is thought that both accounts are sufficiently off-the-wall to merit inclusion in this volume.)

Spanning the Ohio River from Louisville, Kentucky to New Albany, Indiana there is the Sherman Minton Bridge, named for New Albany's most famous resident. This story is about his son, Sherman Minton, Jr., born in New Albany, a little town in southern Indiana. My family moved to New Albany when I was ten years old. The Mintons and the Murphys lived in the same neighborhood but I was not aware of the Mintons and Sherman immediately. He was a year younger than I and we had very different interests.

At ten years old I became the youngest member of a gang called the Mysterious Six. When I joined it became the Mysterious Seven. The gang was very secretive and athletically active. They had meetings in which dire punishment was threatened if any gang business was leaked. This applied without exception to leaking to mothers and fathers, and especially, sisters, of which I had three younger than I. The warning seemed directed at me since I was the new member and very young. I promised to keep a closed mouth and to do anything I was told to do.

The gang played baseball and football, and later, basketball when they discovered that the Williamson twins, not gang members, had a backyard large enough for a basketball court. The Williamson twins didn't have to know anything about the gang who were only nice enough to the twins to be invited to play basketball on their court. Athletics was a new life for me, better than the cowboys and Indians I had played in Jeffersonville, Indiana, where we had lived before.

Being the youngest member, the oldest was twelve, and with no experience, I was awkward and bumbling, striking out the most in baseball, and in football, playing center where I could do the least damage to the team. In baseball the gang took the name of the Main Street Indians and carried BB guns when they entered the territory of other gangs, like the Eighth Street Fencebusters. I carried a BB gun and shot at the Fencebusters from behind a wall but was scared silly when we were supposed to leave the wall and charge them in the open. I hung back but was never punished for my cowardice. The gang was understanding enough to make allowances.

Sherman wasn't interested in sports. Nor did I see him in school. He was a Catholic and went to Holy Trinity School next door to his house. Sherman had a bunch of kids even younger than he who came to the Minton backyard to play with Sherman's snakes. Snakes and the locations of our houses eventually made me aware of Sherman.

The Mintons lived on the next street over from us, facing Market Street. The Murphys lived on Main Street facing away from the Mintons. The unusual feature of the neighborhood was that Holy Trinity School had a large playground separating the backyards of houses on Market Street from those on Main Street, minimizing contacts between the two blocks. At recess the playground was full of screaming Catholics, just as my school a few blocks away was filled by screaming Protestants.

The gang occasionally played baseball in the schoolyard when their own field was too wet. So Sherman and his friends were noticed because he lived nearby. I occasionally stopped and looked over the low fence at the Mintons to watch Sherman and his coterie of small followers, boys and girls, playing with the snakes that were kept in cages. Sherman and his gang seldom looked up and didn't speak when I watched. My family had a picture of my youngest sister, five years old, holding a black snake aloft by the head and letting it dangle toward the ground. She was the only one of the Murphy children to join Shermsn in playing with snakes.

When Sherman was about twelve he made the newspaper, the *Tribune*, New Albany's afternoon paper. It was not really a competitor of the morning *Louisville Courier Journal*, even in New Albany, but a skimpy second paper for some very local news.

One hot lazy day when school was out for the summer I picked up the *New Albany Tribune* because its headline jumped out at me. Across the front page was "MINTON BOY'S FRIEND, POWELL, BITTEN BY COPPERHEAD." It seems that Sherman and his neighbor, Junior Powell, were hiking in the Knobs, the name of the hills surrounding New Albany. The boys had come across a copperhead, common in Indiana. Sherman with his skill in handling snakes had grabbed the copperhead behind the head and popped it into the bag he used for their catch, usually black snakes, garter snakes, garden snakes and other non-poisonous varieties. Sherman was always careful with poisonous snakes, kept them in their own cages, wouldn't let anyone but himself handle them and usually released them back in the Knobs after a few days. On this occasion Junior Powell had poked at the snake through the burlap bag and had been bitten through the bag.

The newspaper continued by reporting that young Powell and Minton had gone to the hospital. Sherman had already made a slash in Junior's wrist and sucked out the venom so that the hospital visit was unnecessary. The newspaper lauded Sherman for his presence of mind and his knowledge of what to do.

What the newspaper did not report was Sherman's mother's part in all this. Unlike most mothers, Mrs. Minton did not object to, at least she tolerated, her son's love for snakes. Sherman was just a kid, of course, and couldn't drive a car. Mrs. Minton would drive Sherman and his friends to the Knobs for their snake hunts and at an agreed upon time and place would drive out and pick them up. She did so on the day that Junior Powell was bitten and drove them to the hospital.

One might think the newspaper did not want to implicate Mrs. Minton out of deference to Mr. Minton, Sherman's father. I was also slow to learn about Mr. Minton. He was a lawyer and an aspiring Democratic politician who might be hopeful of national recognition. I was an avid reader of the Louisville *Courier Journal* that covered Louisville and Kentucky politics but carried very little news of Indianapolis and state-wide Indiana politics.

But the Tribune's omission of Mrs. Minton's name was not necessarily to be expected because the owner and editor of the *Tribune* was a staunch Republican. Many of his readers disliked snakes intensely and had been brought up to kill them, poisonous or not. They would have been aghast at a mother who condoned snakes as a hobby, let alone who cooperated with a misguided son. It was an opportunity for the Republican newspaper to make hay at Democratic expense. But then again, New Albany was a small friendly town, not Washington, D.C. New Albany was the kind of town whose people could lay aside political differences where children and mothers were concerned.

Young Sherman was very different from his father. He did not have the glad hand for everyone as most politicians do. He was serious and uncommunicative about his hobby—snakes. Gradually I became a casual friend of Sherman's. Initially, I thought Sherman was a little odd. I had been conditioned to hate and fear snakes by my country farm relatives. Under Sherman's tutelage I came to tolerate snakes but I never qualified for Sherman's Snake Club. A requirement for membership was to let a blacksnake, at least nine inches long, bite you. Of course, a snake's bite is clean, if it is not a poisonous snake, and it will let go if you just let its tail touch the ground. I was a sissy; I didn't want to be bitten.

I was a junior when Sherman entered high school as a

sophomore. The new high school was too small for the freshman class from the day that it opened, a mistake of city planners. In high school I became good friends with Sherman and began to find other appealing traits in him besides his love of snakes.

Sherman's father had already taken his seat in the U.S. Senate after his unexpected victory in the 1932 elections. Franklin Roosevelt's triumph swept Republicans from office all over the land and the elected Democrats held offices everywhere. Actually, it was the voter's desperate repudiation of Hoover that gave Roosevelt his victory in the midst of the country's unprecedented Great Depression. And the spectre of Communism was seen as a threat to the American democracy. Earl Browder, Communist, later got nine million votes in the 1936 election.

Despite any desires of his own, Sherman was well-known and observed throughout the small town because of his famous father. Any notice was against Sherman's shy nature. He looked at the ground when he talked. He didn't tell jokes. He was just there, and everywhere Sherman was, something very humorous or very interesting would happen. He seemed to have a gift for it, however unintended it might be.

Another thing began to prey on Sherman's mind. He tried to be self-protective of his father. He saw himself as a possible liability for his father's career. Most people would think him peculiar for his hobby of snakes. Sherman knew that he was different. He refused to give interviews to the press; he determined not to be a human interest story. And he didn't want to give up snakes if he could possibly avoid it without hurting his father.

Withal, Sherman was very bright and could not conceal it. Smart genes were showing up in his mind. He was nominated for the Wranglers, the most prestigious boys club in high school. It was a speaking and debating club which I had joined a year before Sherman. Adolescence urges were stirring in Sherman, moving him to mingle with his peers, making him unlike the comfortable loner he had been as he was growing up. Sherman could be sociable, relaxed and friendly with those who appreciated him.

As his neighbor and one willing to vouch for him, I introduced him to other bright boys in high school. The smart guys ate together in the cafeteria, had their own jokes, and felt rather superior to ordinary classmates.

I had a foot in two camps, so to speak. I was on the football team but I preferred my buddies who were scholars and more stimulating. The athletes always looked at me as if to say, "What are you doing with those guys?" But they didn't ridicule me as they did other serious students.

Sherman sometimes did peculiar things to show that he belonged. He once mixed up some horrible unsavory concoction in a glass in the cafeteria—salt, left over food and milk—and on a bet he drank it. Some of the onlookers got almost as sick as Sherman should have been. I had a strong stomach, laughed and congratulated Sherman.

My regard for Sherman did not keep me from participating in an elaborate practical joke on him at Sherman's initiation into the Wranglers. I was abetted, actually put up to it by Mr. Thomas, History teacher who was a favorite, beloved instructor. He taught in New Albany High School despite the law requiring teachers to live in New Albany. For years Mr. Thomas had caught the interurban from Louisville in the morning and in the afternoon could be seen chasing down Vincennes Street to the interurban station to return to Louisville. Mr. Thomas was the faculty adviser to the Wranglers. All clubs required an adviser. In class Mr. Thomas was noted for his interesting stories of history told with a puckish sense of humor which kept students laughing. But his classes while not quite sedate were always orderly and disciplined.

After school hours as adviser to the Wranglers, Mr. Thomas really let himself go. When Sherman made his speech to qualify as a Wrangler, Mr. Thomas was in rare form. He must have stayed up late at night thinking up his joke. Sherman left the room after his speech. It was a formality. The new members had been accepted before they tried out, references and grades checked, evaluation made of their compatibility with other members. I knew of no one who, invited as a candidate, had ever been turned down, whether or not they spluttered and spit and used poor grammar in their speeches. It was well-known who the smart guys were. Good grades and compatibility were the standards for membership in the Wranglers, the elite of all the clubs in high school.

After Sherman's speech he had no such automatic acceptance by the Wranglers. When he left the room Mr. Thomas said, "Of course we are to take Sherman in. We can't do anything else if for no other reason than his famous father. But let's have some fun anyway." Mr. Thomas proposed that when Sherman reentered the room after his speech, that he, Mr. Thomas, would announce dolefully that there was dissension over Sherman's admission. Some wanted him in; others strongly wanted him turned down. Sherman was to stay and listen to the arguments on both sides and help them decide. Then they would take a vote. As president, I would be leader of the accusers and Bill Prosser, vice-president, would be captain of the defenders.

Sherman returned and Mr. Thomas told him of the Club's division. He added that as Club supervisor for many, many years that he, Thomas, thought this was the worst speech a candidate had ever given. Sherman meekly faced the Club. I began by saying I had known Sherman for a long time. "He is reasonably smart," I said, but my own friendship with Sherman did not change the fact that Sherman didn't measure up to Wrangler standards, that his speech was terrible.

Prosser pooh, poohed "those harsh words" and said that he knew that the speech was awful but that anybody could be nervous before this Club, so much was at stake. Prosser further stated that he knew for a fact that I was opposing Sherman because I thought he was trying to get in on his father's reputation.

It was my turn to pooh, pooh. "His father's reputation? What is that, everyone knows he just a stooge for Rusenfelt," giving the name the Republican anti-Semitic twist. Beebe Stein spoke up sharply from the group, "Bull shit, you guys make me sick with your talk of this and that. Murphy, I know you are opposing Sherman because he is Catholic and your father is a Presbyterian minister. A bunch of us Catholics, and I'm one of them, come to this damned school because of the Depression and our families don't have the money to send us to St. Xavier's in Louisville. That's a real high school and can whip New Albany in basketball any day in the week." Joe Moore, also an unhappy Catholic, cheered Beebe Stein.

There was a general uproar. Mr. Thomas tried to quiet the boys by shouting, "Boys! BOYS!!! BOOYYS!!! LET'S HAVE A LITTLE ORDERRR HERE. ROBERT'S RULES!!! WE ARE SUPPOSED TO USE PARLIAMENTARY PROCEDURE INSTEAD OF ACTING LIKE THE NEW ALBANY CITY COUNCIL." The group calmed down out of respect for their advisor and Mr. Thomas continued in his conciliatory way, "I know you boys did not like that speech. Neither did I. But, I suggest to you, there is more to this Club than making speeches. There is general intelligence. That can compensate for a lot of poor speeches."

Some Wranglers were silenced, others still grumbled. Mr. Thomas continued, "I suggest that we give the candidate an intelligence test to see if he qualifies. I have one here which I picked up this morning from my desk." The Wranglers feigned seriousness. Sherman agreed to the test. I whispered to Beebe Stein, "The poor guy is so rattled that he'll believe anything we say."

The test was indeed ridiculous. Mr. Thomas started with a series of questions involving the stars and outer space that no astronomer had ever heard of. Sherman sweated and struggled, confessing manfully, "I don't know, sir." The questions and answers were an unintelligible blur but I do remember the last question, "Do you believe in a wooly devil or a hairy devil?" Sherman stammered, "I haven't thought much about it, sir." I imagined Sherman must be thinking that this is a Protestant question that he didn't know anything about. Catholics are not strong on theology. Their priests take care of theology.

The Wranglers began to giggle. Surely, Sherman would see through this joke and laugh, too. Sherman looked glum when Mr. Thomas announced that he had failed the intelligence test. There was applause, whistles and shouts from Sherman's detractors, groans and curses and threats from his supporters. Mr. Thomas announced gravely, "I hate to see this club broken up by the unqualified, even though his father is a Senator."

Sherman sprang to his feet, "To hell with your damned old club. I don't want to join." Sherman ran out into the corridor and down the hall. The Wranglers pursued him all the way to the boys' toilet where Sherman was hidden in a stall, probably not to show his tears of disappointment. His pursuers laughed and shouted, "It's a joke, Sherman! Can't you take a joke?"

Yes, Sherman could take a joke. He returned to the room and shook hands with Mr. Thomas who was laughing, heartily spitting and foaming at the mouth because of his dentures. They had a good time with punch and cookies for all. Sherman told them, "You had me going with the argument about accepting me, but when Mr. Thomas pulled out his intelligence test with the nonsensical questions, I said to myself, 'Oh no, they are pulling my leg. Fantastic! What jokers!'"

I gave Sherman a sideways glance. Was it possible that Sherman had turned the tables on them and had been enjoying himself all along? Never would Sherman admit now to having been fooled. But he had looked so glum during the intelligence test, I was not so sure.

I became prouder of my acquaintance with Sherman and was amused by *his* practical jokes. Sherman would coil a blacksnake around his arm and pull down his sleeve, grasping the snake's head in his palm, then shake hands with an unsuspecting friend or even a stranger. Instead of a Sherman handshake the shocked and often terrified recipient would receive a snake-shake instead. Shy, reticent Sherman seemed to be emboldened when snakes were involved.

As a minor joke, Sherman would borrow a school book from a fellow student, then cut out a neat square inside, put in a small garter snake and quietly return it to its owner. The reaction depended on how one felt about snakes. Some boys would laugh while some girls would shriek, even throw the book at Sherman. It was a literal example of "throwing the book" at a tormentor.

The Wranglers did not have to wait long for a display of

Sherman's unintended humor. The High School met Male High of Louisville in debate. It took place at a special assembly of the student body in the auditorium. Students liked the principal's once-a-year tribute to the debating team. Debates were usually held in an empty classroom after school. Although the proceedings in the assembly were boring, students were excused from the regular scheduled class for that period.

Sherman presided at the public Male High debate. He wasn't on the debating team. This would give him speaking time in front of fellow students, all types, the tittering girls, the tough guys on the football team who might yell most anything, a few parents who had dropped in for the contest of the smart students. I hoped speaking in public would help Sherman overcome his shyness and to show the sprightly humor that he exhibited in private.

From his list of participants Sherman introduced the first Male speaker, then the second Male speaker. Sherman started to announce the third speaker—but he stopped. He seemed to have trouble seeing the name, he stared at the piece of paper he was reading from, and then tripped over his tongue as he unsuccessfully repressed his guffaws, "Wal-wal-y Buttttts," he dragged out the name. The student body howled. Poor Wally Butts! It wasn't the most embarrassing of names. But evidently it had taken Sherman by surprise and tickled his funny bone.

Sherman recovered his aplomb and didn't laugh again until Wally Butts got up to speak. Whatever Wally Butt's reaction to the mention of his name, he maintained his composure and proceeded to debate. And you might say his name was vindicated. Before the year was out his father, Wally Butts, Sr., coach of the Male High football team, was appointed coach at the University of Georgia. From high school directly to a college coaching job, Wally Butts, Sr. was a legend for his many years of coaching the Georgia Bulldogs.

In my final year in high school, I accomplished, with gusto but basically with due modesty, something that no one else or no team had done. I won a state championship. In Indiana there were state-wide championships of all kinds, basketball being the most prized; the Hoosier basketball tournament got national recognition. It had a unique rule that any high school, no matter how small, could enter the state tournament, one tournament for all. Then there were football, baseball, track, even typing state champions. The competition followed the basketball format, first the sectional, then a regional, and then the finals, usually in Indianapolis.

New Albany competed in all these events but had never won a state championship. Jeffersonville, up the river, was *the* hated rival. Its Red Devils had won a state basketball championship. New Albany had only come close.

In the spring of 1935, I won a state championship in—well, my strong suit, debating. It was a type of individual debating called a Discussion Contest. The topic was the national high school debating topic for the year as promulgated by the National Forensic League: "Resolved, that the Federal Government should equalize educational opportunities by proportional payments to the states, the poorest state receiving the most funds and the richest state the least." The Discussion schedule was the same as for other competitions—sectional, regional and finals. Each speaker was to make a speech of eight minutes presenting the facts. It was a neutral speech. Then each speaker was given five minutes to take a side, affirmative or negative. He was to use the facts that all the speakers had presented, no new ones.

I had no opposition in high school and sailed through the sectional and regional. I had a single judge, a Speech teacher from Indiana University. The professor said he liked my delivery and the "enthusiasm" I brought to the rostrum. The finals were at Indiana U. in Bloomington. Since we had no car Sherman drove my father and me to Bloomington in his family car. We stayed overnight before the contest. Sherman and I shared a room. We talked far into the night about debating, snakes, girls, athletics and our common ideas and attitudes. In the dark our good friendship became a warm intimacy. We went to sleep when I became alarmed that I might get too tired to speak at the contest on the following day.

On the next evening the eight contestants gathered behind a

large table with a rostrum in front, all the other contestants seemed to have large files of notes, index cards, and who knows what to assist them. I had nothing and felt bare. Sherman had a brilliant idea. He suggested that I put my small overnight bag on the table in front of me. I did and then felt like the others. Also, the judges might be influenced by my evident preparation. The bag contained a soiled shirt, an extra tie, and pajamas.

To summarize: I won the trophy; my favorite judge was there, one of three judges this time. I got one first place vote, obviously from my favorite judge, and a third place and a fifth. Two other contestants got a first place vote each, but not enough total points to beat me. The disgruntled losers all fled the hall in a huff, mumbling and cursing. Almost no one was left for the punch and cookies—Father, Sherman, and I, and my favorite judge. The judge beamed and was gratified to learn that I was planning to attend Indiana University and perhaps take one of his courses. I smiled and thanked him but had no intention of taking the professor's speech course. I didn't want to waste opportunities for meatier courses; I did not consider Speech a college subject, or even a high school subject.

Sherman went to college at Indiana University; I went to Harvard. We didn't see each other except in the summer and on Christmas vacations. As often happens we developed different sets of friends, even in New Albany, different double-dating partners, etc. But I always tried to keep up with Sherman's news, and news from others about Sherman.

Two years later, another Democrat, Van Nuys from Ft. Wayne was elected junior Senator from Indiana. Senator Minton thought it would be a nice gesture if the Mintons invited the Van Nuyses to New Albany. Senator Minton could tell his junior colleague what the Senate was like, what to expect, and what not to be surprised by. They would be together for at least four more years, collaborating on programs to benefit Indiana as well as the nation.

The Van Nuyses arrived on a cold day in December. Mrs. Minton, a charming and efficient hostess, warmed them all with an excellent dinner. They had wine legally inasmuch as Prohibition was on the way out, one of the few promises from his campaign that FDR had kept. The Minton children were introduced and then were fed in the kitchen. It was a lovely evening. Mrs. Van Nuys toddled up to bed, slightly tiddly from the third bottle of wine.

Next morning bright and early Mrs. Van Nuys arose and started down to breakfast. She could hear the bacon sizzling in the kitchen, and sang, "Tra la la la la!," as she skipped down the stairs. Suddenly, she began to feel the steps moving under her. She grabbed the railing. Indiana does not have earthquakes like California where she grew up. She looked down. The stairs were full of moving animals, it couldn't be but was—SNAKES! She swooned and fell down the rest of the stairs.

Sherman had feared the cold December night before that his snakes would freeze in their cages in the backyard. Their cages had wooden floors so that the snakes had no place to burrow to stay warm. He put them all in one cage and carried it upstairs to his room for the night. He would take them to the backyard first thing when the sun came up in the morning and warmed the cold night air. Sherman was uncharacteristically careless. The snakes got out and since they seek the ground they were slithering down the steps when Mrs. Van Nuys came down after them.

Mrs. Van Nuys was laid out on the couch and given smelling salts for her fainting spell. The doctor was called and prescribed aspirin for her headache and no breakfast for her nerves. This was not satisfactory for Mrs. Van Nuys. She wanted her own doctor. And further she wanted no more of the Mintons. She gathered her husband and they drove back to Ft. Wayne. In the Senate, relations between the two Senators seemed strained. Senator Minton tried to speak but Senator Van Nuys just looked away. No one could understand it. I am one of the few people, living or dead, who knows why the two Senators didn't get along.

In our separate colleges and across the intervening miles, Sherman still affected my life. One night Sherman was prowling in the countryside around Bloomington, Indiana, at two a.m. Some snakes are nocturnal. An alert police patrol stopped Sherman. They didn't get a satisfactory response from Sherman and so took him in to the station.

"What's your name, kid?"

Sherman tried to protect his father and he replied, giving my full name, "Ralph B. Murphy."

The cops examined the young man and his belongings. "If you are Ralph Murphy, what are doing with Sherman Minton's watch?" they wanted to know. The name was inscribed on his watch.

Again Sherman had no satisfactory answer. The police called my father in New Albany in the middle of the night and informed him that his son was in jail in Bloomington, charged with stealing Sherman Minton's watch. "Sherman Minton is the son of Senator Minton of Indiana, you know," they reminded my father.

Father expressed surprise, "This is news to me, I thought my son was in college in Cambridge, Massachusetts. I thought he didn't have the money to travel to Bloomington in the middle of the school year."

With enough telephone calls and the exchange of descriptions of both young men, the matter was cleared up. But Senator Minton in Washington was unhappy with Sherman. It wasn't very good publicity and the national newspapers had their human interest story about young Sherman after all.

At Christmas when I came home to New Albany a friend who was going to I.U. told another story about Sherman and his fraternity. When Sherman was a pledge the fraternity had played a classic practical joke on the incoming pledges. During the year they told the pledges confidentially that there was one problem the fraternity regretted. They hoped the pledges would still consider them for membership. They named two frat brothers who did not get along. They had been separated after several bloody fights. It got so bad that the brothers felt that they could not leave them in the same room together.

When pledge week arrived the pledges were all sequestered in a room awaiting notice of their fate, accepted or rejected. While they waited there was a slip-up of frat security. The two warring brothers suddenly appeared in the pledge room and began fighting. One knocked the other down and was standing over him crowing happily that he thought he had killed him. Then he turned on one of the pledges and accused him of being friendly toward the fallen brother. It had reached the point where the ruse was to be exposed and all would join in brotherly laughter. But before that could happen Sherman took matters into his own hands. He picked up a handy baseball bat and beaned the attacker. "Cold cocked him," said one brother.

The young man was taken to the hospital but released after three days with the diagnosis of mild concussion. Some people with a certain reputation are given credit, or blame, for something they did or did not do—the halo effect. When I questioned him, Sherman was no help in verifying or denying the story.

After college Sherman's path and mine diverged. Sherman went to Indiana University Medical School in Indianapolis. His family could afford it. I was on my own. I did not have the money for graduate school. But even so, I had a desire to get out into the real world. I knocked about in several jobs in different parts of the country. It was my first opportunity to see that the country had more to offer than New Albany and the East.

When World War II broke out, I joined the Marines and was in San Diego waiting to go to the South Pacific. Surprisingly, Sherman was also in San Diego. Mutual friends told me of Sherman's presence and I looked him up. Sherman had joined the Navy as a doctor and was awaiting assignment.

My wife, Ruth, and I found Sherman and his girl friend, Madge. Sherman and I were both convinced that we were not going to survive the war. I had taken a wartime bride and Sherman was planning the same. Sherman had the use of a borrowed car. It doesn't hurt to have a father with political connections. Sherman Minton, Sr. had left the Senate for a job of Assistant to the President. It was one of the newly-created jobs so bitterly opposed by the Republicans as "interposing non-elected appointees who cut off access to the President by the elected Congress and ordinary voters." Also, among the new assistants were Harry Hopkins and

Tommy, the "Cork," Cochran. The assistants were known derisively as the "Brain Trust."

M.D. notwithstanding, Sherman still had his interest in snakes. Once Sherman and Madge, and Ruth and I, were driving along a mesa outside San Diego when Sherman stopped the car and jumped out. He didn't really stop the car; I had to turn off the ignition from the seat on the passenger side. I was able to brake the car to a stop. Ruth was upset at Sherman's wild gallop through the mesquite. Sherman returned to the car, proudly displaying a five-foot Diamond Backed Rattler that he held by the head. Sherman had not had time to get his bag or his forked stick which he used to catch poisonous snakes so had had to press him down with his foot and take him by the back of the head.

"Isn't she a beauty?" Sherman asked. He always knew the difference between a male and a female snake. "Some beauty!" Ruth shrieked and buried her face in her hands. Madge and I were impassive; we knew Sherman and Ruth did not.

Sherman shortly thereafter was assigned a ship. On the last night the couples were together Sherman made an offer to Ruth, "If you can get your husband to write and tell you what snakes there are where he is on duty, I will tell you where he is."

I never did. I became a censor myself and was trying to catch Marines who evaded the rules. Besides, if Ruth had listened to Tokyo Rose on intercontinental radio, Rose always knew where the Marines were and where they would be going next, even before the Marines had been told of the next blitz.

Ruth and I had more time in San Diego waiting for my ship to be repaired. The ship had taken a hit in World War I and listed ten degrees to port. The two of us enjoyed what San Diego had to offer. We went to the zoo, which was just getting started in this growing Navy town. Ruth loved zoos and she finally found some snakes that she could like, safely in a cage, of course. She drew attention to the plaque beside the cage, "Thanks to Sherman Minton, Jr. for the Diamondback Rattlers that he has donated, the beginning of our reptile collection."

After the war, I didn't see much of Sherman. He lived in

Indianapolis where he was in medical research; I lived a number of places in the East. We did meet in several reunions of our high school class. The reunions were in New Albany, of course, and I could not always get away or stand the expense of the trip. My new wife and I, Helen, were struggling as I tried to get established in the hospital business. At reunions we stayed in the hotel headquarters for a week unless Beebe Stein, a classmate, offered his house and pontoon boat on a lake near Elizabeth, twelve miles from New Albany.

I felt that if we did go to a reunion we should make it a week's visit to see other high school friends who weren't in my class. I also wanted to roam around New Albany and point out to Helen, our house, my school, and old haunts. This was nearly a fiasco. They had paved over paradise. The Murphy house on Main Street had been torn down to make a parking lot for the Holy Trinity clergy. Father's church had been demolished a month ago for downtown parking. The Junior High School was now a Burger King.

We toured the high school and found that the additions and renovations had made it almost unrecognizable. I was able to convince the principal who had escorted our alumni group that the auditorium where the Wranglers had debated had an outside wall with windows. The principal did not believe it until he checked the construction drawings and came back and admitted I was right.

At the reunions when they did see each other, the two couples enjoyed the other's company. Sherman and Madge would invite us to their hotel room for a drink and old times sake. I noted that the Mintons had real leather luggage, a silver flask for whiskey and silver shot glasses. The Cadillac of Sherman's that I saw in the parking lot contrasted with the second-hand jalopies that I drove.

I learned that Madge had flown fighter planes during the war, not in combat, but that she had ferried them from the West Coast to Greenland where the Army flew them overseas. I had new respect for Madge.

The difference in economic status between Sherman and me was attributed to—of course, snakes. Sherman had become a world authority on snakes and reptiles. He wrote about them and his books, he said, had put his four daughters through college. I knew Sherman was an authority when the *Philadelphia Inquirer* had carried a story that Dr. Sherman Minton was directing by phone from Indianapolis the treatment of a local boy who had been bitten by a poisonous snake but had not received treatment soon enough and was in the hospital with serious complications. The boy recovered.

At the last reunion that I attended with him, Sherman was still making news. The reunion that year was at the new Holiday Inn, near the bridge from Louisville. The bridge had replaced the long-gone Kentucky and Indiana bridge and carried an Interstate that went on to Chicago. The bridge had been named the Sherman Minton Bridge in memory of New Albany's most famous resident, Sherman's father. Helen and I checked into the Holiday Inn and had a drink at the bar. Sherman and Madge had not arrived and we were not sure they would come.

I inquired at the desk if a Sherman Minton had a reservation. Hotel chains shift their personnel around and they don't know much about their new communities. This clerk was also somewhat of a smart ass, "We don't accept reservations from a bridge," he sneered.

Sherman did arrive and signed as "Sherman Minton." A flicker of astonishment crossed the face of the clerk but he recovered quickly and put on a reservation clerk's deadpan expression. I learned that three-fourths of the town, maybe ninety percent, did not know the origin of the bridge's name. "Sic semper honorous maximus!"

I retired and moved to the suburbs of Philadelphia. Naturally, I became a frequent user of the local library. It wasn't very large but I found two books in the library written by Sherman about snakes and other reptiles. His father—Senator, controversial Assistant to FDR, Supreme Court Justice—had apparently fallen into the dust bin of Ancient History, hello George III and George McGovern.

There was no mention of him in the library catalogue. I had to utilize the services of the reference librarian, Mary Tobin, to find anything at all about Sherman's father. The information came out of tomes that no ordinary library member would ever find, let alone know how to use. It took Mary Tobin, who knew Wordsworth's poems and Alexander Pope's couplets by heart, to find a skimpy biography of Sherman Minton, Sr.

Sherman published. His father never wrote a book; maybe he was snake-bit.

Sherman Minton's father was New Albany's most famous resident, born in a little hamlet outside New Albany but raised in New Albany. He started as an inconspicuous lawyer in a small town and was elected U.S. Senator in 1932. Minton was a fortunate beneficiary of the most devastating and soul-destroying economic slump in the nation's history. Indiana was usually Republican but the Depression had made Minton a part of the Roosevelt sweep. Instead of the usual Democratic sacrificial lamb to the Republican candidate, the unknown lawyer from New Albany was part of the Roosevelt landslide. As late as the 1920's, the Grand Imperial Wizard of the Ku Klux Klan lived in Indiana, not in Mississippi.

Senator Minton became the Democratic Whip as they called the party's junior leader in those days. His assigned task was to round up the Senators for important votes. He also became the spokesman in answering charges against the administration by the newspapers and radio. The owners of the media were solidly against Roosevelt but the editors, reporters, columnists, as well as the readers were for FDR by huge majorities, particularly after his "first hundred days in office" which set a target for subsequent new successors to the Presidency.

Senator Minton had a way with words—sarcasm, humor, just like his boss, FDR. He used it to effect against the newspapers, their owners, that is. He foreshadowed the later years when Spiro Agnew hurled the epithets of "tattering nabobs" and "effete Eastern snobs" against newspaper editors for their support of liberal Democrats, Spiro Agnew, the convicted Vice-President under President Nixon.

After sixteen years of Roosevelt activism, the country was preparing, according to the pundits, to return to normalcy.

Roosevelt was about to retire after an unprecedented four terms. He had lost much political capital by his four terms, by the recovery of business from the Depression, and by his efforts to pack the Supreme Court.

The Court had not changed its attitudes much since the Dred Scott decision, pre-Civil War nineteenth century. Dred Scott was a slave who was returned to his owner after Scott had escaped to the North. Once a slave, always a slave was the Supreme Court's decision. The Constitution had been amended to free the slaves but Supreme Court authorization of "separate but equal facilities" had negated much of the social impact of freedom.

The 1930's Court had vetoed New Deal legislation to the dismay of Roosevelt and his supporters. The "due process" clause of the Constitution had been used to assert property rights over rights of labor and an economically active Federal government. Roosevelt had tried to pack the Court by the simple expedient of increasing the number of justices all at once, with the intent of appointing new members en masse who were sympathetic to the New Deal. The Democratic Congress turned him down. The Supreme Court was the institution closest to ruling by Divine Right that American politics had seen since they had escaped the kingship of George the Third.

After Roosevelt was rebuffed in his packing attempt, he appointed Senator Sherman Minton to the court, his sole New Deal appointee. These facts of Judge Minton's life have faded from the memories of New Albanians. In those days the sports in town thought that their most famous citizen might be Billy Herman, Chicago Cub's Hall of Fame second basemen. Contemporaries are likely to think that Fuzzy Zoeller, the golfer, is their most famous citizen.

CRIMSON LITE: WITS, JOCKS, AND OTHER HARVARD COMICS

Harvard Selects Murphy

This is not a serious book about a Harvard career. Murphy has the utmost respect for Harvard and the education he received there. This is an account of lighter aspects of Harvard life, of certain adventures and mishaps at Harvard of some of its would-be Renaissance men, and instigators of lighter escapades in their Harvard lives. Harvard athletic teams are the Crimson, contrasting with funky Yale Blue. So this story of Crimson Lite seeks to do for Harvard what Bud Lite does for beer—keep it frothy, bubbly, less potent, and a welcome change of pace. For instance, how can you explain Murphy's selection by Harvard except to say that it was off-the-wall?

On a languorous June day of 1935 in New Albany, Indiana, Ralph Murphy, just graduated from high school, gently rocked in the swing on his front porch. He was thinking of his coming college years with confidence and pleasure. He had had a perfect record scholastically in high school and he had played football without much d1stinction but with great satisfaction. He would head for Indiana University in the fall where his father had gone and was graduated with highest honors. Murphy saw no reason that he couldn't substantially equal his father's academic record. Of course, he knew that he had no chance for the football team. Indiana was in the Big Ten, toughest conference in the country. He wouldn't even go out for football; he recognized his athletic limitations.

Murphy's musings were interrupted by a telephone call that completely changed his future. Murphy got to the phone ahead of his sisters; it was from his high school principal whom Murphy did not particularly like and thought he had seen the last of. The principal was inviting or rather commanding Murphy to come to his office to meet a visiting Dean Bender from Harvard. The dean was not very high on the ladder in the Dean's Office. In Harvard parlance, as Murphy later learned, he was a "baby" dean fresh out of graduate school. In New Albany he was interviewing prospective candidates for Harvard Scholarships. Murphy didn't know much about Harvard except that it had lost its former preeminence in football and was now just another team. He did know that it was a wealthy private school in the East, founded in colonial days and now too expensive for a family of limited means. Murphy's father, a Presbyterian minister said that their family was lower middle-class in income but of the top three percent in brains, both in New Albany and nationwide.

Murphy made the walk he thought he would never take again, trudging the mile or so to high school and into the principal's office. There he met a Dean Bender. The high school principal was beaming at his hypocritical best. It seems that Harvard had decided that its college was too provincial, had too many students from New England and the Midatlantic States. Under a new president, the first non-Harvard alumnus to be president, Conant from U. of Chicago, Harvard was in the second year of offering two scholarships each in states of the Old Northwest Territory, of which Indiana was one. Prosser, who was Murphy's high school chum, was also in the principal's office. Murphy was ranked one and Prosser number three in the graduating class and so both were logical candidates. The second ranked was a girl who had all A's like Murphy but she had only 32 to Murphy's 35 because Murphy had attended an additional half-year in order to graduate in June. The girl was going to attend business college in New Albany. Prosser, with 35 A's and a B was ranked third. He had taken one more course than Murphy.

Prosser and Murphy had separate interviews with Bender and the principal. In his interview Bender spoke optimistically of

Murphy's chances of getting a Murphy Scholarship if he did not get the National Fellowship, "We have lots of Murphys in Massachusetts who have been getting those scholarships and if you do not get an appointment as a National Fellow, I am sure you would be welcomed from Indiana as a Murphy scholar." Murphy left the interview with the strong impression that he would get a Murphy Scholarship.

In a few days Prosser was notified that he has been offered the Conant National Fellowship while Murphy was offered the other less lucrative Murphy Scholarship. Very odd, the Murphy Scholarship; it was awarded only to "men whose last name was Murphy." The Fellowship to Prosser was for $1200, annually and it was said that this would cover all expenses. Murphy's scholarship was for only $800. annually and Murphy saw a gap of $400. which he and his family would have to make up. This cast a new light on the Harvard offer. Murphy consulted with Dr. Buerk, retired Superintendent of Schools, who had received a graduate degree in Education from Harvard. He strongly urged him to accept. Murphy also talked to the son, Evan McLinn, of the current Superintendent of Schools in New Albany. Evan was a few years older than Murphy. He said his father and he both strongly urged him to accept the Harvard offer if it was at all financially possible, even with a sacrifice by Murphy's family.

It was true, Murphy knew, that his father had saved for his children's education; that was the reason they had no car. Murphy's father, a former Classics Professor before he became a minister, was excited by the Harvard offer. Murphy accepted, giving up his intended career at Indiana U. He hoped that he hadn't made a mistake. As he learned more from the material Harvard sent, he too, became enthusiastic about Harvard. One item was a *Confidential Guide to Freshman Courses*, put out by the Harvard *CRIMSON*, the independent student newspaper. It ranked the courses from excellent down through "fair" and even "don't take." Murphy was impressed by the number of courses and the bold evaluations by a student newspaper.

Murphy did wonder why Prosser had been favored over him for the Fellowship. Oh well, that was a way of getting both of them to Harvard which couldn't afford to award Indiana's two Fellowships to students in the same high school. And Murphy was glad for his chum, Prosser. He had the guilty suspicion that Prosser was really smarter than he, despite the faculty vote.

New Albany was a small town, pop. 30,000, like many other midwestern small towns. It was almost ideal for growing up from childhood to youth. It was Murphy's hometown. New Albany was across the Ohio River from Louisville, called "Luavull" by people on the south side of the river. Those on the north side, Indiana, were singularly blest. Indiana had better high school basketball than any other state in the nation. All high schools, no matter how small, could enter the State basketball tournament. Once Franklin, with only ten boys in the high school, had won the state title.

When Murphy left for Boston and enrollment at Harvard, he was put on the train by his family. His mother and three younger sisters cried. His father shook his hand firmly.

"We tried our best to be good parents to you," his mother sobbed. It was almost as if she felt him slipping away into an environment that would be better for him and that he would prefer, and that they had been derelict in not realizing his potential. "Of course you did your best," Murphy assured them. He had a lump in his throat. It almost made him cry.

The train gained speed as it headed out of town past the backyards of Spring Street and the back porches of many high school friends and rivals. There was this feature of New Albany High School. A group of students who were considered smart, ran things, were elected to the class offices, won academic honors, performed in the plays, were rivals in debates and speaking contests, but also were friends who socialized and took each other to their respective club banquets.

Murphy was eagerly anticipating Harvard and being a grown-up away from family but he was also reluctant to leave New Albany, the wonderful little city that would always be his hometown, where his adolescent experience, unique to himself, was also shared with beloved classmates. With this less than original observation, Murphy chugged out of New Albany and on the way to Harvard.

Upward Bound

At eighteen, Murphy, the inlander, caught his first sight of the ocean on the train ride to Boston. It was a beautiful day when the sea was a sparkling azure with jaunty surf pounding the shoreline. It was just as depicted on postcards and in movies. As the New York, New Haven, and Hartford Railroad rocked along Murphy soon felt the magic of the ancient ocean and its relentless assault upon the land. The train darted in and out along the Connecticut Shore, into the stations at Stamford, New Haven, and New London, emerging sporadically to new vistas of breakers and sky.

From his literary heritage Murphy was immersed in the lore of the sea—from the sailing ships of the Phoenicians, the galleys of the Romans, the fearless voyages by sail of Columbus to the New England whalers of *Moby Dick* fame, down to the iron buckets of Kipling and Conrad and then the sleek modern ocean liners imperiously steaming around the world. Until now it had been a static vision, frozen waves on a page, billowing sails that were noiseless.

He stared out the train window, watching the white caps, feeling the rhythm as his spirit caught up to his primeval birthright. Suddenly the train turned northward through the swamps and cranberry bogs of Rhode Island, desolation in the middle of the populous northeast, and made a run toward Boston.

Murphy looked at the passengers his own age, as they came aboard and wondered who would be his fellows at Harvard. He tried to remember faces for he knew they would soon be lost in a student mass. Likely candidates got off at New Haven and Providence. But the Harvard student body, like other urban masses, coalesces in isolated strands, unrecognizable until the last moment when a mass streams into a Yard, a building, or a stadium.

Murphy was discharged into the bawling sprawl at South Station, Boston. From the subway he emerged to face that sheltered Cambridge enclave called Harvard Yard, behind walls of dormitories, full of classroom buildings, a chapel and the dominating Widener Library. Armed with a catalog sketch of the Yard, Murphy went through the gate and sought Thayer Hall, his assigned dormitory.

The Yard cop or maintenance man or professor whom he consulted on the fly cheerfully pointed out Thayer, "Why, it's that shoebox over there." Murphy detected in the man a desire to be witty but at the same time actually helpful. Thayer Hall seemed to have been not so much designed as put together by a committee of carpenters and bricklayers. It was a rectangular, brick building of straight lines, high windows, and a barren exterior, unlike the other predominate and graceful Georgian, red brick, dormitories with their slate roofs and dormer windows. Thayer Hall was a reflection of nineteenth century textile mills; over the building hung the gray pallor of the Industrial Revolution.

Murphy, with his heavy luggage, trudged up the stairs of the middle entry of Thayer to the top or fifth floor where he found his room number, his name on the door, and his roommate who said he was "Daner Huntington Piss." The card on the door had read "Dana H. Pierce." He was from Orleans on Cape Cod, only son of a widowed mother, and an engineering student who was recipient of a small scholarship. Dana was going to work his way through school, had been there for several days, and "waited on" (tables) at the Student Union, the freshman eating facility.

Dana and Murphy found their way through the language barrier and soon were conversing with delightful comprehension. Dana was going to take Engineering for practical reasons but his love was literature. After they had become acquainted, Dana admitted that he liked to hear Murphy roll his "ah's" (r's). He unsuccessfully tried to imitate Murphy's pronunciation, but the hard Midwestern "r" eluded him, unless he could throw it in for free as in "umbreller" "idear" "ioter," etc. In turn Murphy rather enjoyed the New England refusal to acknowledge the "r" where it did occur, producing startling results when there were a number of "r"'s to ignore, as in the name of the college that became "Havad, theah almer mahta." In time Murphy learned to distinguish among the several varieties of Bostonian English, to recognize the hollow honk of Back Bay as opposed to the soft Doachesta Flutta, pronounced Dorchester Flutter by mid-Americans. Murphy decided that upon arriving in the New World, the Puritans had separated from the English tongue as well as from the Church of England.

Prosser showed up smiling. He had been there for two days and had the room just beneath Murphy. His roommate was from Ohio so the two understood each other linguistically but had completely different interests and soon never spoke. The Midwest was well represented in the middle entry. The residents had more in common than geography and that was scholarships. Even the Easterners in Thayer Hall were on scholarship and tended to be like Dana, poor and bright. Murphy learned that it was not as easy for Easterners, rich or poor, to go to Harvard as for these favored scholars from beyond the seaboard who were needed for national balance, courtesy of the new president, James Bryant Conant.

Little Fish

That evening there was a reception for freshman in the Student Union that was the dining room and lounge for freshman. While waiting for a meal of codfish cakes, baked beans and brown bread, they were entertained by a pianist on the lounge piano which was there apparently for anyone to play who might find it available. The pianist was playing a Mozart Sonata beautifully and skillfully, far beyond Murphy's stumbling efforts to conquer the C major Sonata assigned by his New Albany music teacher. It was his last piano piece before he gave up the piano for football. To make conversation Murphy asked the man in line ahead of him if he knew the pianist's name. "He's a guy from New York I am told," was the reply, "Bernstein, Lewis Bernstein, I think, no, maybe Leonard, Leonard Bernstein."

"He plays well," Murphy observed.

"Yes," the other agreed. "He's supposed to be some sort of prodigy, will take Music here at Harvard."

In a few days Murphy had settled in and discovered many fellow students with outstanding credentials and quick minds. He signed an overpriced laundry and pressing contract, signed up for meals, looked through the Harvard Co-op store, pronounced Coop, noted that Harvard Square had a movie house, visited the Elm and plaque on the Cambridge Commons where George Washington had received his sword and commission as General to lead the Continental army. He prowled around the College, Soldiers Field (football), the banks of the Charles, and the Weld Boat House (crew), got used to the booming bell on Memorial Hall sounding the hour, and eventually started to school with a History 1 class in the New Lecture Hall that had been built thirty-four years ago.

After midterm exams in November he knew it would be a struggle to keep his scholarship. He studied but found time in his freshman year to make the Wrestling team, time for trips to Scollay Square in Boston and to the Old Howard burlesque, and for drinking in Boston without being challenged as underaged, which he was.

But, this is not the story of his Harvard career; that is for another day, perhaps. Harvard is a place where students take their studies, that is their "work," seriously. But all work and no play diminishes the Renaissance man that Murphy hoped to be. This is about the initial shock, yes, and thrill, yes, of Harvard for a Midwesterner who had been a big fish in a little pond in Indiana but who suddenly became a small fish in an ocean of talent and brilliance. It's about some of the richly-endowed friends that Murphy made and tried to keep up with, and some of their humorous and "off the wall" capers and adventures.

The Houses

By the 1930's Harvard had outgrown the original confines of the Yard. As a sophomore, Murphy moved to the new residences along the Charles River called Houses, a faint echo of the separate colleges at Oxford and Cambridge, England. In the early 1930's six colonial Georgian Houses were built of red brick with inner courtyards and multiple entries of five floors each. Up the stairways, each floor contained facing suites, singles on some floors, doubles on others, and economy doubles with dormer windows on the top floor. The economy rooms on the fifth floor attracted the scholarship students. A seventh House was established in an older residential structure closer to the Yard, the Gold Coast of old Harvard. The Houses were gifts of a Yale alumnus who contributed substantially all the funds.

Up from the subway at Harvard Square, Murphy, a new sophomore, turned away from the Yard across the street and headed down through two intervening business blocks toward the Houses. He and Prosser had applied and had been accepted for Lowell House in the spring as freshmen. Not all sophomores could be accommodated in the Houses, which had authority to choose members as they wished. Murphy's roommate as freshman, Dana Pierce, did not gain admission. Harvard had made progress away from its elitist past but was as of now, and perhaps might always be, an imperfect democracy.

Murphy passed through the arch of Lowell House from the street and through a second arch leading to an inner courtyard and lugged his suitcase up the tight staircase of J-entry to the fifth floor, and turned into the suite he was to share with Prosser, J-52. The two would be roommates, strictly defined. In a matter of hours Murphy was feeling proprietary like any college student, casually accepting the legacy that he did not know or really care about. Thenceforth, J-52 was his until graduation so long as he maintained himself in good standing.

His friends are the essence of Murphy's Renaissance experience at Harvard. Murphy made new and stimulating friends among sophomores, juniors, and seniors in Lowell House. He made life-long attachments to a remarkable coterie of sophomore classmates who shared extracurricular activities, athletic struggles, and humorous adventures.

Roommates

As expected, Prosser had arrived a day early. Prosser led the way in introducing himself and Murphy to Tobin and Sullivan across the hall in J-51. Tobin and Sullivan from Thayer Hall were speaking acquaintances of Prosser and Murphy from freshman year. The four occupants of J-51 and J-52 were Midwesterners and three were Conant Fellows while Murphy acted as though he should have been. Richard Sullivan was an all-American boy, a scholar, an athlete, an outgoing gregarious leader and lavish with time and energy in cultivating friends, but making no enemies. He was a Conant Fellow from Ohio. He had played freshman basketball and this year was going out for the varsity. He came from Marietta, Ohio where his father was Superintendent of Schools. Sullivan was graduated first in his high school class, was class president, star of the basketball team, an excellent golfer and tennis player, and as the prize catch in town was reluctant suitor to Ruth Kinney whose father owned the Marietta *Times*, the leading newspaper of southeastern Ohio. Among his honors was an appointment to the Army's WestPoint. He had actually enrolled after graduation from high school. Finding the military education wanting and military discipline demeaning, Sullivan, after a disillusioning two months on the plains above the Hudson exercised the delightful option of dropping out and accepting the Harvard Conant Fellowship which he had also won.

Tobin and Sullivan had met each other as freshmen and had applied together to Lowell House. James Tobin was from the college twin-town of Champaign-Urbana, home of the University of Illinois. Tobin had been reared in both an academic and athletic atmosphere. His father, Mike, was one of the first publicists of university athletic programs. He was at Illinois when Red Grange came along. It was mutual good fortune. Red Grange's four touchdowns in the first quarter against Michigan would have received raves in any case but his exploits gained in national fame from the promotion by Mike Tobin. Under Mike Tobin's guiding typewriter Red Grange became the Galloping Ghost and enjoyed immortality even before graduation.

Murphy learned that the rumor he had heard as a freshman was indeed true, Tobin had made all A's, including an A in History 1. He was a gangling sort, a basketball player in high school. Tobin had the modesty and reticence that is the mark of the extremely talented.

Prosser appealed to Tobin and Sullivan with his repartee and his Noel Coward style. Murphy could not match Prosser's wit, such as, "it was raining cats and dogs, and I stepped right into a mud poodle" and "A wet dream is more enjoyable than going to a cat house. In the wet dream you meet a better class of girl." Murphy relied on a bucolic clowning that he had perfected from a number of Latin banquets and other high school affairs. Tobin and Sullivan seemed vastly amused by Prosser and Murphy's New Albany skits, such as the comments on the passing female parade by the guys on the street corner. In time Murphy added a deadpan sarcasm to his humorarium and gained a reputation as a dry wit after all.

Lowell House had supporting facilities for the residences. There was a dining hall and lounge or coffee room, and a second floor comfortable library making unnecessary many visits to the cold, clattering monolithic beast of the Yard, Widener Library, saturated with freshman and postgraduate researchers.

The Housemaster's residence occupied one corner of Lowell House and had an outside street entrance. A number of college faculty were resident tutors in first floor single rooms, ostensibly to be nearby to help students but probably to keep student hi-jinks from getting out of hand. There were squash courts in the basement, a ping-pong room, two small lounges that served as music rooms for an excellent Lowell House record collection, and then, of course, the blue-domed bell tower.

The bells gave Lowell House athletic teams their name of Bellboys. The bells were seldom rung. It took a special person to ring, some said to jangle, the bells. The original bell ringer was a Russian who drank ink, it was reported, and eventually he was sent back to Russia. Members of the music faculty and who knows what wandering minstrels were privileged to try to ring the bells. The ringer with lines and cords attached to arms, legs, and other body parts that could be moved independently looked like a puppet with a mind of its own. Not that many were permitted to glimpse, let alone identify, the intrepid bell ringer in his regalia. Bell concerts were never announced, probably to forestall demonstrations of any kind by the students. Typically, the bells would shatter the unsuspecting calm of a Sunday morning and were greeted much like an earthquake, the Bellboys streaming into the courtyards to gaze at the tower with wonder, amusement, and if visitors happened to be present, with apologies. The pitch of the bells varied from a heavy, leaden, barely audible throb at the lower end of the scale to the slightest of tinkles at the upper end like ice in a glass. Unlike the Liberty Bell in Philadelphia, the bells inflicted no wounds on themselves but did crack the bell tower. The crack was watched by Buildings and Grounds who occasionally imposed a moratorium on bell ringing but nostalgia always got the better of calculation and the concerts resumed. After a few years it was noted that the crack got no worse and eventually the hazard was dismissed as alarmist.

Murphy quickly adopted the chauvinism of his chosen House. From his dormer window looking toward the Charles River, Murphy could see Winthrop House, which was reputed to cater to athletes. Off to the right were Eliot and Kirkland Houses with their inconsequential towers. Eliot House had the Grill and was reported to be a House for history concentrators. Eliot House was socially ambitious but had lots of four, five and even six-room accommodations. When Roosevelt spoke of one-third of a nation that was ill-housed, Murphy was convinced that he had Eliot House in mind. Kirkland House was nondescript and lacked any architectural character. To the left of Lowell House as one looked toward the river was Leverett House. It boasted a Saltonstall, son of a Massachusetts governor who had become a U.S. Senator. Only a few years in operation the Houses could not claim famous alumni, only sons of famous men. Lowell had Welles Lewis, son of Sinclair Lewis and Dorothy Thompson; there was little Bobby Sarnoff whose father headed the new industrial giant, Radio Corporation of America; young Piper's father had acquired Taylor Aircraft and was converting the famous Taylor Cub to a Piper Cub; and there was Earle whose father was Governor of Pennsylvania.

Down the Charles River toward the Cambridge Gas and Electric Co. was Dunster House, in left field so to speak, an afterthought when the original site of the Houses had become crowded and the money was running low. It was rumored that Harvard had tried to raise a few more dollars to build Dunster House to the standard of the other Houses. An alumnus named Hoare had stepped forward, his stipulation being that the House bear the family name of Hoare. Harvard turned down the offer. The residents became known as the Dunster Funsters, taken seriously by no one. They almost always finished last in the athletic competition and were so far from the Yard that no one in Dunster signed up for a course to be given earlier than ten o'clock.

Happily for Murphy, not only did Lowell House have the scholars, the location, the beauty of the spire and the most distinguished master, Julian Coolidge, it was pre-eminent in intramural athletics, a perfect exemplar of sound minds and sound bodies.

The Houses were somewhat like the independent colleges of Cambridge and Oxford, socially, if not academically. All House residents received the one Harvard degree and were part of one college. The House offered a style of living that improved immeasurably, Murphy thought, on fraternities. It took no indoctrination to convince Murphy that he would have been ill at ease in a fraternity, its lack of privacy, the group think, the hearty fraternal handshake and secret rites, the adolescent pranksterism being much against his grain.

The Houses were experimental, a compromise with the exclusive club system of Harvard's past that remained, however, tattered, impotent, but alive. Murphy and his friends did not feel inferior to that odd breed, the Harvard clubmen. After the Houses were established, the clubmen could not live in the clubs, only share a club dining room and social functions. The clubs were clustered along Mt. Auburn St.—the Porcellian, the Fly and the others, some literally on the Lowell House doorstep. The smarter of the clubmen also applied to a House and, if accepted, enjoyed the advantages of House living while indulging their social elitism at their clubs. Other clubmen lived in the frame houses lining the side streets and known as rat houses, three and four-level walkups shared by the clubmen and Cambridge working people. From Murphy's bedroom outward from the House a slice of Cambridge life was laid bare. Lowell House residents on Murphy's side were privy through windows and opaque curtains of the rat houses to witness the joys, heartbreak, and broken heads of Cambridge families who were tenants along with the clubmen. In rank order, the clubmen were the noisiest when they arrived home drunk at three a.m.; the Cambridge wives were next in their shrieks when they got belted by their husbands; then came the kids who quarreled, fought and bled; and last were the husbands sitting in steamy kitchens in their underwear tops, their muttered curses only occasionally rising to audible volume. Murphy was condescending toward the clubmen who, he thought, had traded a good House life for a chimerical independence and even more meaningless social distinction. His real resentment of the clubmen was the newspapers' identification of them as typical Harvard. Their Hasty Pudding Show drew Hollywood glamour visitors who were led to believe that they were experiencing Harvard instead of a snobbish irrelevance.

There were the unfortunate minority, like Dana, who could not be accommodated in a House. A week after Murphy moved into J-52, a somber Dana paid a visit. Murphy was saddened by the brave look on Dana's face; Murphy was genuinely distressed at Dana's tale of finding a room he could afford in a basement somewhere out there in Cambridge. Murphy had Dana as a guest for dinner in Lowell House, signing a chit for the expense, and promised to visit Dana soon. Dana still seemed to be living with a sense of betrayal but Murphy felt helpless both as to the fact and as to Dana's hurt feelings.

The eight residents in the four suites in line on the top floor of

J and K entries of Lowell House came to refer to themselves as
roommates. While not actual roommates, the interconnection by
open doors, and the desire to visit each other daily made the
designation as "roommates" functionally appropriate.

The compatible roommates ranged intellectually from the very
bright to the brilliant. Two of the brilliant were Larry Ebb and
Irving London who lived at the far end of the line in K-52. They
were Jews of poor families in the Boston area, Ebb from Dorchester
and London from Malden. They had modest scholarships and their
presence at Harvard represented family sacrifice. The details were
unknown to Murphy. In their group the subject of family finances,
if not avoided, was not a matter for ordinary discussion.

Many Harvard men were at the privileged pinnacle of a family
broadly defined; they were only sons or cousins, the only ones in
the extended family who had the opportunity and qualifications
to go to Harvard or similar institution. It was embarrassing to
reveal oneself as such a favored family member and to disclose the
degree of sacrifice necessary for one's educational opportunity. The
true state of affairs was likely to come out only when families visited
and an outsider was permitted to overhear conversation or when
one visited a colleague in his home as Murphy had done with
Dana Pierce.

The competition for admission and for scholarship money to
Harvard was keenest in the Boston area, and for Jews whose numbers
breathed hard on the rumored quota, denied, of course, by official
Harvard. And who is to say if the rumors were true or basely false?

The facts are that Ebb and London were winners in the stiff
competition for admissions from Boston and their occupancy of
dormers row on the fifth floor of Lowell House. Demonstrably
compatible, they were soon joining the J-entry circle for meals,
visiting, entertainment, and cultivation of the academic arts and
the soul.

Ebb was the more immediately gregarious, a member of the
debating team, and mentally extremely nimble. In discussions with
Ebb, Murphy was likely to find himself entangled in contradictions
and either "uninformed" or "misinformed," two deficiencies that

could not be lightly dismissed. Murphy objected at times that his points were valid but that he was victim of Ebb's debating "technique." It was the sourest of grapes in view of Murphy's high school debating success and his instinct for the verbal jugular.

Ebb was debonair, witty, and an apparent bon vivant. Of a slight frame he professed no athletic abilities. He differed from London who claimed athletic prowess, particularly in tennis, but he never demonstrated it because of pressure of studies. His tennis was confined to summers and remained a subject of skepticism to his Lowell House peers. Ebb was likely to take pride in his way with the ladies. He claimed to be constantly courting but most of this took place off the Lowell House premises.

Ebb was light-hearted, untroubled, and unassailable. His ideas, which were sound, his politics, which were informed, and his academic excellence spoke for him. He was not inclined to negative comments. Personal problems, if there were any, were private. Ebb preferred to be judged by a public mien that he took care should be cheerful, witty, rational, and solid. He would rather study than become embroiled late at night in earnest probings of the eternal verities and individual wisdom, quirks, longings and humorous misbehavior.

Occasionally, Ebb would exhibit a flash of moral judgment, as in reaction to the latest rantings or actions of Adolph Hitler. He maintained vehemently that racial libel should be a serious crime. Murphy thought that impractical. Racial epithets were a part of the social, and now, the political scene in the U.S. It would be impossible to penalize millions for their everyday speech or to censor Father Coughlin on the radio.

Jewishness was a problem for some Jews at Harvard, a problem Ebb chose to ignore as much as possible. Jewish accommodation was mixed. At least some preferred to be called "Jewish." Those Jews who were loud and aggressive drew the wrath of other Jews. But many were meekly mild. Some said their prayers; probably most did not. Some, like London, were proud and religious.

London was a handsome young man with black hair, flashing dark eyes, a blue beard, and an ascetic and hungry look common to saints and criminals. He alternated between the most serious of observations and the most irresponsible gaiety. He had a keen appreciation of other's humor and good points, but also a ferret-like instinct for their weaknesses and pretensions. Murphy received both kinds of judgments from London, which London expressed without hesitation. He laughed at Murphy's jokes and clowning, he criticized Murphy equally for the false humility that Murphy affected to deflect the judgments of his intellectual superiors in the inner circle.

Like Ebb, London was concentrating in Philosophy and Government. It was a popular combined field for the best and the brightest in the 1930's. The rise of Communism and Fascism and the economic disaster of the Great Depression were calling into question the history, governance and, indeed, the very values of Western civilization. It was a time when to be "informed" was a particular virtue. The world was on the edge of new technologies but the future seemed to be dark with old animosities and the new Teutonic barbarism. What more worthwhile collegiate endeavor than to try to understand, and therefore to influence, the brave new world, perhaps save it. Left to his desires, Murphy probably would have concentrated in a meaty subject like History and Government rather than the frivolous enjoyment of the English novel, but it was a matter of keeping his scholarship and, therefore, his college survival with an eye to the main chance.

London had at one time thought of becoming a rabbi but was settling on Medicine. However, he continued Jewish studies while at Harvard, going downtown to a Hebrew University and receiving his degree. Meanwhile, he was interested in that most rational of ages, the Eighteenth Century Enlightenment, and Thomas Jefferson, to which he combined an interest in the great rationalist and pre-scientist, Aristotle. London was so intrigued by the two that he saw a connection between their philosophies, a symbiosis that had been barely mentioned by scholars up to the present.

Perhaps Murphy felt an affection for London because the latter tolerated Murphy's impious crudities. Murphy's religious moratorium did not enjoin respect for orthodoxy. Perhaps Murphy

saw in London what he, Murphy, might have been like with a less
rationalistic father; Murphy might have been a missionary or a
modern creedless religionist who went to the Harvard Divinity
School.

One morning Murphy broke in on London in the midst of his
morning prayers. London was in his bedroom in ceremonial robes.
Murphy's years of orthodoxy had never encompassed ritualistic
ceremony; in fact, Catholic practice of dead ceremony without
conviction was what the Reformation was all about. Murphy was
taken aback at this evidence of London's apparently sincere,
Orthodox Judaism. It was incompatible with the Enlightenment
and even Aristotle's cold Prime Mover who wished to be
contemplated, not moved like an Old Testament Jehovah to reach
for a thunderbolt when he saw evil-doing.

Murphy was daunted but only for a moment. He recovered
his composure and began heaping scorn on London for his
ceremonialism, close, if not identical, to superstition. Particularly
telling, Murphy thought, was his accusation that London had in
his phylactery the foreskin of Moses and he challenged London to
prove otherwise by opening the box. London suffered the
interruption with grace, smiles, and Christian good humor, proving
that old Jehovah could inspire a gentle forbearance without the
help of the New Testament. Murphy finally withdrew vastly pleased
with his cleverness, leaving London to who knows what resumption
of his prayers in who knows what state of mind. The incident did
not seem to make any difference in their friendship. London only
occasionally lashed out at Murphy's inanities and Murphy's self-pity
that he overlaid with a phony humility.

There were serious discussions between Ebb and London that
Murphy sensed more than listened to. The Jewish religion, it was
clear, occupied different niches in their lives. At the very least, Ebb
did not wish to make a public demonstration of his religion at this
stage of his life and London wanted his Jewishness known. Ebb
may or may not have been an assimilationist who would have
ignored Jewish culture if he could have. There are times to speak
and times to keep silent and the choice of tactics is not clearly an

indication of conviction. Between the two of them Murphy was afforded a feel inside the skin of those discriminated against. He may have obtained the same feeling in kind, if not in intensity, by ruminating on his own status in Boston as Irish. Murphy was not sensitive enough for that and he knew few clubmen or other Boston Brahmins.

Two men from across the inner courtyard, Richard Finn and Harold Stubbs who roomed together, were quickly added to the group in J and K entries. Finn was concentrating in Classical Studies: Greek, Latin, and who knows what else, Sanskrit maybe. Despite his rigorous curriculum, Finn, too, was a Renaissance man, a participant in House athletics, and prominent in House social affairs. He came from the Buffalo area, destroying Murphy's skepticism about Buffalo's intellectual calibre. He had thought it was just a cold, blue-collar, hockey town. Suffice it to say that Murphy did not attempt to converse with Finn in Latin or Greek, despite Murphy's three years of high school Latin. Finn performed a vital function for the group. He was the gadfly, the neigh-sayer, and the dogmatic challenger of Right Thought as exemplified by Tobin. Murphy called him an extremist but Tobin suggested in private that Finn was really a Right Thinker but just liked to be an iconoclast.

Harold Stubbs concentrated in Math and likewise could not converse about his field with Murphy who avoided Math like chess. He was afraid of flunking a Math course and couldn't afford to because of his scholarship. Stubbs also connected strongly with the group because of his athletic prowess. He was accomplished in tennis, played with Murphy and Tobin on the Lowell House basketball team, coached softball, and was a manager of the entire sports program for Lowell House. He played contract bridge and was always good for a lark. He never got mad, at least not explosively so, which set him apart from all others in the group. Leaving out two Conant Fellows on the fifth floor who were juniors that left the eight college sophomores as fast friends.

Occasionally, in athletics or in class Murphy would become sufficiently acquainted with a clubman to exchange pleasantries.

Once on the way to class he met a clubman whom he knew. The clubman was explaining his tolerance, and apparently mistook Murphy for a preppie from the Midwest. "I had a conversation once," intoned Murphy's walking companion, "with a guy who had gone to a public high school. And it was interesting, it really was," except that "really" was more like "rally." Murphy did not resent the clubmen; they gave him a whole class of people at Harvard he could feel morally and intellectually superior to. Murphy hung on to his feeling of being intellectually superior to the clubmen, old Harvard, moneyed sons of Harvard fathers and Harvard grandfathers.

The Great Psychic Hoax

At college Murphy, with help, sharpened the sardonic humor that had served him so well growing up in New Albany. After Christmas vacation of junior year the Great Hoax was quietly born; Sweet Innocence was midwife and Gentle Humor an emollient. Wise Men were present and unknowingly assisted in the delivery but only the proud parents, Tobin and Murphy, were privy to its Conception. Their lusty brainchild depended for its physical reality upon a single Strand of Coincidence. It survived its primal trauma by the merest Quirk of Fate, a fortunate Happenstance suggestive of Psychic Intervention in a Teleological Universe. Of such ephemeral strands are legends made, nourished and passed into folklore.

1938 was an unusual year for psychic phenomena. Orson Welles frightened a sizable fraction of a nation with a radio thriller of an invasion by Martians. The account was so gripping that thousands of people jumped into their cars and drove to safety, wherever that was. Also in 1938 on the best seller list was Duke University's published research indicating that some individuals had remarkable powers of reading symbols, sight unseen, on a series of cards that were turned over in the next room. The psychic receivers consistently made a higher percentage of correct calls than could be expected statistically of a blind choice of five symbols.

To understand the Great Psychic Hoax it is necessary to know that when Tobin and Murphy were alone in Tobin's room after the holidays, Murphy had described and Tobin had recalled a parlor game that Murphy had played over Christmas with New Albany friends. Nine magazines are placed on the floor in three rows of three magazines each and a Swami is asked to leave the room. The group selects a magazine to concentrate on and the Swami is recalled. His confederate in the room then points, using a broom handle, umbrella, anything that will reach, to the displayed magazines in turn, "Is it this one? This one? This?" and when the pointer reaches the chosen magazine the Swami brightly announces it is the correct object of the group's concentration. The secret is in the position of the pointer when placed on the first magazine, the magazine cover being mentally divided into the nine areas of three rows of three, corresponding to the arrangement of the nine magazines on the floor. The pointer resting on the first magazine identifies the area of the selected magazine by pointing to the proper area of the magazine from positions one to nine. He then points at other magazines successively, asking Swami, "Is it this one? This one?" until he reaches the magazine which had been indicated by the pointer on its initial point. Swami's face brightens and he firmly announces, "Yes!" It isn't a particularly difficult game to "see through," most high schoolers catch on quickly. Tobin and Murphy never believed the parlor game would be successful, not for a Harvard audience anyway.

The Unexpected Window of Opportunity Opened Up at Harvard during the January reading period, a time for loafing, roaming to friends' rooms and inviting the soul, Prosser, Murphy and Tobin were visiting John Morgan and Bill Felmouth in their suite on the floor below. Someone brought up the Duke experiments and the book that had been reviewed in *Time Magazine*. This Harvard group had its hard skeptics but also its soft doubters. Felmouth planned to be a minister and perhaps was more inclined than the tough-minded to believe in the human potential for clairvoyance. It was Felmouth who suggested that they should test themselves to see if anyone had extrasensory abilities as reported by the Duke Psychology Department.

Tobin, the intellect, naturally suggested a method for testing. To Murphy's delight, Tobin plopped down nine magazines arrayed three by three and picking up a poker consigned Prosser, as first subject, to the hallway. The group agreed upon a magazine, called Prosser in, Tobin pointed and Prosser failed. Next it was Felmouth and he did not extrasensorily perceive. On a second try Morgan picked out the correct magazine, next Murphy also felt vibrations from the right magazine. To complete the testing, Tobin was sent out but did not succeed. The results were promising in that two of the five, Morgan and Murphy, might have a glimmer of psychic power so the two were tested in extensio. It was soon apparent that Murphy was the one who could be attuned to the thought vibrations of the group because he bettered probability by an astounding percentage and Morgan's performance soon deteriorated into mere guessing.

Felmouth wondered aloud if similar results could be obtained in a different test. Could Murphy whose performance was so impressive with magazines read numbers through concentration of the group? Felmouth was psychologically sophisticated. He suggested that the group by some hidden and unconscious physical sign might be giving away the chosen magazine, even something as subtle as a catch in the breath by someone when Murphy's eyes wandered from magazine to magazine. Numbers would not admit of such a clue.

Murphy was feeling the glow of his unexpected new ability but he was aware that his extrasensorium, if it indeed existed, was a fragile bud and required careful tending. He felt he would like to try a single digit number. He was excused from the room and upon returning he failed to get the number. A promising rival to Duke seemed about to suffer the fate of so many Harvard competitors. Sotto voce, Murphy mumbled to Tobin that the left foot was "the center foot" and Murphy went out to try again. This time he got the number. Tobin had deduced that Murphy was indicating that the left foot, as Tobin sat in his chair, could be the center position as in the magazine game, actually the number five and the right foot could be rotated around it to produce the numbers from one to nine. No pointer was required, just Tobin's two feet. Murphy got a second number, then ripped off a string with only one miss. Murphy was not just defying the law of averages, he was shattering it.

Intelligence Too Eagerly Wed to Enthusiasm can Stumble Over Itself. The bright occupants of Morgan's living room that day, in their eagerness to discover a rising star of human potentiality, neglected to heed Murphy's discreet words to Tobin that the left foot was "the center." With that critical understanding Tobin was able to use his feet to signal. It was Prosser, the cynic, who would not be convinced, insisting that Murphy had a confederate. Felmouth suggested that Prosser, himself, was the most logical confederate and so Murphy and Prosser went to the hall together. Murphy got the number again. Murphy left the room with each in turn and finally with Tobin.

Murphy and Tobin knew the game was over. They chuckled in the hall, ready to confess, but not without heaping ridicule upon their gullible peers. Murphy returned and guessed "four." It was the correct number! Murphy was thunderstruck! For a fleeting instant in his mind's eye he thought he had seen the number "four" light up before he had announced it. Quickly he recovered his sanity and thanked the Gods of Chance for their Unexpected Gift. With Tobin Exonerated from Complicity, the two of them terminated the session as soon as they had consolidated their triumph with a few more of Murphy's perceptions. Fortunately, a second round of absences from the room was avoided. As it was, Murphy had pressed their luck. He had come back in the room on one occasion and after difficulty in perceiving he had turned on Prosser and accused him of not concentrating. Prosser confessed. Murphy then missed a number deliberately and charged the group with not concentrating. That, too, was admitted by the senders. Felmouth pleaded guilty of Sabotaging the Group by "thinking of another number." To Tobin and Murphy's great relief the session was over. Murphy had met all tests but was now too fatigued to perceive. It was a physical strain for the concentrators, too. Prosser had a headache.

Murphy and Tobin were astounded at their success. Now all they needed was Time to Connive. They could not get away for long with perception of single digits. They worked out a system for three digit numbers. The feet would indicate the single digits, the hands the ten's, and the eyes the hundred's. This enabled Tobin to signal all numbers from 1 to 999. With this extension of Murphy's abilities they consented to another and, in the words of Felmouth, "Fantastic Séance." Murphy could perceive "999" just as easily as "3." For Tobin it was a considerable Contortion, of course, and only the Familiarity of the Sight of Tobin on Other Occasions Wrestling with a Problem saved them.

The next day Felmouth and Morgan were enthusiastic. They wanted Murphy to report to the Psychology Department immediately. Since Harvard was so stodgy, they discussed the advisability of immediate contact with Duke. Tobin advised caution. Murphy, too, was uncertain that his psychic powers were real. A Mark of the Man throughout the Whole Affair was Murphy's Seemly Modesty. He was humble about his newfound ability and sought no wider public or academic acclaim. He felt woefully unprepared for exams and his extrasensorium did not seem to handle mundane tasks like remembering historical dates and personages for the exams.

In the weeks to come as it could be fitted into schedules and as Tobin and Murphy could confine audiences to the more gullible, Murphy showed off his extrasensorium to privileged newcomers. Sullivan, Tobin's roommate, was an early convert. Stubbs, McKay, Ringer, Agnew, Ralston and Morton, primarily of J and K entries, attended and were amazed in varying degrees. There were a number of hard-headed realists that Tobin and Murphy made sure were never in the group. They did not want Ebb to attend but he managed it anyway. He smiled smugly at Murphy's feats and said nothing. London was sedulously avoided. Murphy and Tobin refined the system so that Murphy could perceive anything in the room, even find a book on the shelves and an exact page that his hard-working senders transmitted across the ether. It was done by a series of foot, hand, and eye positions and codes for room location and type of object. Tobin worked Hard, Twisting and Squirming, Earning every Bit of the Acclaim Due but Denied him.

Murphy was modest, almost painfully so, about his ability to penetrate other minds. He resisted any suggestion that he abuse his powers by reading the random thoughts of others, declaiming that if that were even possible it would be an invasion of privacy. When pressed he described his manner of working as best he could. A Light seemed to Go On in his Brain, he said, as he ran over digits or objects and zeroed in on the right one. He found certain people to be excellent senders, others not so good. Prosser's brain, when Prosser was really trying, proved to be Especially Luminous to Murphy.

As with many mediums, Murphy was not particularly perceptive in other areas or even smart. He made the same old mistakes in memory, judgment, and common sense that he had always made. It is an observable fact that the ability to read minds is a gift unrelated to powers of reasoning. There have been mediums that were actually retarded. Murphy exhibited a certain ordinariness in his daily functioning. He slipped on his grades at midterm, B's in his English courses and Economics and an A only in Fine Arts.

As college pressures and distractions were renewed and Murphy steadfastly refused to court a psychic duel with Duke or even to present himself to the Harvard Psychology Department, his admirers abandoned their fervent interest and he was permitted to lead a normal life with just an occasional exhibition. Greatness can Not be Thrust upon an Unwilling Genius. On their part, Tobin and Murphy laid low waiting for a day, place, and time when they could, with the most devastating effect, expose the simple-minded naiveté of their friends.

The Junior Eight of the Harvard Phi Beta Kappa Chapter were announced after midterm. Tobin, London, and Ebb all made it. The Junior Eight were the elite of the elite, the eight men out of a class of one thousand adjudged the best scholars in the class. Next September the naming of the Senior Sixteen would be the high distinction of the next rank, and then at the conclusion of senior year, Phi Beta Kappa took in the mob, perhaps eighty or more of ranking members of the class, an honor so mundane that hardly anyone knew who finally made it.

Thus the inner circle on the fifth floor, J and K entries, provided three of the Junior Eight. It was a concentration that defied all probability and made Murphy acutely aware, if he were not already, of the company he was keeping. Undaunted, Murphy continued to debate his intellectual superiors, psychic power or not, Tobin on economics, London on Aristotle and Ebb on politics, absorbing many a bruise for his brashness.

Tobin and Murphy decided that the *Lowell House Chronicle* was the ideal place to expose the muddle-headed innocence of their friends. From its inception, Lowell House had decided it would be worthwhile to record for posterity the memorable events of each year in the House and so the *Chronicle* was born.

The first *Chronicles*, a single copy per year, reposed in unique typed splendor on the shelves of the House library, their literary excellence bursting at the rings of buckram binders, their typed pages in annual increments soiled by assiduous thumbing and rethumbing.

Then Lowell House 1938 had a great idea. That year the House was an aggressive, energetic, creative body as shown by their determined race for the Straus Trophy, the prize given the House which won the intramural year-long athletic competition, to say nothing of having three appointments to the Phi Beta Kappa Junior Eight, and the cocksure certainty that Lowell was pre-eminent among the seven Houses in a University that was the leading bastion of learning in the country. It was decided to print the 1938 edition of the Chronicle for distribution to all House members at $2.00 each. As Gardner Stratton, Chairman of the project, said, "With just a little sense, business sense that is, you can go first class."

Tobin was appointed Chairman of the Editorial Board and promptly added Murphy and others to the staff. The co-conspirators, Tobin and Murphy, rubbed their hands at the *Chronicle's* coming exposé of the Great Psychic Hoax. It would have a maximum audience for the maximum discomfiture of their deluded psychic transmitters, particularly Prosser. By some pretext they got a photo of Prosser, wan and intense as he sat in his morning robe in a chair. He could have been concentrating on the three-digit number being beamed to Swami or he could have been nursing a headache from the night before when Murphy had stretched his cerebellum to the breaking point.

Tobin wrote the text for the Great Exposé appearing under the heading of Indoor Sport. On the bright day in May when the published Chronicle circulated throughout the House, Prosser discovered the Exposé and became as pallid as his picture. Tobin, in his write-up, deftly massaged salt into the wound, "It wasn't hard, Pross, to indicate the number you were straining your brain about by the position of the feet. These simple signals mastered, all the rest was easy."

In a day or two Prosser's smile became less sickly. To their horror, Murphy and Tobin discovered that Prosser was accepting congratulations for his part in the Great Psychic Hoax. Many careless readers were missing entirely that Prosser was the Featured Goat but were casting him as the Nefarious Accomplice, a role that Prosser was now playing to perfection. Tobin with characteristic modesty had not mentioned his own participation as the Satanic Medium Co-Conspirator. His name appeared nowhere in the article. But those whose names did appear knew what Tobin meant when he wrote, "It is really too preposterous that anyone can read minds. But all of Swami's followers believed implicitly that he could. They still do." There were even a few bright Harvard men who misread the Great Exposé; they thought it was a worthy Harvard corroboration of the Duke experiment. With the Great Exposé, Tobin lost forever his reputation, deserved or not, of the one man in Lowell House that you could trust with both your money and your girl friend.

The editor of this first printed *Chronicle* modestly noted, "the verdict on the usefulness of the Chronicle can't yet be passed [sic], for Lowell House hasn't yet produced a President of the United States. When the country does have the great good fortune to be ruled by an erstwhile Bellboy, it will be tragic irony if the sophomores fifty years hence rush to the *Chronicle* only to find that the great man didn't row on the crew or sing in the opera or do any other thing that was Chronicled." Lowell House's tardiness in producing a President was understandable for the House had "risen from the jungles of Cambridge" a scant three years before and its oldest alumnus was far from the requisite age of thirty-five years to be President. However, the editor's ambitions for the House were not beyond reason since the University had graduated three Presidents by 1933 when the editor had not even heard of Tobin. Nor had he ever dreamed of the Fourth Crew. It is hoped that no Presidential aspirant was an occupant of that boat because the saga of the Fourth Crew, complete with names, was a feature story in the *Chronicle* of 1938.

Tobin had a bevy of capable writers who with wit and verve captured the flavor of House life in articles about the bells, the founding of the House and its history, the plays and opera, its institutions of the Master's high table for distinguished guests and the Housemistress's high tea for House members and nubile young ladies. Unfortunately, only Radcliffies and girls in Boston's finishing schools were available on Sunday afternoons.

The Harvard *Crimson*, the student newspaper, wedded to elitist Harvard of the Clubs and inherited wealth, reviewed the Chronicle and observed sourly, "This is by no means an ambitious undertaking and will probably serve only as an interesting comment on the youth of Lowell for the inquisitive of future generations. It has a vague taint reminiscent of boys' club circulars and the bulletins of Ladies' Aid Societies. It is an approach far too obvious for the modern taste."

The Crimson liked to reserve good fun for the inanities of Hasty Pudding and the drunken brawling in the rat houses sheltering the elitists who scorned the Houses.

The Lowell House Fourth Crew

In learning a new sport sometimes it is not the basics that are difficult for the beginner, such as hitting a ball, shooting it through a hoop, blocking and tackling on the football field. Frequently, the little things show up the novice—the customs, the jargon, the etiquette. In Murphy's career with the Lowell House Fourth Crew it was both the basics and the little things that undid him.

Murphy should probably not have tried to row on the Fourth Crew. But Lowell House was behind in the race for the Straus Trophy. They were desperate for points, even seconds, thirds and fourths to overcome archrival Kirkland House. There were eighteen sports in the program ranging from football to fencing and including every form of athletic endeavor save ping-pong. Annually each House met every other House in each sport and there were seven Houses. Harvard had, let's hope, still has, the most ambitious program of collegiate, intramural athletics in the nation. Ah, the power of a huge endowment.

Lowell House was known as the Phi Beta Kappa House; Winthrop House across the street was the jock House where all the Kennedys went, from Joe to Bobby and later, maybe Teddy. The Lowell House Bellboys, so named because of the carillon in their belfry, had won the Straus Trophy every year except last year and derived a certain primitive satisfaction in beating the more "athletic" Houses.

There was no limit on the number of shells a House could enter in the pivotal crew race. Lowell House put on the Charles not just one racing shell but a second boat of experienced scullers. And since there were a few disappointed oarsmen, the athletic managers of the House scurried around and filled a third shell of eight, unprecedented strength for an intramural boat race. Success went to the heads of the managers. As a final intimidation of the opposition they decided to scrape together at whatever cost a Fourth Crew. If the Fourth Crew proved to be hopelessly non-competitive, there was the possibility that it could challenge the Wellesley varsity, not for any prize, of course, just to reward the crew members for their efforts. Murphy, as a leader in intramural athletics, a mainstay of Lowell's football, basketball, wrestling and softball teams, was approached to fill out the last eight. Murphy's roommate, Prosser, rowed for exercise. Murphy had picked up enough of the lingo from Prosser to know what one was supposed to do in rowing. He knew the difference between comps, broads, and narrows, a succession of training boats one mastered on the way to being entrusted with a sleek, fragile, capsizable, racing single on the crowded Charles. Granted, his only rowing had been a few turns in a rowboat on midwestern creeks.

Murphy was convinced by the recruiters that he could pick up enough pointers by watching others in his boat and that he was close to being a natural athlete whose skills were transferable to other sports. Murphy's attitude about his own abilities was called confidence by some colleagues, cockiness by those who did not know him so well. They twisted Murphy's arm. "You can do it," he was told, "Nothing to it," he was assured. Murphy responded, "They need me." He agreed to participate.

Murphy arrived at the Weld Boathouse properly dressed. The coxswain turned out to be John Morgan, his neighbor in J-entry and a reassuring choice. Morgan was experienced in crew from prep school, like Punting-on-the-Tweed Academy in some little New England town. The shells were racked in layers along the walls of the boathouse. The Lowell House crew took its place beside one of the boats; the man behind Murphy positioned him properly. Morgan barked a set of orders, none of which Murphy could make out, and he found himself with a boat over *his* head, supported to this point by others. Murphy extended his arms and bore his share of the load. They marched forward and the bow crashed through the glass doors of the boathouse. This definitely was not Murphy's fault. Either Cox Morgan had not guided them properly or the stroke, the lead oarsman, had not walked straight, or someone should have opened the doors. The Fourth Crew ignored the tinkling shards and carried the shell out onto the dock.

Morgan barked more orders and, for an instant, Murphy thought he was going to follow the boat into the water. He released in time and there was the boat beside them in the water. Too late Murphy realized that he should have asked more questions about the launching procedure. They marched back into the boathouse and got their oars and returned parallel to their shell. At the command "Embark!" that Murphy could understand, he stepped into the boat, that is, into and through it. It is true that a racing shell has a near paper-thin hull of light balsa wood and Murphy discovered that. He extracted his foot, seeing too late that he should have stepped on the solid raised track running the length of the boat for the sliding seats of the rowers. The man in front was looking with dismay at the water flooding in from the slit Murphy had made in the bottom. Murphy found that by pressing the two pieces of the opening together he could conceal the split and do a fair job of keeping the shell from leaking, fair but not perfect. The shell took on water that began to slosh around as they got underway.

Belatedly, Murphy was coached on how to lock his oar in the oarlock. The Fourth Crew pushed off and for a few moments as they glided up river, under and beyond the Lars Anderson Bridge, Cox Morgan had the impression that he was commanding a crew and Murphy had the sensation that he had overcome a start made rough simply by ignorance for which others were responsible.

Murphy enjoyed gliding along pulling his oar in unison. He was rowing, not just watching others row. He continued to enjoy the new sensation of skimming over water until, with a sudden uncontrollable wrench, Murphy's oar dived to the bottom, that is, the business end of the oar, the blade, did and left Murphy clutching the other end that now stood straight up in the air. Murphy later learned that the expression for this was "catching a crab" and it effectively stopped the boat. It was a conspicuous mistake, both to his boatmates and to other boats on the river, and even to those on shore who might be driving along Memorial Drive. Murphy knew that the derisive laughter floating over the water was meant for him.

Cox Morgan did not laugh nor did the remainder of the crew. They were embarrassed and annoyed. Murphy resumed rowing but in five strokes had caught another crab and was again in the awkward position of wrestling with his own oar. Belatedly he realized that there was an art to rowing. He had heard of feathering the oar, that slight twist of the wrist to take it out of the water at the end of the stroke and then, the reverse, to slip it into the water at the vertical. It had to be done in perfect synchronization with his mates and the cox. The penalty for poor timing was catching a crab.

Cox Morgan tried to proceed but each burst of momentum was terminated by Murphy and another crab. The Fourth Crew began to feel abused, and unkindly toward Murphy. He was savoring fully the travesty of his decision to help fill out the Fourth Crew. People tended to think that Murphy was a good athlete when Murphy knew it was all hard-won gain over his natural ineptitude. On the football field or in most any other athletic situation one could be removed, substituted for, put out of his misery. But the Fourth Crew was stuck on the river with Murphy and he with it, or with them, or to hell with grammar, Murphy was in a predicament.

The shell was only a quarter mile or so upriver. This did not begin to qualify as a practice run even for Wellesley or anyone else. Cox Morgan knew defeat when it looked him in the eye. There was nothing to do but come about and head back to the boathouse. The Fourth Crew was jinxed even in such a simple maneuver as coming about. Upstream the Charles River rapidly narrows. The shell did not have all the room an inexperienced cox may have wished. Even so, Cox Morgan was careless in coming about. He drifted too far into shore and after a few strokes, Murphy suffered the ultimate indignity. He got his oar caught in a fence that ran down vertically to the water's edge, a fence of links and guy wires. The oarsman's manual does not provide for such a mishap. It was quite impractical for Murphy or anyone else to go over the side and free the oar. One could not get back into the boat without wrecking it. The crew got the attention of two Cambridge urchins on shore at a distance. Attracted by the plight of the boat, they were prevailed upon, by a variety of pleas and curses, to free the oar, an act of mercy they doubtless wondered about later since they probably had so little use for Harvard.

The Fourth Crew limped home. Murphy found that he could minimize the damage he was causing by not putting his oar in the water. He went through the motions, rowing in the air, and he no longer caught crabs. However, he became victim of a new malfunction. Without the resistance of the water as he pulled his oar, Murphy began "shooting his tail," sliding into the man in front or behind because Murphy's stroke was improperly timed. Murphy gave the back in front of him a beating and had the man in the rear cursing in his ear. The shell did regain the Weld boathouse and was properly stowed on the rack. There were no recriminations except for one crew member's snide pun. He asked Murphy, "Whatsa' matter, man, shell-shocked?" He followed it up with a dirty laugh.

There was no further effort to put the Fourth Crew on the water. Wellesley was not challenged. Murphy's friends were remarkably understanding and the crew members did not even glower when they met him on the street. In fact, by term's end even Cox Morgan laughed whenever he met Murphy.

An Intellectual Joker, Practically

Lowell House had a talented, clever, eccentric—Underwood, who brought practical jokes to a level of diabolic art. Underwood lived in I-entry, a floor below Sullivan and Tobin. He was connected from the back of their room by a fire door and a stairway that led down to the vestibule of Underwood's single room. The glass on the fire door knob had long since been broken permitting access down to I-entry from Tobin's room. The shortcut down to I-entry was a boon to the biddies, the hired Cambridge ladies who cleaned rooms and made students' beds.

Underwood's handiwork came to Murphy's attention one Saturday morning when Murphy was visiting J-51, the room of Tobin and Sullivan. The biddie had finished her work in J-51 and made her usual exit through the firedoor. There was a sudden clatter on the stairway, the sound of a mop bucket bouncing down the steps, then loud wails from the biddie. Tobin, Sullivan, and Murphy rushed to the stairway door. The stairway was dark and the light switch did not work. The woman lay in a sodden heap at the bottom of the stairs, her empty bucket beside her. Sullivan scrambled down the steps toward the moaning biddie, almost repeating her tumble as he grasped the banister of the darkened stairs. Sparks flew and Sullivan received a hard jolt. It was discovered that the biddie had not taken just an awkward middle-aged fall but that she had received an electric shock as she had closed her hand on the banister. Copper strips had been run down each side of the hand rail and at the bottom wired into the adjacent light socket. Hands grasping the banister completed the circuit. The overhead light bulb had been removed and there was evidence that the steps had been wet down before the bucket had been spilled. "Underwood!" exclaimed Sullivan in awe. "Underwood," agreed Tobin matter-of-factly. The electrified stair was certainly Underwood's work although no one could prove it, of course.

A New Yorker, Underwood operated on a national scale. His best-known caper, for which he never received credit, took place in Washington in 1937. A gleaming Grecian temple had been built for the U.S. Supreme Court, moving it out of the Capitol Building and across the square. There was to be a dedication on the outside marble promenade of the new building, a fine day of Periclean oratory in the Washington Acropolis. That morning official Washington awoke to find fluttering from the flagpole of the new Supreme Court Building the hammer and sickle on the red flag of the Soviet Union, sarcastic irony in view of recent anti-New Deal Court decisions. Republicans accused the New Deal of being Communist inspired. The anti-New Deal decisions, therefore, buttressed the country against the threat of Communism. Underwood's humor was satiric; he had raised the red flag sometime during the night for the dedication of a Court that was anti-Communist.

Underwood's politics are unknown, except that he was far from a Communist; his enterprise was completely free. He just had a talent that could not be unexercised. From a grapevine Murphy learned a lot about Underwood. As a teenager, Underwood had perfected his craft in New York City, his hometown. He installed new signs on traffic routes and diverted cars bound for New England to Long Island. He picked up manhole covers in the middle of the night, surrounded them with wooden horses and signs proclaiming "Men Working," creating obstacles to traffic of extended duration since no one knew how to get the manholes recovered.

At Harvard, Underwood found a rich environment for his imagination. It is not known whether he disliked the proctor in his freshman dormitory but, as Elbert Hubbard would say, "he might as well have."

From Boston, trains ran all night on the hour to New York. In the wee hours they were known as milk trains. Underwood once called four cab companies, gave the proctor's name, building, and room number to each cab and arranged for one cab at one a.m., another at two a.m., the third at three and the last at four in the morning. He gave each driver the same story, "I must catch the milk train to New York. I'm a sound sleeper and sometimes I have a hard time waking up. Keep pounding on my door until I get up and then no matter what I say see that I get dressed and on the train. If you get me to South Station and on the train there's twenty-five in it for you . . . plus fare, of course." It was reported that the proctor did not get rid of the one o'clock cabbie until almost time for the second, and that the third driver and the proctor almost exchanged blows. When the fourth arrived the proctor gave up and took a walk to an early breakfast at Hayes Bickford's on the Square.

Underwood's jokes could turn messy. When the proctor in Underwood's freshman dorm was spending a weekend in New York, Underwood captured a crate full of the pigeons that overwhelm Harvard Yard, lowered himself to the proctor's window by the fire rope, opened the window and released the pigeons into the room, and closed the window, The proctor got home late Sunday night, snapped on the light and surveyed his room. The pigeon feathers that swirled in the air at the swing of the door were the least objectionable droppings of the penned up birds.

Underwood seemed to live a charmed life despite his victims' sworn oaths for revenge. He ate alone in the dining hall and rebuffed overtures at conversation. He had dark hair and a face that in literature is described as swarthy and calls to mind castles in Romania. His eyes were deeply recessed. Once Murphy scrutinized Underwood's face from a distance in the dining room and noticed that one eye did not face forward. The socket seemed to have slipped around toward his cheek, or was that just Murphy's imagination?

The Hit Heard Round The Square

Indifference was a sophisticated ennui that was supposed to describe Harvard men and for which Harvard was acclaimed but also vilified. Murphy had mixed feelings about Harvard indifference. As long as it meant concentrating on one's own life and not idolizing athletic heroes, Murphy was for it. The proper Harvard response to the news that someone was on the varsity football squad was "Good enough." Another's athletic accomplishments should be acknowledged but one had one's own college life to live and academic work to do. And Harvard was unashamedly and unabashedly intellectual.

If Harvard indifference meant a balance between athletics, scholarship, drinking parties, dances, and the theatre, without narrow obsessions, again Murphy was all for it. But Murphy's approval of indifference did not extend to a blasé contempt for what college life had to offer. Murphy, and he suspected most Harvard men, did not suffer from the Noel Coward confusion of wit with boredom. Certainly in the Lowell House pursuit of the Straus trophy in the spring of 1938 there was no indifference or boredom.

The Straus Trophy was a recent innovation, inaugurated after the Houses were built. It was awarded first in 1935 to Lowell House that annexed it again in 1936. Kirkland spirited the trophy away in 1937 and Lowell was determined to regain it in 1938.

Kirkland held a narrow lead all fall, winter and early spring over the Lowell House Bellboys in the eighteen-sport marathon. In late April desperate measures were called for. The three Lowell House athletic managers whipped House members mercilessly to the track, the diamond, the squash courts and the river. In the closing weeks, the House went flat out. Even the non-athletic esthetes were impressed as participation in athletics for the year increased to 58% of all House members. Lowell House might have had a shortage of the very best but had numbers of the eager.

In the track and field meet, Lowell House overwhelmed Kirkland and the other Houses by sheer numbers, some thirty-seven Bellboys who took third, fourth, fifth, sixth and seventh in almost all events but no firsts or seconds. Sustained mediocrity was sufficient to win the meet, the last scheduled event of the intramural season. By a steady flow of points in all sports Lowell House was almost able to offset Kirkland's greater number of championships.

The galvanized efforts of Lowell resulted in the most unlikely of championship games. At season's end Samborski, the Director of Intramural Athletics, and his staff poured over the results of the season, calculating and checking over and over. Finally, they announced their findings. Kirkland, in fact, led Lowell by a few points but it had been discovered that the winner of the Straus Trophy would be decided by a Kirkland-Lowell softball game that had been postponed during the regular season because of rain. Kirkland had already sewed up the softball championship with a pitcher who was too good for the House league. Lowell House had been a creditable third. Now if they could eke out a victory in the postponed game they would edge out Eliot House for second in the final standings and would pick up enough points to surpass Kirkland for the Trophy.

Never before had the Trophy been won after the regular season was over. Never had a championship been decided by a minor skirmish. Hell, it wasn't even baseball played by athletes, it was softball played by pantywaists.

Harvard indifference jettisoned, Lowell House proceeded en masse to the softball diamond for the showdown, with marching band, cowbells, Scotch and seltzer water. Murphy stayed away from the proffered Scotch in order to insure a clear head.

The game was played in a corner of spacious Soldiers Field. At the other end the Harvard Varsity hardball team was playing Rhode Island before about two hundred spectators but the winner-take-all House game drew maybe seven hundred, almost all of Lowell and Kirkland Houses including masters, tutors, and a few waitresses and girlfriends. Professor Coolidge, the Housemaster of Lowell was there. So was his wife, the House Mistress, in her ridiculous old-fashioned high top and buttoned up shoes.

Stubbs was the manager and Finn, Sullivan and Murphy were stalwarts of the Bellboy team. Levin was their cocky pitcher who staked a noisy claim to being their best hitter also. Levin was limited only by the opportunity to play just one position at a time.

As sometimes happens, just getting there spends the emotions and energy and the big game is anti-climactic. So it was today. The Kirkland pitcher, a fireballer in a big-time summer league back in his hometown, mowed down the Bellboys methodically. Murphy did not get a loud foul in two times at bat and others were equally futile. Finn's customary gibe at an opposing batter, "He can't hit the size of his hat band!" was true of Lowell House in the big game. Levin pitched creditably except for a brief lapse permitting Kirkland to bring a 4-1 lead into the seventh and final inning. Levin dutifully retired Kirkland in the top half and closed his mouth for the season.

It was all but over. The crowd frayed at the edges and Kirkland supporters were doing anticipatory war dances along the foul lines. The Kirkland pitcher walked the first batter and now Manager Stubbs dictated a new strategy, "Wait him out, don't swing," was the word passed to the Lowell batters. It worked. The pitcher did seem to lose his excellent control. Perhaps even he succumbed to nerves with everything on the line.

He walked the next two men to load the bases. But the next man struck out and the prospects for a big inning dimmed. However, Johnny Weston, the compact little shortstop, got the first real hit of the day for Lowell House, a ringing double to left center. Two runs scored and Bill Shirk with the tying run from first rounded third and may have beaten the relay to the plate. In his reckless dash Shirk would not have hesitated to barrel into the catcher and try to part him from the ball. No one will ever know if Shirk would have made it by bowling over the catcher, or whether the catcher would have held on to the ball. The throw from center field was right on the line and there was no way a collision could have been avoided at the plate. No umpire would have dared to call Shirk out with the Straus Trophy in the balance because Bill Shirk, scorning an attempted slide, would have simply plunged ahead like a fullback. The umpire was spared that decision just as history was spared a second guess whether Shirk should have tried to score from first.

The umpire was spared a decision because Bill Shirk tripped rounding third, did a full somersault and lay sprawled fifteen feet down the line. On the sidelines Lowell House pleaded as one man for Shirk to gather his wits about him, his legs under him and scramble back to third before the catcher's throw should arrive. Shirk moved with agonizing slowness. Hands were extended but did not assist him. The third base coach shouted in his ear but did not touch him. All Lowell House men who were there that day will take an oath that Bill Shirk was in no way pushed or otherwise impelled back to third. Nor was his inert hand lifted and clamped on the bag. The rally was still alive with men on second and third.

Crane, a timely hitter, was next up and could have been a hero by driving in both runs, or a half-hero by plating one on a fielder's choice to the infield that would have tied the game. Or who knows, the way Kirkland was coming apart the second baseman might have thrown the ball over the catcher's head allowing the winning run to score and undoubtedly touching off one of the wildest celebrations that Soldiers Field had ever seen. Alas, it was not fated to end in such wonderful fashion. Crane popped up for the second out. The Kirkland pitcher still had his stuff.

Murphy, circling in the background while these heroics were transpiring in the foreground, realized that his worst nightmare was occurring in broad daylight. He was due up with two out and he had not been able to get around on the pitcher's fastball yet. The Lowell House *Chronicle*, the yearbook, later recorded the scene: "there emerged the well-built frame of one of Harvard's star intramural competitors, captain of the House football team and a standout on the basketball team, the pride of New Albany, Indiana." Murphy let two balls go by and when the pitcher had to come down the pipe with a strike, Murphy lashed it over the second baseman's head and cleanly to center. Murphy dashed to the first base bag, collapsed and hung onto the bag for dear life as the tying and winning runs scored. What Frank Merriwell was to Yale, Murphy today was to Lowell House. The Straus Trophy had been recaptured!

Murphy had a long ride on bony shoulders back across the bridge over the Charles River, the traditional route of conquering heroes, varsity and all, from Soldiers Field. The triumphal procession got almost to Lowell House before the small wiry guys who had formed Murphy's mount in a moment of ecstasy came to the panting end of a hot May journey with 175 pounds of beef cradled in midair. Murphy was glad to dismount, hurry on to his room for a leisurely shower and make a grand entrance to the full dining room and a thunderous ovation. He accepted the thanks and congratulations of all with that magnanimity he hoped to be noted for.

The Straus Trophy had already been reclaimed. It was polished and shining on a table with a tablecloth at the front of the hall. Mrs. Healey, the affable hostess of the dining hall, knew how to set a hero's welcome. The carillon in the belfry chimed in a special concert for the winning of the trophy.

Murphy basked in the glory for a full week. He gave a silly quote to the Harvard Crimson about taking aim at the pitcher by sighting down his bat and letting fly. He should have confessed that the unlikely prospect of his getting a turn at bat had come so quickly that he had not had time to get nervous. But whether in a daze or fully conscious, Murphy enjoyed his mighty blow for the trophy. It was the winning hit heard around Harvard Square, also reported by Boston's *Herald*, a metropolitan daily newspaper. Only Sullivan had a wry, no doubt envious, reminder for Murphy, "If Bill Shirk hadn't fallen down you never would have come to the plate."

A legendary Harvard coach had once said to his football eleven as they left the locker room to play Yale, "Nothing you ever do in life will be as important as what you are about do this afternoon on the football field."

Following his Harvard spectacular Murphy was back in New Albany in a month schmoosing with former high school classmates from Indiana U., DePauw, Louisville U. and Kentucky. They spoke of athletic victories of their colleges and listened patiently as Murphy related the winning hit for the Straus trophy. His hit was one story among their many. To others in New Albany, those who hadn't gone to college at all, to his neighbors, to members of his father's church, Murphy said nothing at all. Sic semper heroicannus!

Murphy never equaled his feat in athletics that day on Soldiers Field. Of course, team sports were basically over after college. He played some pick-up basketball before and after World War II but his real sport was tennis. In his tennis career there were some exultant come-from-behind victories, there were other times of bitter defeat when he was carried off the court on his shield, metaphorically speaking. But he never was again carried off on the shoulders of others, never received another ovation, and almost never had spectators.

His greatest athletic feat was oddly enough performed in silence with no witnesses. It was when he was working at the University of Pennsylvania Hospital. At noon for exercise there was a time when he would go the Gimbel Gymnasium at 37th and Walnut Streets, check out a basketball at the desk and go up to the court on an upper floor and shoot a few hoops. There was almost no one on the court at noon. One day Murphy was hitting shots from all over the court, couldn't miss. He decided on the ultimate challenge. He would shoot one from the center of the circle at midcourt. It was a shot that in many cheering, crowded arenas some designated spectator, maybe someone who had practiced a week for the part, would throw/sling/jump shot the ball from the center line toward the basket for a reward of a million dollars if he should make it. It was known to happen but rarely. In the noiseless gym that day except for the swish of Murphy's shots and the bounce of the ball on the floor, Murphy accomplished the same feat not once but three times, not in total, but on three consecutive tries. His usual old-fashioned chest shot would not carry to the basket from the centerline so he put the ball between his legs and heaved. The first one he banked off the backboard with a thud and it went in. The next two swished right through the net. Murphy was so impressed that he asked his wife that evening to make a note of it so that she could verify it if the question ever came up.

Campaign Kickoff

In Murphy's junior year the Winter Dance Committee engineered a real coup for Lowell House. They obtained one of the most sought after bands in the land, Tommy Dorsey. All tickets were bought by Lowell and the other Houses as soon as they were offered. Only the eagle eyes of the ticket takers at the door spotted counterfeit tickets in the hands of men from Winthrop House across the street. Prosser, recognized as a coming social lion, was on the band subcommittee and was instrumental (God, what a pun) in holding out for a name band and landing Dorsey.

The dining hall and the waitresses were transformed for the six o'clock candle light dinner, the hall into a midwinter Greek pine glade with white columns and boughs of evergreen, the waitresses from wan Cambridge housewives into passably sparkling colonial dames. Murphy was surprised at the social graces of the middle-aged waitresses, usually in black uniforms with white trim.

It was a cold night and at parties in rooms before the banquet good cheer was a necessity. Prosser had lovingly concocted his unique punch and made sure that the supply would last. The base of lime and lemon juice had been mixed the day before for proper aging. The rum and cordials in the secret recipe were added before drinking. The punch was cooled by dry ice, its foaming mist raising thoughts of MacBeth and witches brew. Prosser's punch was known for its "virtuous" potency.

Murphy's date was a darkish Radcliffe girl, one of Ebb's string of dates from his little black book, a date for the asking by a grateful classmate. He knew just the girl for Murphy, he said, and so it was arranged, sight unseen. Murphy had taken a cab to pick her up just in time for the party before the banquet. Though petite, the girl, Jamie, did not stand out in a group of Radcliffe women that meant she was pretty nondescript.

The parties were lengthy before dinner. Tobin had a date from Wellesley, a Peggy Coble, his former classmate at University High back home in Illinois. She was a striking brunette, gay and bubbling, a typical honey from the Midwest that towns like New Albany and Champaign-Urbana turned out in bunches. Murphy engaged Tobin and Peggy around the punchbowl. Tobin was not much of a drinker but he had heard, perhaps Murphy had bragged, that Murphy could down his liquor. Tobin was always encouraging Murphy to prove it. Murphy flitted to and from his date, Jamie, who seemed to have her own circle of admirers. Back to Tobin and his glamorous date, Peggy, Murphy informed Peggy of Tobin's accomplishment in making the Phi Beta Kappa Junior Eight. She was not at all surprised. She and her classmates at University High had known that Tobin, she called him James, was destined for great achievements. It was an accepted fact in Champaign-Urbana. It was odd to hear Tobin called "James." At Harvard almost all men were called by their last names.

Murphy agreed that there should be no limits on James' aspirations. At the requisite time he would be superbly qualified for the Presidency of the country. His field was Economics and that was becoming critical knowledge for modern statesmen.

As Prosser's punch performed its wondrous magic, Murphy became firmer in his resolve that Tobin would and should indeed be an ideal President. Politics was changing for the better. Harvard professors were running for the Massachusetts State House and even for the U.S. Congress. Roosevelt's reliance on his brain trust had injected a new dimension into politics. By the time Tobin and Murphy's generation came on line, the country would be seeking unusual intelligence in its elected leaders.

At the hour of six the parties adjourned and couples arrived for the banquet. Dorsey and his band provided low mood music during dinner. After dessert the waitresses promptly cleared the floor for dancing. Prosser, Murphy and a few others scurried back upstairs to the punch bowl for a quick pre-dance libation.

Arriving back on the dance floor, Murphy found Jamie for the first dance. It was obligatory to have the first dance with one's date for the evening. Thereafter, one could exchange partners with friends, or as Murphy preferred, roam the floor like any stag cutting in on the girls who looked appealing. Murphy was becoming specific in his ambition for Tobin. Tobin should run for President in 1964, and Murphy would be his campaign manager as of this very night. While a jammed dining hall shuffled, glided, squeezed, and applauded to the swinging strains of Tommy Dorsey, Murphy kicked off the campaign, "Tobin for President in 1964!" Murphy was absorbed in his theme, "Tobin for President!" He covered as much of the hall as he could, buttonholing a wandering stag, cutting in on friends and shouting, "Tobin for President in 1964!" Drinks were available at side tables. With a few drinks, Murphy tended to be rough, overbearing, and physical. He began pushing people, spinning them around, grabbing.

Somehow the kick-off of the campaign became a literal action. Murphy would peer into a male face and shout, "Tobin for President!" Then as a clincher he would spin the prospect around and administer a kick or knee in the rear. It was an odd way to win friends for Tobin's candidacy and it won no friends for Murphy. At the twelve o'clock break for refreshments, several concerned friends like Sullivan and Morgan attempted to remonstrate with Murphy. To no avail, he stiff-armed them both and continued the campaign.

The Dorsey band was worth the cost. They played until three with Tommy's mellow trombone and Edythe Wright's torchy ballads giving everyone his money's worth. Murphy courted disaster when he spun around the Head Tutor, David Worcester, resident in the House, and planted his foot hard on the tutor's coccyx. In a momentary rage Worcester paused—then thought better of his first impulse.

The triumph of the band, a tradition of leniency and hard

drinking, and probably a certain amount of good will that Murphy had engendered in Lowell House combined to keep him in one piece until the punch fumes died in him and he observed his folly. However, no one was much the worse for it except Jamie who had a miserable time.

Tobin who had begun the evening with a modest appreciation of a compliment tossed his way ended with considerable chagrin but no real guilt. He was not the first political contender to be done in by an uninhibited campaign manager. Murphy got Jamie home in a cab and she dashed into her dorm, disconsolate and unaware that the Dorsey dance had been a Lowell House masterpiece.

After they had returned their respective dates to dorm or hotel, Murphy and several friends returned to his and Prosser's room for a nightcap. Prosser had indeed made a sufficient supply of his punch of "virtuous" potency. The dry ice had kept it cold without dilution. Stubbs, Finn, Sullivan and several unknown sophomores joined them. Tobin, never a big party man, left them and went to bed.

The long dance and the cab ride to Radcliffe and back had begun to clear the alcoholic fumes from Murphy's head. Before lifting his cup to imbibe again, Murphy had a slight momentary twinge of his Protestant conscience, to wit, that there was a dark corner of his psyche that he could never come to terms with. Why had he behaved so badly as he had done on the dance floor? But even so, even now he could not suppress a chuckle at Satan's handiwork.

Perhaps, subconsciously Murphy's conscience had been eased by the fact that he had studied very hard all day before the dance for the Fine Arts exam, which was to be on the morning after the dance. What timing in his exam schedule! No one else, Prosser certainly not, nor Tobin, Sullivan or others had mentioned a final exam the morning after the dance.

The punch's "virtuous" potency soon renewed and enhanced their inebriation of the evening. They all felt like singing and somehow went down the four flights to the courtyard without breaking any limbs. Arms draped around each other in the best barbershop style, they loudly resounded throughout the inner courtyard. Winter dawn was breaking bleakly over Cambridge and the Houses when Dave Worcester, Senior Tutor, shouted obscenely from his window for the singers to knock it off or he would call House Security. Murphy, remembering the kick of the tutor at the dance, advised the group to disperse quietly.

Upstairs in their roam, Murphy stared in disbelief at Prosser's empty punchbowl. Prosser lurched off to bed and in ten seconds was snoring like a pig. Murphy's brain was aware enough to remind him of the Fine Arts exam. There was not time to take even the briefest of naps. He could not be sure of waking even with an alarm if, indeed, he could set it properly. Nor could he afford the luxury of missing the exam as the wealthy sons of Harvard sons might. His scholarship was always at stake. He had to show up and try for at least a D.

In the gray morning he stumbled up the snowy street and safely across Massachusetts Avenue and on through the yard to the Fogg Art Museum and got there by nine, the time for all morning exams. The entire exam consisted of slides on a projector of sculpture, paintings, and architecture. The exam was to identify the art and artist and to write a justification of the answer. Murphy felt he *was* recognizing the slides. His intuitive brain must have taken over or the remaining alcohol relaxed all anxiety. He nailed it. He got an A+. That was the only exam and so it determined the grade for the course, the best grade by far that he ever received at Harvard.

The Great Dehallucination

In the late fall of 1938 Murphy and friends had an engagement with the Psychology Department but it was not to display Murphy's psychic powers. It did result in a psychic aberration, however, that has come down in the lore as The Great Dehallucination, or more popularly, The Gulls Gulled or even The Silent Sirens. It had an impact on Psychology and Murphy heard it quoted some years later in a remote event, a fire in Baltimore when women were trampled to death by men trying get out of a burning building at a bull roast.

Tim Tonkenow was a sophomore member of the Lowell House basketball team when Murphy and Tobin were seniors. He was a Psychology student and he recruited the Lowell House basketball team for an experiment in his department. It was a study of group performance in problem solving, specifically, how an established organized group went about a task compared to an unorganized group of similar individuals brought together ad hoc just for the experiment.

The Lowell House basketball five—Tobin, Stubbs, Storey, Murphy and Tonkonow—came to the lab one Saturday morning. Not only was the department getting five sterling collaborators but this five had exceptional intelligence as well. They were taken to an inside room, no windows, just a skylight above, and told to choose among three puzzles and work to solve one or more. The time limit was one hour.

The group would be observed through a one-way glass window in one wall behind which three observers could listen in and take notes. The study subjects were not to have any conversation with the observers whom they could not see. The researchers were interested in, among other things, how leadership is exercised. Murphy was captain and the acknowledged leader of the basketball team. Murphy directed attention to the first puzzle on a table. It consisted of a mass of wooden pieces, boards, slats, and strips, a confusing pile like Lincoln logs, and a picture of what they should build. Murphy saw immediately that five people would be in a hopeless muddle with this project so he suggested they look at another puzzle.

The second puzzle consisted of a large wooden cone like a circular pyramid, with an outside track spiraling to the top. The cone was mounted on a board with handles so that it could be lifted, held and tilted. The task was to start a marble at the bottom of the inclined track and with the group holding and moving the cone by the wooden handles to roll the marble up and around the track to the top without touching the marble. The spiral incline had no groove or restraining lip. Murphy saw that this also was hopeless. It took a quick trial of starting the marble up the incline and having it fall off after a roll of several inches. Three tries and all agreed it was a trap for a disorganized group that could waste its entire time with this impossibility.

Rather quickly, Murphy noted proudly, the group under his direction settled on the only project of the three that was divisible and also suitable for group effort. It was the mathematical four four's problem. The task was to formulate equations using the number "four" four times in each equation and in successive equations to derive all numbers from one to one hundred. Thus, number one could be obtained by: 4 minus 4 Plus 4/4 = 1. Two could be: 4/4 Plus 4/4 = 2. One could multiply, divide, square, perform all mathematical functions with the four fours. Stubbs was a math concentrator. Tobin was brilliant in math as well as everything else so the team set to work around the table, dividing the task by blocks of ten numbers, Murphy was to work on equations for numbers 1 through 9, Storey 10 through 19, etc., the higher and presumably more difficult numbers assigned to Stubbs and Tobin. Stubbs came up with the information that there was a mathematical function called "factorial" that was highly useful. Four factorial, 4x3x2xl, equaled twenty four and was written with a dot, as "4.". This was probably necessary to develop equations for all numbers through one hundred especially the higher ones.

Murphy wanted to know how four factorial was derived and what it meant. The group was hard at work on the assignments that Stubbs had handed out. Murphy was told to shut up and work on his equations. It was a reasonable rebuke. Fifteen minutes of the hour had elapsed in determining the right problem. Intellectual curiosity was a luxury. It was right that temporary leadership pass to another, more qualified for the specific task.

The observers undoubtedly noticed this functional shift of leadership to Stubbs. Old leaders in new situations are sometimes swelled with pride and may not recognize when the mantle should be tossed to another, if only temporarily. The observers may or may not have detected that Murphy spent the next forty-five minutes in a rather peevish snit, solving few equations and feeling generally abused. While Murphy was brooding about four factorial, others had to help him with his assigned equations. Stubbs, Tobin, et. al. tried to complete the series to one hundred but fell a few numbers short at the expiration of time. It was apparent who had failed to hold up his end.

The director terminated the experiment and gave them bluebooks in which to describe their reactions and answer a set of questions. The investigators then left the room.

After a few minutes of silent work, Murphy sniffed and smelled a trace of smoke from someone's pipe. In a few minutes others were sniffing. It was not pipe smoke. Somewhere in the building a coffee pot may have burned dry. The University was always warring without success on hotplates in old buildings. Murphy imagined that in the still air of the closed room he saw just a wisp of hanging smoke so he got up and went to the door to get some fresh air. The door was locked; it was easy for absent-minded researchers to forget to fasten open the spring latch. Someone remarked that smoke seeming to be seeping under the door. Murphy looked and there was no mistaking the little swirls of bluish smoke. It was preposterous but could someone's carelessness in this old building actually have started a trash fire that was filling the corridor with so much smoke that it was infiltrating under the door? The group left its work at the table and began milling about.

The door was a monstrous oak slab with heavy-duty hinges and would not yield, if need arose, to the ram of a shoulder, or even many shoulders. The skylight was far above head height even if one stood on the table. It was left for Tonkonow, psychology student, to gently recall them to the real world, "These psychologists will do anything to prove a point or just to have a little fun."

Murphy chuckled, the group was reassured. They had been close to losing their calm and their sense of humor. Then Storey remarked that he heard fire engines. "Listen," he commanded. Stubbs heard them, then everyone as the clanging came down the next street. A fire company was only a half block away from the building, a wise location by the City of Cambridge. Some old buildings, like Memorial Hall, were veritable firetraps and often were unoccupied for long stretches.

The occupants of the inside room with no windows began pounding on the one door but there was no response, "Had these damned Psychology instructors panicked at the sight of a trash fire and left their charges to inhale smoke or even worse in this old building?" Tonkonow put Stubbs, lightest of the group, on his shoulders and elevated him toward the skylight. If, indeed, they had to save themselves, as unlikely as that might be, could the skylight be reached for possible exit?

The door was flung open and a gleeful band of investigators ambled in displaying the pipettes they had used to blow smoke under the door. It was really bizarre that Murphy and his friends, so smart, so blase, had been taken in so easily. Tonkonow attempted to justify himself and them, "I didn't really believe it until I heard the fire engines," he said. "Yes," they all agreed, "it was the fire engines that did it." How had the researchers managed to win the cooperation of the Fire Department?

"Fire engines?" the chief investigator inquired. He cocked his head on one side, "You heard fire engines?" The investigators were impressed and then elated as one after another, Murphy, Stubbs, Tobin, Storey and Tonkonow affirmed that they had heard fire engines. They insisted so strongly that an investigator thought that he must be scientifically thorough and record the denial from the Fire Department. He checked with the fire company by telephone and returned crestfallen. The operator had verified that the equipment had responded to an alarm and had gone down the street a few minutes ago. Murphy felt better, his grip on reality restored.

Murphy learned that the experiment in group dynamics went into the literature. The Lowell House basketball team completely outshone the disorganized group in cooperating on the puzzles, also in succumbing to panic when smoke was blown under the locked door. The unorganized group had just laughed at the smoke.

Of course, there were no fire engines for the unorganized group who had been tested on another day.

The literature records without regard to hurt professional pride the Great Dehallucination of the three investigators who were so intent on scaring the hell out of the Lowell House basketball team that they could not hear fire engines. 1938 was, indeed, a vintage year for extra-sensory perception and misperception. The investigators ordered beer all around. It was illegal, of course, but it was Saturday and there were no classes in the building. And Security could be counted on to stay out of an empty building.

New Harvard Replies in Expose of Snow White

Tobin and Murphy, avid New Dealers and pioneers in the evolution of Harvard into a university with national appeal and admissions, were moved to reply to an attack on the New Deal by Walt Disney. They sent off a satiric letter to the New York Times:

To the Editor,

IS SNOW WHITE A REPUBLICAN?

In the acclaim for *Snow White*, the latest offering by the Great Animator of a fairy tale supposedly for children, the hidden Republican propaganda directed at moviegoers has gone unnoticed, or, at least, unremarked. Is the message so hidden? Given Mr. Disney's well-known and anti-Roosevelt and Republican bias, it takes no leap of the imagination to see that Snow White herself is pure symbol for the American Way in Republican terms. She is protected and nourished by dwarfs who obviously represent Small Business and all its virtues—unflagging industry and uncritical acceptance of the work rules of the capitalistic system. It is hard to imagine a more cheerful band of miners engaged in the their dangerous and crippling occupation. In real life, Mr. Disney is known for his studio sweatshop of low paid animators. Hunched over dwarfs, maybe? Snow White loses her way in the Black Forest, which can only stand for the Great Depression. The twin vultures of Communism and Fascism perched on a limb croak in anticipation as Snow White is torn by the brambles and thickets of entangling economic theory. Snow White falls into a sinkhole, which threatens her extinction, an obvious Republican assessment of the public debt.

Her pretended savior, the Wicked Witch, with jutting jaw and angular face even looks like Franklin Roosevelt and leaves no doubt of the malevolent Republican characterization when the Witch asks, "Mirror, mirror, on the wall, who's the fairest of them all?" The apple presented to Snow White is attractive on the outside but poisonous within. The apple is clearly the New Deal nostrum of spending (consumption) as a cure for the Depression. But the apple, that is, deficit spending, induces in Snow White the deep sleep of economic stagnation.

Snow White is rescued by Prince Charming, patently the Republican Presidential hopeful of 1940, identified presently only as Prince Charming. He rides in on a trusty steed, the Republican Party, of course. After the kiss of life, an infusion of sound economic policy, the American Way and Prince Charming ride off to the Castle of Prosperity.

No, Mr. Disney, we are not beguiled or hoodwinked. The tracks of your reactionary politicking are a mile wide. New Dealers beware!

HARVARD JUDGES FDR

The following editorial in the Harvard Crimson on the occasion of President Roosevelt's address at the Tercentenary celebration of the founding of the college is typical of the tone and substance of the paper's political commentary during the presidential campaign of 1936:

Harvardman Speaks

President Roosevelt orated a vital Truth in Friday's harangue. "In the hands of political puppets of an economic autocracy, such power" (the new instruments of public power created by his administration) "would provide shackles for the liberty of the people." Also, such power bodes danger when any sort of inexperienced demagogic President and Administration hold it. That is why such added power seems scandalous when combined with wholesale corruption of the Civil Service. That is why those who do not hold as high opinion of Mr. Roosevelt as, judging from the self-righteousness and continual self-quotation of his address, Mr. Roosevelt seems to himself take the still present liberty of calling him the . . . (unprintable). The disillusioning thing is that this man, believe it or not, the same who delivered Friday evening's guff, graduated from Harvard College, in good standing, about thirty-two years ago. Perhaps those who have repeatedly told us that educated men should go into politics were on the wrong track. Not that intelligent youth should shy from public service. Not that the problems of government are too narrow to challenge the gifted. But that, judging from our eminent example, and from Abraham Lincoln, perhaps brains and character are more important than, and not essential to, education, good family, and wealth.

Mr. Roosevelt came of a good family; he had wealth; he passed through the best and most expensive education in the country. After twenty-nine years, he found himself in a position where the richest and most powerful nation in the world was at his feet, begging for leadership, for strength, for intelligence. He yielded to the entrenched stupidity of special interests; to capital he gave monopoly, to labor he gave crooked unionism and class bitterness. Only borrowing on a back-breaking scale floated the country off the rocks of disaster. Let us not perhaps propose the repeal of all Roosevelt measures, although (sic) the A.A.A., the Guffey Act, the Wagner Labor Bill, the Social Security Act, and the Neutrality Law might go with great good effect. But let us, above all, repeal unreliability and treachery and flibbety-gibbety in government; let us this fall, repeal the Roosevelt Presidency. In the midst of our great Three Hundreth Anniversary Celebration, let the presence of this mans serve as a useful antidote to the natural overemphasis of Harvard's successes.

Harvard Rejects New Albany High School
and its Unprincipled Principal

With his thesis on Jane Austen accepted, Murphy was graduated from Harvard, A.B., magna cum laude, and elected with the mob to Phi Beta Kappa. It did not hurt that Tobin, Sullivan and other friends were by then voting members of the Harvard Phi Beta Kappa Chapter. Ironically, Prosser, Conant Fellow, was not elected. Murphy received his gold Phi Beta key and pin and promptly lost them. He never replaced them and Tobin never forgave him.

After the graduation which his parents attended, Murphy returned with them to New Albany where Murphy spent a brief vacation before going out into the world to find out if it was as cruel and as cold as it was said to be. It had developed that the Murphy scholarship of $800. was much less of a help than a Conant Fellowship. For his sophomore year Murphy's stipend was reduced to $600. Murphy had only himself to blame because his grades were only Group III. For his last two years the scholarship was reduced to $400. annually. For these years Murphy was Group II. So it may not have had to do with grades but was a game played by "little" Harvard. "Little" Harvard was the niggling administration of Deans and baby Deans who tried to save money.

"Big" Harvard was the Faculty responsible for making the college a pre-eminent institution. Murphy was obliged to borrow money for his last two years, a debt he did not discharge until he was in a foxhole in World War II.

Murphy's father showed him a letter which he had written to Harvard at the time of Murphy's admission and which he had withheld from him until now. The letter explained many things that Murphy had wondered about. In the letter, his father wanted to know why his son had obtained only a lesser Scholarship and Prosser a Fellowship when Murphy was first in his class and Prosser only third. Father had enclosed a copy of the high school graduation program listing Murphy as Valedictorian and Ruth Mazey as Salutatorian. Prosser's name did not appear.

Harvard replied to the letter and stated that they had been misled by the high school principal who had written that Prosser was first in his class and Murphy second. The Harvard letter added that never again would a New Albany High School student receive a scholarship from Harvard. Murphy wonders if that ban still applies. Or is it like so many threats, a forgotten file in the mausoleum of history.

In retrospect the principal's strategy is apparent. He had a son in Murphy's high school class who finished sixth in the rankings, a good record certainly but not one that would qualify him for a Conant Fellowship. Nor did the principal expect his son to go to Harvard. But Prosser had also applied for a Rector Scholarship to DePauw, a school highly thought of in Indiana. The Principal wanted the Rector for his son. It became all-important that Prosser receive the Conant Fellowship, and if Murphy also got a Harvard scholarship, so much the better. However, Murphy's boyhood chum, Strickland, upset the strategy by winning the Rector. The principal's son had to settle for a modest Floyd County stipend to Indiana U. The hypocritical betrayal of trust by the principal availed him nothing. Sic semper hypocriticus.

"The world moves and Harvard College moves with it." Who said that? Maybe Ralph Waldo Emerson, sounds pretentious enough for him. The college days and the uncomplicated Harvard that Murphy, Tobin, Sullivan, London, Ebb, Finn, Stubbs and the rest had enjoyed quickly eroded. Shortly, Tobin defected to Yale and spent a long distinguished academic career there. It was unsettling for Murphy, his wife and family to go to the Tobins in New Haven for Thanksgiving, as was their tradition, and find Tobin and his children rooting madly for Yale.

Murphy had occasion to visit Cambridge now and again through the years. It was terribly confusing. Harvard Square was a nightmare of honking, entangled traffic, tunnels under Massachusetts Ave., and God knows where the subway was. The Houses had doubled in number, built in modern architectural style instead of the colonial red brick. The blue dome of Lowell House could still be picked out and on one visit Murphy headed for it on foot. At the archway he had to sign in.

Murphy very much wanted to see his old room again. It was impossible, the House was being renovated and under summer construction. Security couldn't care less. A wandering contractor saw Murphy hanging around in the archway and thought he might be a sub-contractor. Murphy explained that he just wanted to see J-entry in the inner courtyard. It had been his residence in the '30's. The contractor saw no harm in accompanying Murphy up the steps and to his fifth floor bedroom, taking care that Murphy kept out of the way of the workmen. The fifth floor was being gutted, many walls between rooms were down and electric wires dangled dangerously here and there. Murphy saw that the back wall of his and Prosser's living room was still standing. He squinted into the dust and saw a familiar sight. He saw the gouge in the wall where Prosser as a sophomore in a rage had thrown an empty whiskey bottle at Murphy's head. Murphy had ducked and the bottle took a gouge out of the plaster. The gouge had never been fixed while Murphy and Prosser spent three more years in J-52. Maintenance still hadn't gotten around to it fifty years later.

Murphy himself in time transferred his loyalties to the University of Pennsylvania, via its Hospital where he worked and participated in shared programs with the University. In sports Murphy roots for Pennsylvania most of the time, only switching to

Harvard when they have a chance at an Ivy League title and Penn is out of the race. Penn is usually in the race.

Murphy has even expressed criticism of Harvard's elitism and questions whether there should be elitist universities instead of a mix of student capabilities and economic levels in all universities.

Sic semper vainglorious nostalgiannus.